"You a[re] aren't [...]"

Lisa shook her head and gestured for him to follow her into the kitchen. The trouble was, she realized, she was only half kidding when she said that.

"Yes, ma'am, I am." Kevin grinned down at the straight back and softly rounded hips of the intriguing woman before him.

He had a lot to think about in the next few days. Important decisions to make that were going to affect the entire course of his life. But now, this morning, he found he was far more interested in Lisa Emery and getting to know her better, much better. She was lively and intelligent, interesting to be around. One moment she was defensive and wary, obstinately independent and self-reliant; the next moment as soft and enchanting as a meadow flower.

For the first time in months Kevin found himself interested in someone, something else other than his own dilemma. He wasn't about to question the reason. Or analyze too closely the deeper implications of his attraction for this woman. He only knew he was far more inclined to concentrate on Lisa Emery than he was to dwell on his own uncertain future.

ABOUT THE AUTHOR

Marisa Carroll is the pseudonym for a writing team of sisters, Carol Wagner and Marian Scharf. Mutually supportive and proud of their novels, the women penned their first romance in 1983. Today they live about two miles from each other in Deshler, the small Ohio town where they were born and raised. They share shopping trips, duties at the family oil-jobbing business, long walks and stories about their four teenagers when they aren't busy collaborating at the word processor. Readers may already be familiar with the hero of this novel, Kevin Sauder; he was the brother of heroine Laurel from Harlequin American Romance #256 *Come Home to Me*.

Ties that Bind
Marisa Carroll

Harlequin Books

TORONTO • NEW YORK • LONDON
AMSTERDAM • PARIS • SYDNEY • HAMBURG
STOCKHOLM • ATHENS • TOKYO • MILAN

To my son, Samuel,
and to my daughter, Lisa.
For all our summers past
and all our summers yet to come.
—M

Published March 1989

First printing January 1989

ISBN 0-373-16286-3

Chapter One

Kevin Sauder looked at the sleeping infant cradled in his sister's arms. One tiny fist was curled against his three-day-old nephew's cheek, the other wrapped tightly around his mother's little finger.

"You do good work, sis." Kevin smiled, reaching out to touch the soft, brown hair on the baby's head.

"I know," Laurel Norris replied with justifiable maternal pride. She was wearing a pretty pink flowered robe and gown and a pink ribbon in her brown hair. She looked happy and content, if still a little pale and tired after her recent ordeal. "Isn't he beautiful?"

Beautiful wasn't the first word that came to Kevin's mind as he gazed at the baby frowning fiercely in his sleep, but homely was. His nephew looked like a wizened little gnome of a man, toothless and bald except for a wispy bit of brown fluff on top of his head. Still, Kevin wasn't foolish enough to state his thoughts.

"He's beautiful," Kevin replied, loyalty and family pride winning out over honesty.

"Hey, what about me? Don't I get any of the praise?" Kevin's brother-in-law, Seth Norris, sat down on the edge of his wife's hospital bed and took her free hand in his. He was wearing a hospital gown patterned with small pastel-colored teddy bears over a casual cotton shirt and jeans. Somehow on Seth the hospital-issue cover-up didn't look as ridiculous as it would have on anyone else, himself included. Kevin looked down at his own teddy-bear-decorated gown and grimaced. Maybe looking confident and in complete control of the situation, no matter what you were wearing, was something they taught ex-Secret Service agents—which Seth was.

"I have to admit, I couldn't have done it without you." Laurel's tone was light and teasing, but the look that passed between the couple was anything but casual. It was charged with so much love and caring that Kevin found himself uncharacteristically envious of his sister and his best friend for what they shared.

Seth and Laurel's courtship had been unconventional, even scandalous, by small-town Bartlow, Ohio, standards, the wedding held barely two months before the birth of their son. It had been a trying year for all of them. Seth had been badly wounded eight months earlier in an assassination attempt on the President's life, nearly dying before he realized what he wanted most in the world was to come home to Bartlow and farm the land that had been in his family for generations.

And Laurel. Kevin shook his head. She'd wanted exactly what she had today: a husband to love and cherish, a child of her own; she'd just gone about obtaining them in a very unorthodox way. But no one could deny how much they loved each other. And that love would last until the end of their lives, no matter what the future held. Kevin was willing to bet his last dime on it.

"At least he doesn't have your nose." Kevin glanced at Seth's commanding hawklike profile and a grin turned up the corners of his mouth, but he found he couldn't meet his brother-in-law's probing steel-blue gaze when he turned his head. The sharp glare of light from the lamp above Laurel's bed stabbed into his eyes and he had to look away. Kevin turned on his heel and walked across the small, cozily decorated room to stare out at the rainy midsummer morning without another word.

Behind his back Seth and Laurel exchanged worried glances. Laurel handed their sleeping child to her husband. Seth took his son in strong competent hands and transferred him to the transparent plastic bassinet near Laurel's bed. For a long contented moment he watched the baby sleep, then turned to help his wife off the high bed.

Kevin could hear Laurel's slow movements as she paused to tuck a corner of the blanket more closely around her son. The silence stretched around them, comforting and familiar, strained only by the barricades he was building around himself. Outside in the hallway, the sounds of a busy county hospital could be heard, but they didn't really intrude on their solitude.

"Have you decided on a name?" Kevin asked, still looking out over the wooded hospital grounds toward acres of half-grown, pale green corn and soybeans and the dark golden stubble of newly harvested wheat fields. Outlines and colors were softened and blurred by the misty rain like an impressionist painting. Except that Kevin knew it would look the same to him, dull and unfocused, even if the sun were shining high and bright in the sky.

"Samuel Kevin," Laurel said, as Seth's strong arms came around her and held her close. She leaned back against the comforting wall of his chest and felt him kiss the top of her head ever so lightly, telling her without words that he was there for her, now and always. Just as Kevin had been there for her when they were growing up, the handsome successful older brother of every young girl's dreams; just as he'd been there for her last winter when she was so undecided about Seth and the baby and risking her heart at love again. She wanted to be there for her brother now, but he wouldn't let her come close enough. Stubborn, stubborn man, she thought, then smiled a little to herself, because they were so very much alike in that respect.

"I like that." A twist of a smile curved his mouth as Kevin recalled a conversation he'd had with their cousin Elinor Mieneke the winter before. He'd boasted then that Seth and Laurel would probably name their firstborn son after him in gratitude for his successful matchmaking. His prediction had come true, and he felt honored and touched. "It's a good strong name."

"It was Great-grandpa Sauder's name," Laurel reminded him. "And Seth's mother's uncle was named Samuel, too."

"Elinor will be pleased." Their favorite cousin, high-school classmate to both Seth and Kevin, had a teenage son who was also called Samuel. The silence grew heavy again. A flicker of movement caught Kevin's eye as he continued to stare out the window, but he couldn't make out the source. It might have been a robin or a bluejay or even a curious squirrel. In another time and place he would have grabbed a high-powered lens for his camera and zeroed in on the telltale flutter of leaves, maybe even getting a shot he could use in his next book. But no longer. He couldn't even be sure what he was looking at from this distance—from any distance, he added to himself in silent disgust. The equipment he depended on most, his eyes, had betrayed him. Traumatic cataract. Six weeks ago he'd never even heard the words; today he was an expert on the subject of the star-shaped rupture and clouding of the lens of the eye.

"We asked Elinor to be godmother last night." Laurel's voice was unusually hesitant. Seth tightened his arms around her. She knew that Kevin was thinking about the deterioration of his vision caused by the injury to his eye again; that was why he was so distant and reserved.

Laurel's heart ached to be able to undo the damage, ease the pain, but she could not. Kevin's whole life was his photography. What would he do without it?

"We're asking you to be the baby's godfather," Seth added with quiet pride.

Kevin still didn't say anything. Laurel moved out of the circle of Seth's arms, taking a step toward her brother but not coming close enough to reach out and touch him, the rigid set of his shoulders, his air of having cut himself off, holding her back. She glanced over her shoulder at her husband, the expression in her brown eyes hurt and confused.

"Don't you want to be his godfather, Kev?" Laurel wished she didn't sound so emotional, so near to tears. Having a baby, she'd discovered, was a major shock to the system. "We don't want to put you under an obligation you don't feel able to accept."

Kevin spun to face her, dark blond brows pulled together in a scowl above his green eyes. "I'm sorry, sis," he said, his voice harsh and ragged with suppressed emotion. "I'm behaving like an ass." He was ashamed of himself, of dwelling on his own dark thoughts and fears instead of sharing in the happiness of the two people he loved most in the world. "Of course I want to be his godfather. Just try and stop me."

He smiled, and the sharp rugged lines of his face smoothed out, making him look less like an angry blond giant and more like the easygoing, fun-loving brother she adored. Laurel threw her arms around him, burying her

face against the soft cotton weave of the hospital gown.
Seth extended his hand, and Kevin loosened his hold on his
sister long enough to grasp hands with his friend. "I'll do
my best by him." Their eyes met and held over Laurel's
head. Seth nodded, satisfied.

"I know you will."

Laurel sniffed once and smiled up at her brother, who
towered almost a foot above the top of her head. "He's
going to grow up to be a famous wildlife photographer just
like his uncle." Her voice cracked a little on the last words,
but she didn't let herself cry. Kevin must have been to see
the eye specialist again today, she thought. Apprehension
made her heartbeat fast and uneven.

"That is, if we can chain you down in Bartlow long
enough for you to give the kid some pointers now and
then." Seth's words were facetious, but he was watching
Kevin as closely as his sister.

"You won't have much trouble finding me, or chaining
me down." Kevin's tone was bitter and he couldn't do
anything about it. "Dr. Marsden's just grounded me."

"Grounded you? I don't understand." Laurel spoke
only to give Kevin an opening to continue. She was very
much afraid she knew exactly what he was trying to say.

"I'm not going anywhere for a long time. Certainly not
to Hudson Bay or anywhere else in the subarctic to start
work on the polar-bear migration shots for my new book."
Kevin held Laurel a little away from him, her hands
clasped between his strong palms. "She's heard from the
other specialists. The guy at the Cleveland Clinic and the
German ophthalmologist she sent me up to the medical
college to see."

"Kevin, is your vision getting worse?" Laurel didn't
want to hear the answer, didn't want to think of what
might lie in store for him. What would he do if he couldn't

continue the career in wildlife photography that had made him famous, and, more to the point, was the most important thing in his life?

"No—" he shook his head sadly "—but it's not getting any better. The doctors all concur. Surgery isn't indicated as yet. The vision in my right eye isn't compromised by the injury."

"That's a great deal to be thankful for." Laurel didn't feel as certain as she sounded.

Kevin shook his head in impotent rage. "And the vision in my left eye is as good as it might be after removing the damaged lens. The surgery is the same as they'd use on an elderly person with ordinary cataracts, except I have an irregularity in the shape of my eye and a lens transplant probably won't work. They say: 'for the foreseeable future, the loss of acuity and clarity of vision doesn't outweigh the surgical risk.' How the hell do they know if walking around half-blind is worth the risk of being able to see enough to use my camera again? They don't earn their living taking pictures. I do."

He dropped Laurel's hands and spun away, resting both arms on the smooth curved edge of the baby's bassinet, watching his nephew sleep with an infant's total concentration. He tried to ignore the dullness of his vision, the stabbing pain behind his eyes that was due almost solely, Dr. Marsden said, to his struggle to focus with his damaged and dominant left eye. "God, all this trouble because I got smacked in the face with a tree branch. I wouldn't even have remembered doing it except that's how that special new lens of mine got broken last fall."

Kevin looked up. Laurel was watching him with a frown between her eyes. Seth had stuck his hands in his pockets and was staring down at his shoes. Maybe, Kevin thought, he should ask his brother-in-law how you went about changing your life one hundred and eighty degrees; going from a glamorous, dangerous career as a Presidential Secret Service agent to the simplicity and never-ending hard work of life on a farm in Ohio.

What was he going to do with the rest of his life if he couldn't make his way to the ends of the earth, capture on film all the strange and marvelous wild creatures of the world, make people aware of the threats of extinction? He had a sudden mental vision of himself, middle-aged and bad tempered, holed up in a musty store on Main Street, taking silver-wedding-anniversary pictures.

"Listen, sis, I have to get home." A feeling of claustrophobia, almost of panic, beat inside him, rising to his throat, making his breath come short and shallow. "I have to get home." In reality he had to get away somewhere, anywhere. Suddenly the small cheery room that smelled of powder and babies and slightly of hospital antiseptic seemed to be closing in around him. "Mom and Dad will be worrying about me. It isn't supposed to be raining much longer, and driving in strong sunlight, even with sunglasses, is something Dr. Marsden doesn't recommend. At least not until I get used to the haziness and adjust to it."

"Kevin..." Laurel didn't finish what she started to say. Kevin had pulled away from her again, shut himself inside with his own pain and uncertainty. She didn't know yet how to help him. "We'll see you tomorrow? It's really awfully boring here without company."

"Sure, sis." Kevin gave her a quick absent peck on the cheek. "He really is a great-looking kid." He turned to face his brother-in-law.

"Take care." Seth was watching him closely. He knew, obviously, something of what was going through his mind.

"I will." Kevin slapped his friend on the shoulder and left the room.

"I'm worried about him, Seth," Laurel confessed, seeking the safe haven of her husband's strong arms.

"He'll be all right." Seth's voice was wonderfully confident. Laurel relaxed in his arms, unable to see the worried frown between his dark arching brows. "He'll come to terms with this thing. He's still the same old Kevin, his head in the clouds and his feet planted firmly on the ground."

Laurel lifted her delicate stubborn chin to search her husband's blue eyes. All signs of uncertainty were wiped clean from Seth's rugged features when he smiled down at his wife. "He'll be all right."

"I know," Laurel said, smiling through a mist of tears. "I know."

Chapter Two

A beat-up, midsize blue Chevy hardtop with Ohio plates was parked in the graveled space beside the small two-bedroom cottage she sometimes rented to tourists. Michigan State Conservation Officer Lisa Emery, drove by slowly, noting the make and model, committing the license number to memory without even being conscious of what she was doing. A single light was burning through the sheer white curtains of the main room of the cabin, but no fishing gear, hiking equipment, children's water toys or even an ice cooler was leaning against the porch railing beside the back door. Unusual, if the new tenant were a family and planning to stay in the cabin for a week or ten days; not unusual, if it were a couple or single person stopping over for only a night or two.

Lisa gave the cabin one last considering look, double-checked the license plate and drove along the shore of the lake for another hundred yards to her own driveway. She got out of her mud-spattered patrol car and rubbed the tight aching muscles in the small of her back. The lake beyond the grassy clearing where her two-story log home was situated was still and smooth as a pewter mirror; the last dull grays of a rainy twilight fading from its surface into the thick velvety black of a north-country summer night.

Lisa slapped at a mosquito singing past her ear and headed across the sparse grass toward the house.

The steep-roofed, two-story structure, built entirely of local cedar faced west, and the beauty of the sunset over the lake was one of the things Lisa liked best about living there. Except that tonight there was no sunset; only the promise of more rain to come. Rainy days always seemed to bring out the worst in the trout fishermen trying their luck in the cold, fast-moving streams in the rugged countryside around Marquette, which was her principal area of supervision. And today had been no exception. She didn't know why they acted the way they did in this kind of weather, but what she did know was that she'd been up since six chasing down fishermen to check their licenses and make sure they were properly issued and carried a valid trout stamp.

She'd talked to dozens of impatient, sometimes uncooperative anglers, ticketed three for keeping undersized fish and lost two more violators, probably unlicensed, when they were able to outrun her Dodge sedan in a four-wheel-drive Jeep that was so muddy she couldn't even make out the license plate.

In the movies or on television, Lisa had no doubt she would have whipped out her trusty service revolver and put a round in one of their back tires, bringing the perpetrators to a standstill and triumphantly making an arrest. In reality, she'd done no such thing. She'd punched the steering wheel with a small but strong fist, radioed in the best description she could give to the Marquette post of the Michigan Highway Patrol and watched the Jeep disappear down a graveled country road in a cloud of dust that even a day of fairly steady rain couldn't lay. Working alone, thirty miles from any kind of backup, on roads that were for the most part only faint ghosts of the heavily used logging trails they'd been seventy-five years earlier, you simply did not make that kind of grandstand play. Instead she'd gone back to work, trudging through miles of alder thickets and peat bogs for another eight hours.

Lisa caught a glimpse of the light from the cottage through the trees that screened her home from the smaller building. Her strongly arched cinnamon-brown eyebrows came together in a frown, one that also thinned and stiffened the generous curve of her mouth. She was dirty and wet and tired to the bone. She had all her regular paperwork to take care of, not to mention writing up her report on the violators who had given her the slip. The last thing she wanted to deal with was a stranger, or strangers, taking up residence in her cottage.

"Brad. Katie. I'm home." Lisa stopped just inside the back door, stepping into the utility room to unlace and pull off her high-topped hiking boots. She frowned down at the muddy legs of her pine-green, standard-issue fatigues. Filthy. She'd have to put them to soak before she went to bed. Her sneakers were lying beside the washer. She put them on, not bothering to tie the laces, and walked through the kitchen into the high-ceilinged, cedar-paneled living room. Her sixteen-year-old sister, Katherine, was nowhere to be seen, probably shut away in her bedroom listening to Bon Jovi tapes. Her brother, Brad, almost nineteen, was parked in front of the TV watching a Detroit Tigers baseball game. He loved baseball and followed the Tigers avidly.

"Hey, can't you tear yourself away from the game long enough to say hello to your sister?" she complained goodnaturedly, but with the authority of her seven extra years. "What's the score?"

"Hi, Lisa," Brad answered obediently, waving a negligent hand over his shoulder. "It's tied in the bottom of the eighth."

"What's the score?" Lisa repeated her question patiently as she scooped up a handful of popcorn from the coffee table in front of the couch. Popping corn was one of Brad's latest achievements. He made a batch every evening he was home and would, Lisa knew, until he learned a new culinary skill to replace it with. She wondered if he was ready to try mastering the recipe for pizza dough?

"Nothing, nothing," Brad replied with a cherubic look on his round face and a decidedly wicked gleam in his tilted brown eyes.

"That's a scoreless game, not a tie game," Lisa explained as she had before, repetition being the easiest way for Brad to remember abstract concepts.

"Both teams have nothing." He made a circle with his thumb and index finger to emphasize his point. "That's the same score. That makes it a tie game." He grinned at her just as he always did when he defended his reasoning in a manner she couldn't readily dispute.

"You win, little brother." Lisa smiled back. He was so dear to her and he tried so hard. She'd made the right decision three years ago when she'd gained their mother's permission to bring Brad home from the special school he'd been attending in Ann Arbor. Brad suffered from Down syndrome, and while he'd benefited a great deal from intensive speech therapy and the language-skills training he'd received in the Lower Peninsula school, he'd been lonely and frightened so far from everyone he knew and loved.

It hadn't been so bad when Lisa was attending junior college nearby and her mother, stepfather and Katie had been living in Jackson and could visit often. But after Mike

Whitson's company transferred him to Florida and Lisa
was hired by the state and left to begin on-the-job training
as a conservation officer, Brad was very much alone.

When Lisa was permanently assigned to the Marquette
district in the central Upper Peninsula where they'd all
grown up, Brad moved with her into their grandfather's
home, still in the family fifteen years after his death. Eight
months later, Katie finished her last year in junior high
and, disenchanted with central Florida's scorching summers and damp cool winters, begged to be allowed to return to Michigan, also. So, at the very young age of
twenty-three, Lisa found herself both mother and father
to her teenage brother and sister.

Lisa knew it had been especially hard for her mother to
give up her youngest child, as well as deal with the guilt
about leaving Brad and Lisa behind. But Jessica Emery
Whitson had never coped well with conflicting loyalties
and obligations. She was very much in love with her second husband. She wanted to be with him more than she
wanted to be with her children. It was as simple as that.
Lisa didn't hold it against her.

Jessica had been married too young, a teenager still,
when Lisa was born. She'd worked hard all her life and
suffered many disappointments. She deserved the new
happiness she'd found with Lisa's stepfather. Lisa loved
her mother, but she was honest enough to admit that in
some ways it was easier for all of them without Jessica
nearby.

Her mother had never reconciled herself to Brad's
handicap or the fact that he would never be able to live
entirely on his own. When Lisa's father was killed in a
hunting accident shortly after Katie's birth, Jessica had
distanced herself from Brad and his problems even more.
And to a certain degree her withdrawal had extended to

Lisa and Katie. She contributed what financial help she could, called often and sent quirky and unexpected presents whenever the spirit moved her, as well as for birthdays and Christmas. Yet she seldom ventured beyond that surface involvement in their lives, content to leave Lisa in charge.

The responsibility was frightening sometimes, difficult and challenging always, but Lisa wouldn't have traded her life for anyone else's in the world. And if at times she was lonely and tired and longed for someone to share the long cold winter nights with, and knew that she probably never would have that someone... Well, no one had ever said that life was fair.

"Hey, Lisa, quit daydreaming." Brad had left his favorite chair near the TV and stood in front of her, looking perplexed. He topped her five feet, six inches by several more, but he'd stopped growing in the past year and a half. He was wearing a bright red-and-blue plaid shirt he'd picked out for himself in the Sears catalog, and a pair of running shoes that had definitely seen better days. She'd have to drive him into Marquette on her next day off and get him a new pair. There went the "incidentals" budget for the month.

"I'm not daydreaming. I was thinking you need a new pair of shoes."

"Yep, these are pretty bad," Brad agreed, looking down at his feet. "But that's not what I want to talk to you about. I rented the cottage." He walked over to her desk beneath the casement window next to the fireplace and pulled out an envelope carefully lettered in his laborious handwriting. "He's a real neat guy. Katie says so, too. He wants to stay a week. He wrote me a check. Is it for the right amount?" He looked anxious and, as usual when upset, began to run his words together.

"Slow down," Lisa soothed him with a smile. She tore open the envelope, a frown chasing away the smile as she looked down at the document.

"Is it okay?"

"It's made out for the correct amount."

"Good. I thought I remembered right." Brad was proud of his memory for numbers. "Katie took him some sheets and towels and a blanket. I started the fire," he announced, his attention wandering from the subject at hand. "It's a good one," he boasted, indicating the roaring fire in the floor-to-ceiling stone fireplace that dominated an entire wall of the room.

"Feels great. It's going to be cold tonight." Lisa studied the check in her hand. It was a standard bank check, drawn on an Ohio bank—someplace called Bartlow. She'd never heard of it, but that didn't signify anything. The name, Kevin Sauder, and the address, 635 West Maple Street, were filled in by hand. There was no phone number, social-security number or driver's license registration listed. The signature was a bold strong slash across the bottom, a decided contrast to the printing at the top, which sloped drunkenly toward the center of the check.

"I think I'd better go introduce myself to Mr. Sauder before it gets any later." Lisa sat down at her desk and bent to tie the laces on her sneakers.

"I'll go with you, Lisa," Katherine Lenore Emery volunteered, coming out of her bedroom in time to hear her sister's last statement. "He's an absolute hunk. We are talking major shoulders here." Katie held up her hands, spreading them to an improbably wide distance. Lisa gave her baby sister a disbelieving irritated look. "I mean it," Katie stated with a great deal of emphasis. "He's tall—" Katie was five eight and height was a top priority when considering which boys to date "—real tall. Six three or four, at least. And blond. His hair's all streaked like he's been out in the sun a lot." She tilted her head, cinnamon-red curls the exact color of Lisa's bouncing on her shoulders, her hazel eyes taking on a dreamy, faraway look. "It's a little long for my tastes, but it curls around his ears and at the back of his neck. And his eyes." She flopped down on the couch as if her legs would no longer support her. "Lisa, you will positively die for those eyes. Emerald. There's no other word to describe them."

"Green will do nicely," Lisa said dryly, running her fingers through her own less artfully styled curls.

"Hmm, maybe jade would be better." Katie sighed and rolled her eyes heavenward.

"Geez." Brad looked disgusted, turning back to the ball game when a roar from the crowd signaled an important play.

"That's exactly what I say." Lisa pointed her finger at Katherine. "You stay here."

"Lisa, men like that don't come along every day of the week." Katie was on the verge of pouting.

"Stay here." Lisa used her most authoritative tone.

"I'll take him breakfast in the morning." Katie looked very pleased with her new strategy.

"You'll do no such thing." Lisa was flustered. This might be serious; usually Katie couldn't be pried out of bed before ten-thirty on lazy summer mornings.

"He doesn't have anything to eat. I asked." Katie's blue-shadowed eyes were shining with an excitement and new awareness of the opposite sex that Lisa had been noticing more and more often lately. Katie was growing up, becoming interested in boys—and now it seemed, grown men. Lisa wasn't quite sure how to handle it.

"No food? What about his luggage?" She chose to ignore the disturbing hint of emerging sensuality in Katie's speech and concentrate on the matter at hand.

Katie shrugged. "He didn't have much luggage. Just cameras."

"Lots of them," Brad interjected from across the room.

Lisa picked up the envelope that held the stranger's check. Holding it between her thumb and forefinger, she tapped it against her palm.

"Lisa, you aren't going to send him away?" Katie's voice rose almost to a wail. Brad looked over the back of his chair, his round face screwed into a frown.

"Should I have told him no? Katie was still at softball practice and he seemed like an okay guy..." Brad ran his tongue across his lips the way he did when he was nervous or upset. Lisa noted the telltale sign of anxiety and automatically gauged her reply accordingly.

"No, you handled it just right. I'm not going to send him away unless there's a good reason." She didn't mention her unease at seeing the wobbly handwriting on Kevin Sauder's check. What if the stranger in the cabin was a drunk, or on drugs? And why didn't he have any luggage? Even if this Bartlow was in the northern part of Ohio, it was still more than five hundred miles away. No one undertook that kind of trip without a good reason. If he didn't have an adequate explanation she was going to send him packing. It was only twenty-five miles to Marquette. He could find a room for the night there. "If he checks out okay, I'll let him stay. We haven't had a tenant since the Fourth. We can use the extra money."

"Amen to that," Katie replied with happy irreverence. "Anyway, once you see him you'll let him stay—no questions asked." She pretended to study a chip in her bright pink nail polish. Her expression was partially hidden by her hair, but her tone was smugly certain.

"Good Lord, Kate." Lisa let the old-fashioned, wooden screen door bang shut on the rest of her sentence. Had she been that sublimely boy crazy at sixteen? A sad little smile curved the corners of her mouth. She was certain she had not.

Lisa walked down the dark sandy path that connected the main house to the cottage, her footsteps firm. She played the beam of her flashlight ahead of her, on the lookout for roots and rocks that lay in wait to trip the unwary traveler. Overhead, giant fir trees leaned toward each other so that their branches almost touched. The spicy tang of crushed needles was heavy on the wet night air. It had started to rain again, but fitfully, only an occasional drop or two penetrating the overhanging canopy of branches. Despite the past two days of cloudy, rainy weather, the summer had been unusually dry, and the threat of fire in the enormous Hiawatha National Forest to the south and east of their small lake was an ever-present danger.

She'd have to make absolutely certain that the man in the cabin was aware of the tinder-dry conditions and that, under no circumstances, would she permit any kind of open fire on her property. If he expected to sit on the beach and roast hot dogs and toast marshmallows all week, he was going to be sorely disappointed—at least until it rained a lot harder than it was doing at the moment.

Lisa took her sense of resolve with her right to the back door. She flicked off the flashlight and clipped it onto her wide leather belt. She knocked firmly and then, out of habit, stepped off to the side. Conservation officers dealt with more armed suspects than any other branch of law enforcement. Statistics showed that in the course of her duties she was five times more likely to be assaulted with a deadly weapon than any other type of law officer. With those odds it made good sense to take the little extra precautions that might someday save her life.

The main door opened and the porch light came on. Lisa blinked in the glare. The man on the other side of the screen door seemed to be far more disoriented by the sudden brightness than she was. He put his hand up to shade his eyes and swore softly, vehemently, under his breath.

"Mr. Sauder," he heard a woman's voice begin without preamble, "I'm Lisa Emery. I own this cabin and I'd like to know what you're doing here." The female figure standing on the porch seemed to be wearing some kind of uniform, but Kevin couldn't be sure. "Mr. Sauder, did you hear what I said?" Her voice was low and even and surprisingly authoritative, yet still unmistakably feminine and, to Kevin, very appealing: light and musical, but with a lot of character.

"I heard you." Kevin lowered his hand, but beyond the fact that the person outside the door was female, all other details were lost in a rainbow-edged blur.

Did she have red hair, or was that a trick of his newly untrustworthy eyes? He couldn't be sure and the uncertainty was infuriating. If she'd only move out of the half shadows, the contrast between light and dark wouldn't be so acute. He'd be able to make out details of her face and figure with a lot less difficulty. For all his thirty-five years he'd taken his excellent vision for granted; now that it was compromised, the frustration he felt was so great he sometimes wanted to put his fist through the nearest wall.

"I'd like to know what you're doing here." Lisa made the statement an order, thinly veiled as a request. "My brother and sister said you have no luggage, no supplies. Only a great deal of camera equipment." He was very tall, as Katie had said, and he did have broad shoulders. Kevin

Sauder, if that indeed was his name, was a very good-looking man. No wonder her baby sister had been impressed.

His face was ruggedly handsome, his chin square and strongly angled. He had high cheekbones and a nose that was neither too large nor too small for the rest of his face. His hair was blond with a slight curl at the edges. He was casually dressed in a brown cotton shirt and jeans. At the moment, he was also barefoot. It was too dark to see the exact shade of the green eyes that Katie had found so devastating, but Lisa was beginning to belive her sister was right about them, too.

"I have a great deal of camera equipment because I'm a photographer." *Or at least I used to be,* Kevin added silently to himself with a bitterness he seldom let creep into his speech.

"That doesn't answer my question, Mr. Sauder." He didn't sound drunk, Lisa decided. She couldn't smell liquor on his breath or clothing. The wire screening separating them made it impossible for her to detect any subtle visual clues that might reveal if he were indulging in any illegal recreational drugs.

"No, I guess it doesn't," Kevin conceded. The woman was tenacious, he'd give her that. Was she wearing a gun on the wide leather belt at her waist? Again it was hard to tell in the fuzzy glow that surrounded her figure. Even though the cataract affected only his left eye, the cloudy haze it produced seemed to fill his entire field of vision at times.

"Mr. Sauder." He was stalling and she didn't know why. Lisa's right hand had been resting casually on the butt of her service revolver. For a moment she considered freeing it from the holster guard. His next words changed her mind.

"Why don't you come in out of the rain and the kami-
kaze mosquito barrage." If he weren't so tired and if he
didn't have such a blazing headache, he might find this
single-minded interrogation an enjoyable challenge.
"Would you like to see some ID?" He let a small trace of
his growing amusement creep into his words, but she didn't
rise to the bait. He could feel her eyes on him, studying,
appraising. He wished he'd combed his hair and tucked his
shirttail into his jeans before coming to the door. Kevin
opened the screen and stepped back, beckoning her inside. He tried to remember her name. Lisa? Was that how
she'd introduced herself? He wished he hadn't taken that
second pain pill on an empty stomach. It made him feel
light-headed and slow-witted. "I have my driver's license
and credit cards right here."

She stepped inside, swept the kitchen with a quick, en-
compassing glance. She held out her hand for the driver's
license he fumbled to produce from his back pocket.
Lisa—he decided that was indeed her first name—took it
without a word. She studied the plastic-covered rectangle
intently for a few moments. The picture in the right-hand
corner was almost three years old and his hair had been a
lot shorter then; but he didn't think he'd changed enough
to make her even more suspicious of him than she obviously already was.

"Do you want to see my library card, too?" She looked
up from her appraisal of his driver's license. She almost
smiled; then apparently thought better of it. Kevin found
himself a little disappointed.

"That won't be necessary." Lisa relaxed slightly. He was
studying her just as intently as she was studying him. She
wondered briefly what he saw—an ordinary-looking
woman in her mid-twenties, with red-brown hair, hazel
eyes that were more gold than brown and a passable fig-

ure; nothing more, nothing less. Was he disappointed? Lisa was surprised that the purely feminine thought even crossed her mind. She handed back his license in a jerky movement. "Thank you."

Kevin nodded and returned his billfold to his back pocket. "You're a cop?" He leaned his hips negligently against the scrubbed wooden table that sat solidly in the middle of the kitchen floor. The overhead fluorescent fixture didn't bother his eyes nearly as much as the porch light had. He could see details of her face and figure much more clearly.

Her appearance didn't quite match up to her voice. Lisa Emery wasn't a beautiful woman; her eyes were too big, her mouth too generous, and her chin could only be described as determined. In some ways, her wholesome prettiness reminded him of his sister, Laurel. Lisa Emery was taller than his petite sibling, her figure was less rounded, more angular and athletic. She also seemed very young to be some kind of duly appointed officer of the law.

"I'm a conservation officer," Lisa clarified.

Kevin started to chuckle. He couldn't help himself. He was being given the third degree by an employee of the Michigan Department of Natural Resources. "You're a game warden?"

"That is correct." Her face remained serious, her tone businesslike. "Your papers seem to be in order, but I still want to know, Mr.—"

Kevin's amusement faded away, and he cut her off abruptly. "Of course they're in order. And don't call me Mr. Sauder again. My name's Kevin." She was beginning to get under his skin with her questions about his identity and his reasons for being in this godforsaken part of the world.

She set her chin stubbornly and looked him straight in the eye. "Look. You still haven't answered my question. Why are you here? Is this a vacation? A fishing trip?" She looked pointedly around the empty kitchen, then past him to the couch in the small main room of the cottage where he'd piled all his camera equipment. "Or are you just passing through?"

"I gave your brother a week's rent in advance."

She'd made him angry again. For a split second Lisa let herself wish he'd smile at her instead of frowning as he was, then pushed the thought aside. "My brother is very trusting. Surely you noticed...he's handicapped." Sometimes, even after all these years, Lisa found it difficult to say the words aloud. She accepted Brad the way he was. She loved him for both his weaknesses and strengths, but with strangers, she felt awkward and defensive when speaking of him.

"Of course I noticed." The angry frown left Kevin Sauder's face. It was replaced by one of understanding and interest, but interest that held none of the morbid curiosity many people showed about Brad's condition. "He has Down's syndrome, doesn't he?"

"Down syndrome is the proper term, now," Lisa corrected automatically. An English doctor, Langdon Down, had been the first to describe the symptoms over a hundred years ago. But that didn't give him rights to the affliction.

"Down syndrome," Kevin repeated obediently. He wanted to smile again but didn't. Did she champion all her causes with such intensity? "Your brother did very well. He showed me where the fuse box is, how to operate the valve for the hot-water heater and the propane tank. How to light the pilot on the stove and the heater in the living room. He told me which boat I could use and that a motor would cost me fifty dollars a week more—"

"All right, all right." Lisa held up a hand in surrender. She couldn't help smiling at the tone of his voice, and even more at her satisfaction that Brad had absorbed so much of her standard lecture to the tenants. "He covered all the important points, but—"

"I'll take the motor, by the way," Kevin interrupted.

"What?" Lisa felt her mouth drop open and shut it with a snap.

"I'd like to rent the motor to do some fishing. Do you want me to write you another check right now?"

He was looking at her with a teasing challenge in his green eyes. Lisa felt her pulse rate jump and her breathing quicken. He was certainly persistent. Lisa smiled again and lifted her shoulders in surrender. "Tomorrow will be fine, but—"

"That still doesn't answer your question of why I'm here." Kevin Sauder leaned forward slightly so that Lisa had to tilt her head even further to see him clearly. Jade. His eyes held far too many silvery lights in their green depths to be described as emerald. He had sexy eyelashes, too, spiky and dark-tipped. His eyebrows were thick and slightly arched, his lips very kissable.

Lisa caught her breath and stepped back, bumping against the frame of the screen door. "Do you want me to go?" The question caught Lisa off guard.

"No..." She hesitated slightly. "I only want to know why you're here, three miles from the highway, twenty-five miles from town..."

"What if I tell you it's none of your business?" The teasing light was gone from his compelling gaze. There was a bleakness, an emptiness, deep within those green eyes that was very much at odds with the casual toughness Kevin Sauder chose to project to the world at large.

"I'd have to ask you to leave, then. I'm away a great deal of the time. I have my sister and brother to think of." She didn't know why she felt obliged to explain. "You don't have any luggage, or any fishing gear, even if you do want to rent a motor. You're certainly not the ordinary, run-of-the-mill tourist. Why are you here?" Lisa lifted her chin, unwilling to show any sympathetic response to the haunted look, the flicker of vulnerability she'd seen so briefly in his expression. Perhaps she spoke too sharply, too belligerently, because the warmth left his eyes and the hint of a smile that lurked at the corners of his well-shaped mouth disappeared.

Kevin was tired. He'd driven five hundred miles in thunderstorms and summer traffic on the interstate; followed caravans of lumbering campers over rain-slick, two-lane highways once he'd crossed the Mackinac Bridge into the Upper Peninsula; dodged skunks and porcupines and even a deer that decided to cross the pavement directly ahead of his car. His head hurt so badly he could hear, as well as feel, each drumbeat of pain. "I haven't any luggage or fishing gear, because sixteen hours ago I had no intention of coming to the north woods."

He wasn't certain himself why he'd turned north onto Interstate 75 after he left Laurel and Seth and the baby at the hospital. He'd only known he didn't want to go south, back to Bartlow and his loving, overprotective parents. And north was the direction he wanted to be traveling, all the way to Hudson Bay and on up into the Arctic to work on his new book. His stomach rumbled its own protest at being neglected, loudly and unmistakably, reminding him how rash and probably foolish he'd been. This woman's badgering was just about the last straw. "And I don't have any supplies because I couldn't drive the rest of the way into Marquette tonight to find a store."

Lisa couldn't back away from him any further without opening the door, but her hand returned to the butt of the revolver at her waist. Kevin found it incredible that she was questioning his integrity; she should know that he was so hungry he could eat a horse, and he'd just told her he couldn't even drive himself into town to get a burger, or find a camping store to buy a loaf of bread and a quart of milk. He was on the verge of becoming really angry with her, something he seldom allowed to happen with women.

He reached out one long arm and rested his palm flat against the doorjamb just about level with the top of her head. Lisa didn't flinch, just looked at him with her big golden eyes, alert to his every move, her gaze filled with apprehension and intelligence and deeper understanding—and with what Kevin was very much afraid might be a touch of pity. He backed away, stuck his hands into his pockets and put into words for the first time the reality he'd been trying to deny for so many endless days and sleepless nights.

"I have thousands of dollars worth of cameras because up until six weeks ago that's how I earned my living. I told you I was a photographer. Or, dammit, at least I used to be. Now I'm only a guy who happens to be losing his sight."

Chapter Three

Kevin lay on his back, arms folded behind his head, and stared at the pitch-black rectangle of the cabin ceiling. It was less frustrating than staring at the luminous dial of his watch as the hands crawled slowly around the face.

He closed his eyes. A shimmering negative image of the ceiling's shape appeared behind his eyelids, sparked with a whirl of colored lights. The dancing pricks of light made him dizzy. He opened his eyes and they disappeared, but so did any hope of falling asleep.

Was he losing his mind, as well as his eyesight? What other reason could there be for his having told Lisa Emery why he was here? He'd known about the cataract for almost two months, yet only Seth and Laurel, his parents, and his cousin Elinor were in his confidence. He hadn't felt compelled to confide in any other friends or relatives. Then why had he blurted out the truth to a total stranger like Lisa Emery?

He hadn't even told his publisher, although the contract for his fifth book was waiting for him to sign back home in Bartlow. In addition he was going to have to come up with a pretty damn good excuse for why he wasn't already on his way to Hudson Bay. The book on arctic and subarctic mammals was going to be—or would have been—the companion to the best-selling study of antarctic species he'd done three years earlier. He'd only been putting off the inevitable, refusing to admit he wasn't up to the trip, couldn't make the shots, by not canceling the project.

At least he'd wiggled his way out of the series of TV talk shows and radio interviews his publicist had planned to promote his South American rain-forest book due out for the Christmas rush. He'd leave that end of it up to Carrie Granger, his stay-at-home biologist partner. Carrie hated the fieldwork Kevin loved, but she knew her business; the text she composed to accompany his photographs added a dimension to his books that Kevin knew he'd never be able to achieve on his own.

He rolled onto his stomach and punched the hard pillow with his fist. He'd have to tell Carrie pretty soon. With a groan he flopped onto his side and stared at the wall instead of the ceiling. He owed his friend that much. She had to be given time to adjust to the fact that her major source of income, the money that allowed her to stay holed up in her research lab at Cornell, was fading into the mist just like his sight.

But what exactly was he going to say? "Hey Carrie, old girl, remember when I came home last fall to get that wide-angle telephoto lens fixed by the guy who made it for me a few years ago?" His voice echoed slightly in the empty cabin. "Well, I never told you how it got broken, did I?" Kevin shut his mouth with a snap. Now, on top of everything else, he was talking to himself.

It had seemed such a minor incident at the time. He wouldn't even have recalled it if his favorite lens hadn't been cracked by a broken branch, dislodged by a gust of wind, that struck him a glancing blow on the side of his face. Things like that happened when you were dangling from a harness in the canopy of the Brazilian rain forest a hundred feet above the ground. Hell, he hadn't even gotten a black eye out of the deal. Only a cracked one. Just like the camera lens—only a damn sight harder to fix.

Kevin gave up even pretending to sleep. It was close to morning anyway. His stomach rumbled loudly, the way it had been doing all night, unwilling to let him forget the only thing he'd eaten in the past eighteen hours was a Hershey bar and some stale peanut-butter cookies he'd found stashed in the glove compartment.

He swung his long legs over the side of the bed and swore as his bare feet made contact with the cold wooden floor. Gooseflesh popped up on his bare arms and legs. Even though it was the middle of July and sleeping in only his briefs was pretty common practice in most places, he was just a few miles south of Lake Superior and willing to bet the temperature wasn't more than ten or twelve degrees above freezing. Kevin stood up, walked into the living room and turned up the propane heater, then wandered into the kitchen for a glass of water in the hope it might fool his stomach into submission until dawn.

He had no business being here in the Upper Peninsula. Kevin watched the stream of silvery tap water run into the sink. He was running away from reality, and he hadn't even packed a razor or a change of clothes to do it with. He ought to go back to Bartlow, face the future. He could open a portrait studio on Main Street, take those silver-anniversary pictures, those family portraits. He was good with kids, he could coax babies into smiling for the camera. Posing newly engaged couples in front of murals of wooded glades and blossoming cherry trees didn't require any kind of superhuman effort, either. He could surely manage that kind of sedentary, hack photography even with one bad eye. Kevin set the water glass down on the metal drain board so hard the glass cracked. The prospect was no more acceptable today than it had been yesterday.

Kevin remained standing at the kitchen sink, staring out the small square window above it, watching as lights winked on in Lisa Emery's house. From this distance they looked like earthbound stars twinkling through the lacy branches of the tamarack that rimmed the lakeshore. The Emerys were early risers, it seemed. It wasn't quite six; dawn was just beginning to color the eastern sky in shades of rose and gray. The radio had predicted another overcast day for much of lower Michigan. Easy driving, if he wore his sunglasses and took his time.

Kevin made up his mind. He had to face the future sooner or later. It might as well be today. He'd shower and dress and head back home. But first he'd stop and tell Lisa Emery he was going. She deserved that much consideration after his display of bad manners last night. The ghost of a grin curved the corners of his mouth. Besides, this way she wouldn't have to wonder for the next three weeks if his check was going to bounce.

Of course, if he stopped to tell her he was leaving, she'd probably demand to know exactly why he was going. He'd tell her. She'd look at him with those intriguing golden-brown eyes and say nothing, but somehow he knew she would understand. And she would probably insist on returning his money.

Or most of it, at any rate.

His ghost of a smile turned into a full-fledged grin. He owed her something for the aggravation he'd caused her last night, and he intended to see she accepted payment.

Still grinning, Kevin headed for the miniscule bathroom beside the back door. He anticipated an argument about the debt he figured he owed her. And just now he couldn't think of a more enjoyable way to start the morning than by crossing swords with Lisa Emery.

LISA WAS ALMOST as surprised to see Katie coming out of her bedroom, dressed and smiling brightly at seven o'clock, as she was to see her younger sister awake at that hour of the morning at all.

"You're up early."

"Couldn't sleep." Katie shrugged narrow shoulders beneath her best mint-green cotton sweater. Lisa tilted her head and regarded her sister shrewdly.

"Big plans for today?"

Katie blushed. "Not particularly. Matt Swensen called last night before you got home. He's driving into Marquette around lunchtime. I need to get some things at K-Mart. Is it all right if I go with him?" Katie wasn't due to take driver's training until school started in the fall. She'd been saving her own money, and their mother had promised a loan to buy her a secondhand car, but Lisa didn't look forward to the added worry of having Katie driving. Yet, at the same time, she couldn't deny how much more convenient it would be to have another licensed driver in the family.

"I don't know why not, if you promise to be home early."

"Matt has to work at Gilson's Marina at six."

"Could you take Brad with you and help him pick out a new pair of shoes? Or is this a real, for sure, date?" Lisa smiled, but sadness and anxiety tugged at her heartstrings. Sooner or later she'd have to tell Katie the secret she'd kept hidden so long. Her baby sister was growing up. She wasn't a child any longer. Her increased interest in the opposite sex was proof of that.

Katie looked mutinous for a moment, then relented. "Sure. But can you give me an extra five dollars? Matt said something about taking in a movie. I don't want him to have to pay Brad's way, too."

"Then it is a real, for sure, date." Lisa's tone was light and teasing, but her amusement was bittersweet.

"I guess it is." Katie laughed and ran her fingers through her curly, shoulder-length brown hair, which caught and held the morning light in its auburn depths. "Hey, Brad." Katie raised her voice to carry into the kitchen where Brad was busy making breakfast as he did every morning before catching the bus to the sheltered workshop and school he attended in Marquette. Brad never slept in, not even now, during summer vacation. "Want to go to a movie?"

"Movie?" Brad's round face popped into sight around the edge of the kitchen doorway. "What are you doing up so early?"

"Never mind." Katie's tone was huffy. "Do you want to go with Matt and me or not?" She never treated her brother as special. Katie was responsible for a lot of the social skills Brad had mastered, because she always expected him to do his best, assuming he could do something until it proved too difficult. Then she would step in and coach and bully and encourage him, and more times than not he eventually mastered the task.

"What's playing?" Brad didn't like surprises. He planned his day methodically and liked to stick to it. But he loved movies and never missed a chance to go. In addition, he almost single-handedly supported the video-rental section of the general store. At least twice a week he rode his bike six miles there and back, along the store's unpaved gravel road to where it bisected the highway that ran along the shore of Lake Superior.

Katie made a face. "Some kind of Ninja-warrior thing, a new Harrison Ford movie—" Katie paused dramatically, leaving no doubt as to which film she intended to see "—and one of the old animated Disney flicks. *Cinderella*, I think."

"Disney. I like cartoons," Brad decided, and disappeared back into the kitchen where the sound of bacon frying in a skillet could be heard.

"Here's the money," Lisa said, pulling a slim leather billfold out of the back of her dark green uniform slacks.

"Thanks, Lisa." Katie shoved the bill into the pocket of her jeans. "Want a cup of coffee before you leave?"

"Dying for one." Lisa picked up the twelve-gauge automatic shotgun she carried in the trunk of her car to check it over one last time before placing it in its zippered case. She was still holding it in her hands when she looked up to see Kevin Sauder, hand upraised to knock, standing outside the door. She walked over to him, holding the shotgun cradled easily in the crook of her arm. "Why, hello."

If Lisa Emery was surprised to see him, she didn't look it. At least not as surprised as he was to see her in uniform, cradling a shotgun with easy familiarity. She looked very professional and businesslike with her hair pulled up on top of her head in a no-nonsense bun. But at the same time still very much a woman, as soft, wispy cinnamon-brown tendrils escaped to curl around her ears and the nape of her neck. The sage-green of her uniform shirt suited her golden skin and eyes, Kevin decided with the expert judgment of color and composition that was second nature to him now.

Yet it wasn't as a photographer, but as a man, that he noted how her dark green slacks hugged the curve of her hips and the long sweep of her legs; that the wide leather belt she'd been wearing the night before was once again cinched tightly around her slim waist; that the faint coral blush on her cheeks was natural and that it darkened becomingly as his gaze wandered over her face and figure.

"Won't you come in?" Lisa swallowed hard to get her voice under control when she heard it come out breathless and strained. She wasn't used to men looking at her that way, as though she were somebody interesting and exciting and even, possibly, desirable. When it did occasionally happen, it flustered her, made her nervous and tongue-tied. But with Kevin Sauder, it was different. She liked the warm touch of his jade-green eyes. She'd like to feel the strong touch of his hands on her skin even more.

Lisa pulled her bottom lip between her teeth and bit down hard. That kind of thinking got her nowhere. She took a deep breath and forced her too-vivid imaginings to the back of her mind. "You're up early this morning."

Kevin opened the screen door and stepped inside, ducking his head automatically, although the doorway was high enough to accommodate him. "Actually," he confessed, sounding more sheepish than he'd intended, "I'm not exactly up early. I . . ."

"Haven't been to bed yet . . . or at least to sleep," Lisa finished for him. She continued watching him without a hint of a smile, her golden-brown eyes warm and bright with interest. But deep within the honeyed depths, just as last night, Kevin could detect another emotion, a wariness, a hesitancy, that told him she found him attractive—and dangerous. The attraction he accepted as that fabulous chemistry between the sexes that made life a lot more exciting and enjoyable than it would be without it.

But why dangerous? He'd had his share of love affairs, pleasant interludes, some more intense and longer lasting than others. He liked women, they liked him, but few found him threatening or tried so hard to keep him at a distance. Lisa Emery was different.

"Let's just say I didn't get much sleep and leave it at that, okay?" Kevin rubbed his hand across the day-old stubble on his chin and immediately contradicted his words by continuing the discussion. "What gave me away? The beard?" Again he found himself listening to the sound of her voice more intently than her words, just as he had last night.

"The circles under your eyes." Lisa tilted her head in a gesture he already recognized as characteristic. "It was probably the quiet that kept you awake. Silence can be pretty unsettling for city people."

"It's pretty quiet where I come from, too," Kevin replied, dismissing her explanation with a wave of his hand. "Look, if this is too early for company I can come back later." He surprised himself with the suggestion. He wouldn't be back later; he was leaving, that's what he'd come to tell her. He was going back home, to face facts, face reality. He'd made up his mind, hadn't he? Unsettled by his conflicting thoughts, Kevin turned the statement into a joke by looking pointedly at the shotgun.

Lisa glanced down, confused, saw where his gaze was resting and laughed. She couldn't help it. Her unpredictable tenant was eyeing the weapon with speculation and exaggerated alarm. He hadn't been teasing a moment earlier, but he certainly was now. For a fleeting second she'd seen that same look of trapped, cornered bewilderment she'd noticed at their first meeting—the look that darkened his jade-green eyes with fury and frustration. She was certain of what she'd seen, but already, only a heartbeat later, the dark emotions were gone, replaced by a breezy self-assurance and sense of humor she found hard to resist.

"We're used to early hours around here," Lisa said, no more willing to acknowledge the unbidden link of understanding that seemed to have sprung up between them, as fragile and tenuous as a spider's web, than Kevin was. The inner pain he was wrestling with pulled at the strings of her heart, that part of her that wanted to love and protect and care for those around her. But the man himself? He called to a vastly different Lisa, the very feminine, adventurous, sensual core of her being that seldom was allowed the freedom to soar outside her most private and intimate dreams. Daydreams, and love dreams, had no part in her world. That was simply the way it was; the way it had to be. With an effort that was as much physical as mental, Lisa brought her mind back to matters at hand.

Kevin made it easy. "I suppose you know how to use that thing?"

Lisa bristled indignantly, just as he hoped she would, breaking the spell that seemed to hold them there together, in a small intimate space of their own while the rest of the world sped around them. He braced himself for her angry reply, but she was too quick for him. Her eyes blazed with golden fire, then softened as she caught and held his gaze once more.

"My skill is adequate, Mr. Sauder." She turned away before he could reply and zipped the shotgun into its case. That task accomplished, she returned to stand in front of him, her feet planted firmly on the wide-planked floor. "Did you come about renting the motor?"

"The motor?" Kevin found he was having a hard time getting his brain to function normally. Her scent was as evocative and intriguing as the rest of her—light, airy, like wildflowers in a meadow.

"The motor for the boat," Lisa explained, watching him carefully. "Last night you said you wanted to rent it for the week, remember?"

"I remember everything about last night." He surprised himself as much as Lisa by speaking the words. Immediately the soft curved line of her jaw hardened, her expression became guarded and remote. Kevin wanted to kick himself and wasn't altogether certain why. He only knew he'd much rather see her smile than frown.

"Perhaps you'd rather..." Lisa began, convinced she should offer to return Kevin Sauder's check and send him on his way before he destroyed any more of her hard-won serenity and peace of mind.

"I'm staying," Kevin said, as if reading her mind, "and I do want to rent the motor." He looked down at her from his imposing height, and the expression in his green eyes was definitely challenging. And exciting.

"I don't think that's a good idea." Once again Lisa let her words dwindle into silence as Kevin Sauder leaned closer.

"I'm staying." As quickly as that he made up his mind. The detested portrait studio on Main Street, and all the changes it would make in his life, could damn well wait another week or two. His parents knew he was safe. Later today he'd call and let them know of his exact whereabouts. He'd get in touch with his publisher and Carrie Granger. But not today. Today he was going to concentrate on getting to know Lisa Emery better.

Lisa's mouth tightened into a thin straight line. "What if I tell you I'm calling the sheriff's department to have you escorted off the property?"

Kevin was silent for a moment. He was sure she would carry out her threat if he pushed her too hard, but he wasn't about to let the situation get that far out of hand.

"I'd go peacefully." His stomach growled once again, loudly, despairingly. "I'm really too weak from hunger to be any kind of a threat." He smiled forlornly, hoping to look pathetic and contrite. He had a strong hunch that Lisa Emery was a sucker for stray kittens and puppies, and maybe even wayward photographers who turned up on her doorstep.

"I seriously doubt that." Lisa couldn't contain the smile that curled the corners of her mouth. She really was beginning to like this man. "All right. You can stay."

"Good." Kevin straightened to his full height, satisfied for the moment with the way things were going. "Now, could you give me directions to the nearest restaurant? I think I have just enough energy and gasoline to get that far." His stomach growled again, as if seconding the plan.

"Why don't you have breakfast with us?" The suggestion came not from Lisa but from the slender young girl standing in the kitchen doorway who resembled her so strongly. She smiled brilliantly in Kevin's direction, then turned her eyes to her sister. "There's plenty. Brad always fries more bacon than we can eat."

"Do not." Brad's face, with its tip-tilted eyes, appeared over Katie's shoulder. "I make eight slices. Three for you, three for me, and two for Lisa."

"Yes, but I'm on a diet. And so is Lisa," Katie replied with a hint of defiance in her voice, as though she expected her older sister to contradict her words. "So you see, Mr. Sauder, there's plenty."

Lisa turned slightly to give her sister a reproving glance, but good manners forced her to go along with the invitation. "Of course there's plenty, but I'm sure Mr. Sauder has plans of his own." She turned to face Kevin and found his eyes on her once again. "Gilson's Marina and General

Store is only three miles farther down the road. Right on
the highway. You can't miss it."

"Thank you," Kevin directed his words and a devastating smile at Katie. "But I'd love to stay for breakfast."

"Great. How do you take your coffee?" Katie turned
around, shooing Brad back into the kitchen ahead of her.

"Black," Kevin replied, but the doorway was already
empty. "I guess I'm staying for breakfast." He grinned.
Lisa frowned. "Come on," he coaxed, "I'm not that bad
to have around, really. My mother and sister think I'm a
great guy, actually." He was a little desperate. All of a
sudden, staying here on the shores of the small secluded
lake, away from everyone and everything he knew, seemed
very important. "Look, I apologize for the way I acted last
night."

"I don't know what to make of you," Lisa said frankly.
"Last night you said you were losing your sight. Forgive
me, but you don't seem to be having any difficulty with
your vision this morning."

"That's because the sun isn't shining," Kevin said
roughly. Try as he might, he couldn't keep the anger and
bitterness completely out of his voice. He'd asked for this
interrogation. He might as well get it out of the way.
"Have you ever heard of a traumatic cataract?"

"I've heard of cataracts, of course. Everybody has. But
a traumatic cataract, no." Lisa tilted her head once again,
the frown easing away to a look of perplexity.

"I got whacked on the side of the head with a tree
branch and broke the lens of my eye," Kevin said starkly.
His voice was as flat and hard as the expression on his face.
"You can't even see the damage without one of those
special light machines ophthalmologists use. But it's there,
all right. I can't see in bright light. I can't see in the dark.
I can't see to take photographs, and that's how I earn my

living. Or it used to be. Now I have to find some other way to make ends meet.''

"Isn't there some kind of surgery, medication, anything that can help?"

Kevin watched her face as first horror, then compassion was mirrored in her expressive features. "Eventually. Possibly. It's usually a fairly routine procedure, but my eye is slightly abnormal. I never even knew it before the accident. The doctors are very cautious.''

"You did get more than one opinion, didn't you?" Lisa couldn't think of anything else to say. How hard it must be for a man like Kevin Sauder to be faced with any kind of physical weakness, but to be threatened with the loss of sight? Lisa couldn't imagine how she would react to such a sentence.

"Three. All experts. They all say wait and see. At least three years. Maybe five. Maybe never. The improvement has to outweigh the risks.''

"I see." Lisa was silent for a moment, listening to the sounds of dishes being taken out of the cupboard, of silverware rattling in the drawer, the familiar sounds of Katie and Brad bickering in the kitchen, and suddenly she felt very lucky indeed. "You want to stay here and make some decisions about your life.''

"Yes." *And I also want to stay long enough to get to know you better, Lisa Emery.*

"You'll be needing supplies and extra clothes and toilet things," Lisa said, surrendering without a struggle. "Katie can tell you the best places to shop in Marquette. Gilson's doesn't carry clothes, or underwear—'' She broke off, color mounting in her cheeks. "Well, you know what I mean.''

Kevin laughed. "Sure. I'll get started for town as soon as the breakfast dishes are done. I don't have too much trouble driving when it's overcast like this. But I'd just as soon not be out on the highway if the sun comes out.''

Lisa responded to the statement that was easiest to answer. ''You don't have to help with the dishes.''

''Oh yes, I do.'' Kevin held up his hand to stop her protest. ''My mother was way ahead of her time when it came to raising boys and girls equally. My sister, Laurel, is one heck of a mechanic, and I can wash dishes, do laundry and set up an ironing board just as well as the next guy, that is, girl.''

''You are a wonder, aren't you?'' Lisa shook her head and gestured for him to follow her into the kitchen. The trouble was, she realized, she was only half kidding when she said that.

''Yes, ma'am, I am.'' Kevin grinned down at the straight back and softly rounded fanny of the stubborn, intriguing woman before him.

He had a lot to think about in the next few days. A lot of decisions to make, important decisions that were going to affect the entire course of his life from this point forward. But now, this morning, he found he was far more interested in Lisa Emery and getting to know her better— much better. She was lively and intelligent, interesting to be around. One moment she was defensive and wary, obstinately independent and self-reliant, the next moment as soft and enchanting as a meadow flower.

For the first time in months, Kevin found himself interested in something else, someone else other than his own problems. He wasn't about to question the reason. Or analyze too closely the deeper implications of his attraction to this woman. He only knew he was far more inclined to concentrate on Lisa Emery than he was to dwell on his own uncertain future.

Chapter Four

"I knew he was something special," Katie announced, gliding across the room. She dropped into an overstuffed armchair near the fireplace with a gusty sigh.

"I've always liked Matt myself." Lisa kept her expression noncommittal. She continued to study the report she'd been working on when Katie entered the room, but she could feel the intensity of the dark look the teenager bestowed on her.

They both knew the youngest Emery wasn't speaking of Matt Swensen.

"Lisa, don't be dense." Katie let three plastic bags, filled with clothing and sundries, slide to the floor with a noisy rustle as she leaned back in the worn, brown tweed chair. "I'm referring to Kevin Sauder."

Lisa laid down her pen. Her brother and sister had returned from their trip to Marquette only a few minutes after Lisa herself had arrived home to catch up on some of the endless paperwork that the Department of Natural Resources and the state and federal governments demanded of her. Brad had gone straight to his bedroom with the latest issues of his favorite comics and his new running shoes, so the sisters were alone in the big main room of the house.

Turning in her seat to face Katie, Lisa asked, "Did you see his picture on the bulletin board at the post office?"

"Of course not." The teenager shot Lisa a disgusted look. "Nobody with eyes like that could be a criminal."

Lisa let that one pass. She wasn't altogether certain it wasn't a crime for any mortal man to possess eyes that particular shade of green.

"I just knew he wasn't your average, run-of-the-mill tourist." Katie sighed again, but her tone of voice was extremely self-satisfied.

"Okay." Lisa propped her hand on the desk and rested her chin on her knuckles. "How did you come across the solution to this particular secret of the universe?" She didn't even try to hide her smile. Katie wasn't about to allow her to get on with her work until she'd had her say. And Lisa was honest enough with herself to admit she wanted to hear what her sister had learned about Kevin Sauder as much as Katie wanted to divulge the information.

"We stopped at the mall after the show. Do you think he looks a little like Harrison Ford?" Katie asked, switching tracks so abruptly Lisa blinked in momentary confusion. Hazel eyes narrowed to dreamy slits as Katie considered the possibility in greater depth.

"Not really." Lisa's tone was repressive. She thought he was even better looking than Katie's film idol.

"Yes, he does. He's got that same kind of square jaw and those little laugh lines around his eyes."

Lisa interrupted her sister's rambling comparison of the two men. "Is that the only hard evidence you can produce to back up your theory that he's something out of the ordinary?"

Katie scowled across the room at Lisa's slender figure, haloed by the glare of sunlight. She laughed a bit sheepishly. "No, it's not. He's a photographer."

"He told me that." Lisa didn't say anything about the other more painful and private revelations Kevin Sauder had made about himself that morning.

Katie's tone was exasperated. She wasn't smiling any longer. "I mean he's famous. We saw this book at the B. Dalton store at the mall. It was one of those big fancy things full of pictures. It was about Antarctica. There were seals and penguins, glaciers and whales. Lisa—they were beautiful." She shook her head in admiration. "They were so real you felt you could almost reach out and touch each and every animal. And Lisa, that's not all. There were two other titles of his listed in the front. He must be rich, too. That book cost forty dollars," she added with what sounded very much like awe in her voice.

"Are you certain it was the same name?"

Katie nodded. "His picture was on the back cover. We all saw it. Brad recognized him, too."

"I see." Lisa's tone was thoughtful. It helped explain a lot of things, the flashes of rage and frustration she'd encountered in Kevin Sauder's jade-green eyes, the desperation and the fear he'd almost, but not quite, been able to hide when he told her about the injury to his eye.

"I wish I had enough money to buy the book. Then I could ask him to autograph it for me." Katie looked wistful.

"I'm sorry, honey. This month's budget is pretty well stretched to the limit."

"I know. I guess I could use some of the money I've saved for my car." A frown appeared between Katie's strongly arched brows. "But forty dollars is two weeks baby-sitting for Mrs. Crawley's three monsters. I don't suppose I could withdraw some money from my college fund . . . ?'' Her words trailed off into silence.

"No." Lisa answered automatically, without thinking. Katie and Brad received money each month, survivor's benefits because their father had died so young. Lisa put as much as she could spare from each check into savings accounts to help ensure both their futures. "He's going to be here a week. Maybe something will come up between now and then." It wasn't a very good solution and they both knew it.

"I don't believe in miracles," Katie replied with a huff as she bent over to retrieve her scattered packages. "At least not money-type miracles."

"I don't see any reason that you can't ask him for his autograph though, even if all you have for him to sign is a piece of paper." Lisa wasn't sure how much of Kevin's problem she should reveal to her young sister. "Just pick a time and place that won't be inconvenient for him."

"I won't pester the man, Lisa." Katie's voice was sharp.

Lisa gave Katie a long, considering look. "Sorry. Sometimes I forget you're almost sixteen." She made a decision. "This morning Kevin told me the reason he showed up here last night." Lisa picked up her pen, rolling it between her fingers, uncertain exactly what to say. "Evidently he suffered some kind of injury to his eye. He's losing his sight gradually. The damage may be reversible someday, but he doesn't know how long it will take."

"Wow." Katie looked out the window in the direction of the hidden cottage. "That's a bummer."

"Yes, it is." Lisa turned back to her neglected report, unwilling for Katie to see how hard it was for her to speak about Kevin's dilemma. "Anyway, that's why I asked you not to pester him. It wasn't because I don't think you're old enough to act like an adult."

"I won't even mention it unless he brings it up himself," Katie promised.

"That's probably best." Katie turned and started toward her room. Lisa looked up once more. "Katie?"

Her sister looked back over her shoulder and said, "Brad has the change from the money you gave him for the shoes. He picked them out and paid for them himself. He did great, too."

Lisa smiled. "That's good, but it's not what I wanted to say. I think a copy of Kevin Sauder's book would be a legitimate expenditure from your college fund. I have to be at the regional office tomorrow afternoon. I'll withdraw that much and stop by the mall on my way home."

"Thanks, Lisa. It really was a great-looking book. Educational, too," Katie went on gilding the lily just a bit. "It wasn't all pictures."

"I'd like to see it myself." Lisa didn't smile. She meant what she said. Perhaps if she could study Kevin Sauder's work, the photography that obviously meant so much to him, she could learn something more about the man himself. A man she'd known less than twenty-four hours, but one she already found to be more compelling than anyone else she'd ever met.

KEVIN SETTLED HIMSELF more comfortably against the wooden post supporting the dock jutting out into the lake in front of the Emery home. A wooden rowboat rocked gently at anchor to his right. On his left bulrushes nodded in the breeze, their stalks bending slightly toward the tightly furled buds of yellow and white water lilies resting on the surface just beyond the reach of his arm. The water was calm and clean, but stained a dark gold from tannin released into it by the trees on the shore, making it impossible to see more than three or four feet below the surface.

Pure honey gold, Kevin thought as another breeze disturbed the sunset calm. Amber. The exact shade of Lisa Emery's eyes. They were definitely her best feature, large and clear with thick silky lashes. He closed his eyes and let the memory of her face take shape before his mind's eye.

She probably wouldn't photograph well. Kevin opened his eyes again, still concentrating on her mental image. He crossed one foot over the other and appeared to study the toe of his shoe. Her bone structure was all wrong, he decided with professional detachment. Her appearance was too feminine, the contours of her face and mouth too rounded, too soft and touchable-looking to catch the play of light and shadow that challenged the artist in any photographer.

No, Lisa Emery wouldn't photograph well, except perhaps when she was completely taken out of herself. The way Laurel had been when she'd first held her son in her arms.

Or the way Lisa might look after making love, after giving herself wholly and completely to a man who could touch the hidden recesses of her heart and soul, the uncharted landscape of passion and commitment he sensed beneath the calm no-nonsense exterior she presented to the world.

Kevin snorted and laid his head back against the rough wooden post. What the hell made him think he could tell all that about a woman he'd known less than twenty-four hours? A woman he'd never made love to, never held in his arms, never even touched. He wasn't only losing his eyesight. He was losing his mind.

"Hi."

Kevin turned his head and blinked. He'd been so lost in his thoughts he hadn't even heard her footsteps on the wooden planks of the dock. Lisa Emery stood beside him, hands in the pockets of her snug-fitting jeans, shoulders tensed beneath the thin material of her burnt-orange shirt. She smiled down at him, but she looked uncomfortable, uncertain, as if she didn't really want to be there beside him. Kevin didn't blame her. He certainly hadn't given her any reason to seek out his company. Suddenly it was very important that he do something to remedy the situation.

All he said, though, was "Hello." And he smiled.

For a moment Lisa was convinced the sun had reversed its course and popped back high on the western horizon. She found her own smile widening in return. She hated to admit it, but Katie was right. When he smiled and the laugh lines fanned out from those incredible green eyes, he did look a little like Harrison Ford. "I hope I'm not disturbing you?"

Kevin shook his head. "No. Just watching the sunset and waiting for the mosquitoes to drive me into the cabin."

"It won't be long." Lisa put one hand on the opposite pole and dropped down to sit beside him. The movement was unstudied and graceful. The firm roundness of her bottom and the curve of her hips were outlined provocatively beneath her jeans. Her legs were long in proportion to the rest of her body. And her waist, even without the cinch of the wide leather belt she'd been wearing the other times he'd seen her, was slender, hardly wider than the span of his two hands. "Up here they're so big some people want to have them declared the state bird."

"Up here a lot of people want the Upper Peninsula declared a separate state," Kevin pointed out, drawing one leg up to rest his hand on his knee. A pair of mirrored sunglasses lay on the dock beside them. He picked them up and let them dangle from his fingers.

"How do you know that?" It was true a lot of people felt alienated from the Lower Peninsula, whose geography, resources, and economy were so vastly different from the northern reaches of the state. But most casual tourists never seemed to notice the discontent, certainly never after having been in the area only a day.

Kevin looked serious for a moment. The last stray beams of sunlight turned his hair to bronze, the strongly angled lines of his face seemed to be carved of stone. "Just a feeling," he said, then laughed, dispelling the weighty atmosphere created by his sudden serious turn of mind. "And the bumper stickers." He drew a rough outline of the Upper Peninsula in the air with his finger, then swept his hand across the imaginary sketch, and quoted "'Superior: it's a state of mind!'"

"We are a pretty independent bunch." Lisa smiled and raised her hands in mock surrender. It was chilly. She drew her knees up beneath her chin and folded her arms around them.

"I've figured that out already." Kevin spoke so quietly she wasn't sure she'd heard him correctly. She looked up hurriedly. He was wearing the same jeans and brown shirt he'd arrived in. He'd rolled the sleeves down to cover his arms, and Lisa found her attention caught and held by the strong graceful movements of his wrist and hand as he twirled the sunglasses between his fingers. "Do you have everything you need at the cottage?" He looked at her from the corner of his eye. She decided not to beat around the bush. "Did you have any trouble driving into Marquette?"

Kevin turned his head, looking out across the lake. "Not a bit." Once again his voice was cold, the words mechanical, warning her away from becoming too personal. "There and back an hour before the sun came out from behind the clouds this afternoon. Piece of cake, with my handy-dandy aviator shades within reach at all times." He looked at the sunglasses in his hands, folded them and shoved them in his shirt pocket.

"I'm glad it went smoothly."

His eyes held hers. "Are you, Lisa Emery?"

It was hard to keep her gaze from skipping away from the sudden darkness in his. It was there again, that momentary shadow of anger and fear. He hated being weakened in any way. He hadn't come to terms with his limitations, had only begun to acknowledge them, she suspected. He wouldn't easily accept another's help or advice. But she cared about his welfare, even though she'd known him so short a time, and she wasn't about to hide her concern.

"Yes, I am." Her head came up, and she squared her shoulders. He looked at her for another long moment, one that seemed to stretch toward infinity, the same way the last rays of the sunset stretched across the lake from the horizon to the far shore. It was very quiet. The small ripples breaking against the pilings sounded loud in her ears. In the distance a lone Canada goose honked forlornly.

Kevin stood up and Lisa found herself staring at his knees. He reached down and held out his hands. Lisa hesitated only a moment before placing hers within his grasp. He pulled her to her feet.

"Why did you come out her tonight, Lisa?" The question caught her off guard.

"I...I forgot to tell you not to light any fires," she said at last, grateful she'd remembered something of her reason for seeking him out. "Even though it's rained a little the past few days, the rest of the summer has been very dry. We can't chance—"

He reached out and placed the tip of his finger against her lips. "I promise, no fires. Although I must admit the thought of sitting out here at a campfire with you—" he swatted at a droning mosquito that was making strafing runs around their heads "—and a giant-size can of repellent, is very tempting."

"The mosquitoes are already here," Lisa said lightly, while he reached out and tucked a stray wisp of cinnamon-brown hair behind her ear. "And I can furnish you with the repellent. But I'm afraid you'll have to do without the campfire."

"We could substitute moonlight and starshine," Kevin suggested, his voice low and rough around the edges.

"Huh-uh. I have a ton of paperwork to do tonight."

"Couldn't you spare just half an hour?" He was smiling again, and Lisa found herself wavering. "Please."

Above them a small flock of Canada geese honked in noisy disharmony, answering the plaintive call of the lone goose beyond the trees. They made one sweeping circle directly overhead, then glided east and south, the sound of their wings loud in the stillness as they disappeared to land with a series of splashes just out of sight beyond the curve of the shoreline.

"Enoch must be setting decoys again." Kevin had taken both her hands in his. Lisa looked down and her breath caught in her throat at the sight of his long strong fingers folded so warmly around hers. "I knew he was working on a set of Canada geese for some rich collector back East." She said the first words that came into her head, anything to take her mind off the jolting pleasure of his touch.

"Decoys?" The disturbing sensuality in his gaze was gone, turned off, banished, as quickly as the darkness had gone earlier. Lisa relaxed a fraction, but not completely. He still hadn't released her hands.

"Enoch Spangler, our neighbor. He carves duck and water-bird decoys. Mostly the decorative kind people put in their dens. He does that to keep food on his table. But he also makes working decoys. The way they used to in the old days, completely by hand. Two of them are even displayed in museums. He's probably finished the geese and now he's testing them, seeing if they'll attract the real thing."

"Sounds like an interesting guy."

"He is. I'll take you to meet him one day if you'd like. He was great friends with my grandfather." Lisa stopped talking abruptly. She was beginning to babble. In another minute or two, at this rate, she'd start to sound just like Katie—if she didn't already.

"I'd like to meet him."

Lisa chanced looking straight into his eyes once again, and this time saw that he meant what he said.

"Kevin?"

"Yes?" He released her left hand so that they could start walking toward the shore. The other one he still held within the strong confines of his own.

Lisa hesitated, feeling her courage slipping away. She hurried into speech. "Why didn't you tell me who you were last night?"

He looked puzzled and slightly defensive. "I did."

She shook her head, watching the sandy path at her feet. "Not really." Lisa took a quick breath and plunged ahead. "Katie saw one of your books in Marquette today. Your picture was on the dust jacket. You're famous."

There was more than a hint of accusation in the words. Kevin tried not to laugh. He decided he was in for a scolding. He tried to inject a note of humility into his voice. "That's not a crime that I'm aware of."

"You know what I mean." There was an edge of sharpness to Lisa's tone that did nothing to detract from the lilting quality of her speech. "I would never have questioned you the way I did last night if I'd known who you were."

Kevin spun her around with a jerk. Surely she wasn't that naive? "Don't tell me if I'd shoved an autographed copy of that damn book in your face you wouldn't have been a bit suspicious of the way I looked and acted! I could have been some psycho straight out of the violent ward and bent on—" Kevin stopped talking abruptly. There was just a hint of a smile at the corner of her mouth. She was laughing at him. He didn't know whether to be angry or amused. One thing he did know for certain—he liked the way her lips curved upward, and the faintest hint of a dimple that appeared in her right cheek.

He held her by the upper arms and his eyes were dark with silver fire. Lisa lifted her chin and gave him look for look. "You're right. I would still have been suspicious, but I'd have been more polite." She held her breath, wondering if she'd made him angrier than ever with the flippant remark. She tried as hard as she could to keep the smile she felt tugging at her lips from breaking out into a full-fledged grin.

For a moment the silver fire flared more brightly, then died away into laughing sparks in eyes that were almost pine green in the fading twilight. "I don't usually go around introducing myself to people as a famous wildlife photographer." The words were self-mocking. "I did tell you I earned my living with a camera," he reminded her gently. If he lowered his head a few more inches their lips would touch. Lisa's heart began to beat more quickly. She felt a pulse leap to life high in her throat. The hands on her arms were no longer harsh, but warm and excitingly strong.

"I thought you took pictures of babies and wedding anniversaries." The bantering quality of her words faded into the darkness like the last golden rays of the sun.

"I probably will from now on." He spoke without self-pity, but the pain and bewilderment showed in his eyes, in the tense look on his face. "I can't do, physically, what's required to get the kind of shots in those books. My ability to capture that kind of detail, that—whatever it is—set my work apart from all the rest, is being destroyed just like my sight." It was even harder to say the words aloud than he'd imagined it would be. His ability to capture every detail and nuance of his subjects on light-sensitive paper, to be preserved for thousands of people who would never see them otherwise was a thing of the past. His career was a thing of the past.

"I don't believe that," Lisa said suddenly and decisively. She didn't want it to be so. He had said the damage to his eye could probably be corrected—eventually. Her life hadn't been easy, but she hadn't let it overwhelm her. Kevin would have to do the same. "There are always alternatives, different routes to the same goal. Sometimes we just have to search a little harder to find them."

Kevin didn't say anything for what seemed like a long time. Was she right? He hadn't tried to use his cameras for weeks. He just continued to carry them around with him like icons, waiting for some miracle to happen, waiting to wake up some morning with his vision clear and undamaged. It hadn't happened. It wouldn't happen, but that didn't mean the rest of his life had to come to a grinding halt, too. His interest in Lisa Emery had been strong from the very beginning. It had only continued to grow during

the hours he'd spent with her. Now the interest was focusing on what was between them, the basic elemental pull of
man to woman.

She had a very kissable mouth, he noticed not for the
first time, and he wanted very much to kiss that mouth. He
wanted to think of what Lisa would feel like in his arms,
not how much courage it would take to start working with
his cameras again. His photography was yesterday. Lisa
was today, the present—and a sweet hazy dream of tomorrow.

"Lisa?" Her name came out rough around the edges.
She was staring at him wide-eyed, a little apprehensive. He
slid his hands up over her shoulders, the curve of her neck,
to fan out on each side of her face, his fingers buried deep
in the auburn glory of her hair.

She didn't pretend to misunderstand what he was asking of her, even though he spoke only her name. "I don't
think this . . ." she began, but he didn't let her go any further.

"I do think." He lowered his head and tasted her lips.
She stood quietly, but he felt the tightness in the muscles
of her neck and throat, the trembling in her arms, as she
lifted them to his chest to balance herself on the uneven
sandy ground.

Her lips softened under his, parting slightly, allowing the
tip of his tongue to tease the moist softness of their inner
surface. Desire burned through him so fiercely it made his
ears ring and his heart hammer against the wall of his
chest. He couldn't remember the last time kissing a woman
had affected him like this. Maybe it never had. *And she
wasn't even kissing him back.*

Kevin lifted his head. Her eyes, with their dark curling
lashes, flew open and she stared at him, still with a shadow
of apprehension darkening the honey-gold irises to am-

ber. "Lisa, I'm sorry." Kevin stopped and swallowed hard.
His voice sounded as if it were coming from the bottom of
a well. He didn't know what else to say. He'd kissed her
because at first he'd been touched by the sincere attempt
she was making to help him through the quicksand of
starting to come to grips with his physical limitations. But
he'd ended by simply kissing her because it was like finding the sun itself shining inside him.

"No, I'm the one..." Lisa bit her lip in confusion. *Id-
iot. You don't apologize to a man because* he *kissed you.*
She wasn't going to blush. She wasn't going to cry. She
certainly wasn't going to ask him to kiss her again, which
is what she really wanted to do.

Kevin lifted his hands from the high smooth curve of her
cheekbones. "No." He made his voice stern. "I'm the one
who's going to apologize. I don't usually go around kissing women who don't want to be kissed." She opened her
mouth to protest. He let a smile touch his mouth and slide
into his words. "At least not by me."

"It's not that." Lisa started, then halted, because her
denial would have sounded halfhearted. She could feel
heat start to color her face and wished she could dig a hole
and crawl into it. How could she tell him she wasn't in the
habit of kissing *any* man? That she seldom even dated?
"It's..." He reached out one long tapered finger to smooth
it over her upper lip. Lisa felt a rush of fear and pleasure
that went all the way to her toes. She forgot what she
meant to say next.

"It's what?" He was still standing very close and she
could smell wood smoke from the fireplace of the cottage—and something else, faint and exciting and elemen-
tally male, the essence of Kevin himself, in the warm air
between their bodies.

"Nothing." She just couldn't bring herself to tell him the truth.

"It won't happen again, Lisa. I promise."

That definitely wasn't what she wanted to hear. "Oh," she said, and before she could add anything to the single betraying syllable, he turned, stuffed his hands into the pockets of his jeans and walked off down the darkening path toward his cottage.

"Good night." Lisa was surprised she got the words out at all. They sounded so small and forlorn hanging there between them in the night air that she wondered if he even heard them.

"Good night." The words drifted back to her through the trees, but he was already out of sight.

Lisa stared after him. What was the matter with her that she couldn't even accept a kiss from a man she found as attractive as Kevin Sauder? What must he have thought of her childish response? She might as well have slapped his face and run off in a huff. He probably hadn't been turned down like that since junior high. She felt like a fool.

But if she was honest with herself, and she usually was, she'd have to admit her overreaction was caused by the fact that she did find him so devastatingly attractive. And more than that, much more...

He might even understand if she could bring herself to tell him what had prompted her to react the way she did. Or would he understand?

For how could she just come out and tell him point blank that she generally avoided any but the most casual of relationships with men because she couldn't take the chance of falling in love? That she was afraid of loving someone enough to want to be married to him, to bear his children when she knew of the weakness she carried in her very genes.

She'd realized she could never marry and have a family or Katie, either, from the day she was sixteen and her mother had told her that Brad's condition was a rare kind of Down syndrome that could be handed down in a family from one generation to the next. Young as she was, she'd realized it wasn't fair to ask any man to share that risk. It was a reality she'd come to terms with, learned to accept, as Kevin would have to learn to accept his loss of vision.

Lisa turned and started up the path toward the house. She shouldn't feel this disappointed, this sad over not being able to share a single casual kiss. But she did.

Still, she might have been able to reveal her secret—painful as it was—if the time was right, and the man was right. And in her heart she knew Kevin Sauder might be the right man. But how on earth was she to tell him one last, most personal secret of all? For who, especially someone with Kevin Sauder's obvious expertise with the opposite sex, would believe that in this enlightened day and age there could exist such a creature as a twenty-six-year-old virgin?

Chapter Five

Kevin topped the rise of a small hill a quarter of a mile be
yond the cabin. He'd been running hard, but now h
slowed his pace to a fast walk, as much to enjoy the view
as to catch his breath. To his left the pine and hardwood
second-growth forest crowded the shoulder of the grave
road. At his feet, ferns rustled in the breeze, their frond
prematurely yellowed by the unusually dry summe
weather.

To his right the land sloped sharply down to the smal
lake, rising just as steeply on the far side. The lake itsel
was almost circular, nestled like a sapphire against
backdrop of crushed green velvet, its deep cold waters re
flecting the clear blue sweep of cloudless sky above it.

Three or four small fishing boats dotted the surface. A
least they looked like fishing boats from where he stood
It was hard to make out details from this distance. Kevi
found himself squinting against the bright sunlight
straining to focus. A warning twinge of pain stabbed be
hind his eyes. He gave up the attempt, shaking his head i
disgust. It was no use. The only thing he was going to ge
out of the effort was another blazing headache.

Kevin started down the hill at a trot. He was too close t
the cabin to get back up to running speed. Besides, he wa

still out of shape. He'd spent too much time this spring and summer sitting in his parents' home in Bartlow feeling sorry for himself and letting his muscles go soft.

Jogging around a curve in the road, Kevin saw Brad Emery ahead of him, trudging along, head down, as he pushed his bike along the sandy road. As he got closer Kevin could see why Brad was walking. The rear tire of his bike was flat.

Kevin slowed to a walk as he came alongside Lisa's brother. He hadn't seen much of the youngster in the past two days. His first day at the cabin had been spent laying in supplies and supplementing his wardrobe. Yesterday he'd slept the clock around, got up, fixed himself something to eat, watched the sunset and gone back to bed. He didn't know whether to give credit for his extra energy and sense of well-being to the uninterrupted hours of sleep, the crisp, clean pine-scented air, or a gift from the gods. He only knew that today he felt better, more like his old self, than he had for weeks.

"Hi." He grinned at Brad as he matched his pace to Brad's plodding walk.

"Hi." Lisa's brother smiled shyly. "My bike's got a flat."

"I see. Need some help patching it?" Kevin surprised himself with the question. He'd never been around a mentally handicapped person before. He had no idea of the limit or extent of Brad's skill in such simple matters as patching bicycle tires. To tell the truth, he'd felt slightly uncomfortable renting the cabin from Brad that first night, and listening to the young man's enthusiastic conversation at breakfast the next morning.

"I can fix it," Brad assured him, rushing his words, "but I didn't get to Gilson's to get my movie. Mr. Gilson is saving the new Michael J. Fox movie that just came out. I'm the first one to get it. There's a waiting list.''

Brad was talking so fast Kevin had to listen closely to make out what he was saying. He remembered the matter-of-fact way both Lisa and Katie had treated this behavior yesterday morning at breakfast. Kevin decided to use the same approach. ''Hey, slow down, buddy. We'll get this worked out. Will Lisa be home in time to drive you out to Gilson's?''

Brad considered a moment. He looked at his wrist, but he wasn't wearing a watch. His tongue snaked out to wet his lips and Kevin realized something else. Concepts of time were hard for Brad to deal with. ''I don't know,'' he said at last shaking his head. ''I forgot my watch.'' He looked at Kevin expectantly. ''She won't be home until after supper. Maybe even not till it's dark. She had to go to court today,'' he explained, pleased to display his knowledge of Lisa's schedule. ''It doesn't get dark until about nine-thirty.'' He squinted up at the sun, still high in the sky. ''That's a long time from now.''

''Does Katie have a driver's license?'' Kevin asked next, thinking that he could lend his car to the teenager.

''Not yet.'' Brad looked more dejected than ever. He scuffed the toes of his running shoes in the sandy gravel as they walked.

''How about you?'' Again Kevin wasn't sure he was asking the right questions. Perhaps Brad's skills weren't developed enough to allow him to drive a car.

''Lisa won't let me get a license. I could though.'' Brad nodded his head vigorously to add emphasis to his words. ''You don't have to write real good to take the test. I learned that in school. I could do it. I can learn the rules. But the car belongs to Lisa's boss.'' He grinned wickedly in Kevin's direction. ''He's the governor. It's department property. I can't use it to practice. But sometimes when Lisa isn't here, Matt and Katie let me drive Matt's truck. I'm good.''

Brad's speech was still thick and slurred on some words, but he was speaking more slowly and Kevin didn't have any trouble at all understanding him. The youngster really wanted to learn to drive, just like any other teenager. Again Kevin found himself uncomfortably aware that he'd never considered that the needs and hopes of someone with Brad's handicap might be very similar to his own.

"Hey." Brad stopped dead in his tracks. "You won't tell Lisa I drive Matt's truck sometimes, will ya'?

"No way," Kevin assured him with a grin. The driveway appeared on their left. They turned into the cool, tree-lined tunnel of green. Kevin pushed his sunglasses onto the top of his head, no longer needing them in the dusky green light filtering through the branches overhead.

"Good. She worries too much."

Coming out from under the trees, Kevin once again found the sunlight in the yard uncomfortably strong. He shoved his sunglasses back onto his nose. "Listen, give me a chance to shower and change clothes and I'll drive you out to Gilson's. I need to pick up a couple of things I forgot in town anyway."

"Gee, thanks." Brad propped his bike against the door of the huge, barnlike two-story garage at the rear of the clearing. He walked over and held out his hand. Hesitating a moment, wondering what Brad wanted, Kevin held out his hand, too. Brad pumped it enthusiastically. "Thanks a lot, Kevin." He grinned and his almond-shaped hazel eyes sparkled with excitement. "You're my friend."

"I'm glad." Kevin said, surprised at the small lump of emotion that tightened his throat. "You're my friend, too. Do you need help fixing your tire?"

"No. Matt and Katie will help me later. I just want to get
the movie," Brad reminded him none too subtly.

Kevin laughed. He recognized something of Lisa'
stubbornness in Brad's single-minded pursuit of his goals.
"Fifteen minutes. Meet me at the car."

It wasn't until he was standing in front of the bathroom
mirror toweling his hair dry that he began to wonder i
Brad would have difficulty understanding how long fif
teen minutes was. He needn't have worried. Three min
utes later, still buttoning his shirt, Kevin hurried out of the
cabin to find Brad leaning against the fender of his car
thumbing through the bills in his worn leather wallet.

"Just enough," he pronounced, counting the money a
second time. "Running kind of short this month." H
flashed Kevin another infectious grin, pushing a wave o
cinnamon-brown hair out of his eyes. "I mow lawns fo
extra money, but it hasn't rained for a long time." Bra
halted and frowned, furrowing his brow in concentration
"Except the day you came. But that wasn't enough t
make the grass grow so I don't get any money again thi
week." He shrugged in exactly the same way Kevin ha
seen Lisa shrug.

Brad Emery resembled his sisters a great deal. He ha
the same cinnamon-brown hair, and hazel eyes like Ka
tie's. He was tall, slightly stoop-shouldered and just a lit
tle overweight. His features, while showing th
characteristics of a person with Down syndrome, wer
more distinctive and clearly defined than other similarl
afflicted individuals Kevin had seen.

The drive to Gilson's Marina and General Store wa
punctuated with a running commentary from Brad on th
names and life-styles of the families in each and ever
cabin they passed along the way. His observations wer

ively and in many cases surprisingly astute. Kevin was hard-pressed to keep a straight face.

When they passed a battered and dusty GMC pickup heading in the opposite direction, Brad waved until it was out of sight, turning in his seat to do so. "That was Enoch Spangler, our neighbor. He's a neat guy. He's teaching me to whittle. I made a duck," he said with pride. "'Course it's not nearly as good as the stuff Enoch carves. He's real good. Katie says he makes a bundle of money. Or he would if he'd just work faster at it."

Kevin hid a smile. The youngest Emery obviously had a sound grasp of economics, even if it was at the expense of artistic considerations.

"He was my grandpa's friend." Brad was obviously reciting something he'd heard many times. "He got shot in the Korean War. He came here to get well and never left."

"Lisa told me a little about his work." Kevin told him about the goose calls they had heard from the dock on the second night of his stay.

He hadn't seen Lisa since then. Since he'd kissed her. She probably thought he'd lost mind and it was better to avoid him. In a way he did feel a little crazy. He couldn't forget the taste, or scent, or feel of her. He didn't want to forget. He wanted more.

"I'd like to meet Enoch sometime," Kevin added, dragging his mind back to the subject at hand, replacing the mental image of Lisa's curving mouth and honey-gold eyes with a vague image of the middle-aged giant of a man in a yachting cap he'd glimpsed through the pickup's dusty window.

"I'll take you over to his place. There's a path through the woods." Brad settled back into his seat with a satisfied grin spreading over his features. "We'll go tomorrow."

He was still chattering away when they pulled into the dusty parking lot in front of the sprawling, gray-stained log building that housed Gilson's. A good-sized stream, its waters as dark and foamy as root beer, ran alongside the building and crossed the highway beneath a concrete bridge to empty into Lake Superior from between high, grass-covered dunes.

In the opposite direction the stream disappeared into the woods to emerge in a small lake about two miles farther west. A couple of aluminum canoes were stacked on a short dock near the bridge. A hand-lettered sign with a list of daily and hourly rental rates was propped against them.

Kevin hadn't been in a canoe for a long time. He wondered if Lisa might like to go for a paddle with him? Kevin parked the car alongside a Volkswagen and a couple of pickups that had seen better days. Brad was silent as they threaded their way past the gas pumps and several fishing boats, a pontoon raft, one or two paddleboats and a trio of powerful snowmobiles that were displayed haphazardly in front of the long low building.

"It won't take very long," Brad said as he entered a room where Kevin could see an impressive array of video cassettes.

"I'm going to pick up what I need in the store." Kevin pointed toward the middle of the building that was outfitted as a small but surprisingly well-stocked grocery. "I'll meet you back here."

Brad stared apprehensively into the video room. "Okay." He stayed where he was.

Kevin noticed his wary stance. "Something wrong, buddy?" He glanced into the movie room. Two couples were sorting through the titles. They seemed to be about Brad's age. They were all dressed in jeans, flannel shirts nd T-shirts. The boys were big and brawny and looked nough alike to be twins.

"That's Lonnie Bruss and his cousin Jed," Brad said as that explained everything. He glanced at the counter at ie front of the display area. It was vacant. "I don't see Ir. Gilson, but I know where he keeps the movies that are ived for somebody." He squared his shoulders and alked into the room.

The two couples were grouped around a display of adult ovies. The boys were making low suggestive remarks and ie girls were giggling. Brad looked suddenly very alone id vulnerable to Kevin as he searched through a low flat ick of tagged cassettes, looking for the one with his name i it. Maybe he should stick around?

Kevin shrugged off the uneasy feeling with a spurt of ir- tation. Brad could take care of himself. He did a good •b of it. A hell of a lot better job than Kevin probably ould with the same handicap. He turned and walked into .e grocery section of the store.

Five minutes later, standing at the counter, he heard ised voices coming from the video room. The girl be- nd the cash register looked past his shoulder with con- rn. Kevin pocketed his change and quickly crossed the en space that separated the two sections of the store.

A car door slammed and two figures appeared in the te-afternoon sunlight streaming in the open door. Kevin inked against the brightness. The figures moved out of e direct sunlight and resolved themselves into Katie nery and a tall young man whose dark blond hair and e-blue eyes proclaimed his Scandinavian ancestry. Kevin ve them only a fleeting glance before returning his at- ntion to the scene in the video room.

Brad was standing with his feet planted far apart, hold- g on to his videotape with both hands, while the larger

of the Bruss cousins tried to wrestle it away from him. "It
mine," he panted. "I r-reserved it." He stuttered over th
long word, then repeated his first statement for emphasi
"It's mine."

"Come on, dummy. The girls are going back home t
morrow. We want to celebrate tonight and they want to s
Michael J. Fox. Give it to us. You can have it tomorro
You ain't got nothin' else important to do, eh?"

"Lonnie, quit teasing him," one of the girls urged, la
ing her hand on his arm. "He's not right in the head
Behind him Kevin heard Katie's sharp intake of breath, b
at a quiet word of warning from her companion, she r
mained silent.

Lonnie shrugged off his girlfriend's hand. He yanked
the contested tape again, but Brad held on even though h
tormentor outweighed him by at least thirty pounds.

"Give it to me, dummy," Lonnie ordered, and h
cousin echoed the rude demand.

"No." Brad pulled his bottom lip between his teeth. H
face was pasty white under his tan. His voice shook. "L
me go. I have to meet my friend."

Kevin dropped his small sack of purchases on top of a
oil display rack beside the door. In two swift strides he wa
standing directly behind Lonnie Bruss. He put his hand c
the younger man's shoulder and squeezed hard enough
make him yelp and release his hold on the tape.

"You heard him," Kevin said in a voice filled with qui
menace. "He's reserved the tape. Back off."

Lonnie turned with a snarl, only to find himself stari
at Kevin's chest. He stepped back, nearly colliding with h
less-belligerent cousin.

"Who the hell do you think you are, eh?"

Kevin usually enjoyed the musical and faintly inqui
tive extra syllable a lot of north-country natives added

nearly every sentence they spoke. But coming out of Lonnie Bruss's sneering mouth he found the practice highly annoying.

"I'm his friend." Kevin slid his thumbs into his belt loops and splayed his hands across his hips. "And I happen to want to see that movie, too. Tonight. Got any objections?"

Lonnie continued to stare aggressively into the icy green eyes a good five inches above his own. Kevin wondered if he was going to have to pop him one after all.

"It's nothin' but a damn kid movie anyway. Come on, Jed." He gave Kevin one last defiant glare. "You won't always be here to defend that creep." He grabbed his girlfriend and pulled her past Kevin, whose hands had balled into fists, only to come face-to-face with Katie and her friend.

"You're right, he won't always be here. But we will," Katie said in a low angry voice. Her hands were on her hips, her hazel eyes flashing sparks of fire. She looked very much like her sister, and Kevin caught himself wondering how Lisa would have handled this same unfortunate situation.

"You can count on it." Katie's friend moved in close behind her and put his hands on her shoulders. Lonnie Bruss opened his mouth, said two short ugly words and marched out the door, but Kevin noticed he kept his girlfriend angled between Katie's friend and himself.

Kevin swiveled on his heel. "Let's go, Brad."

Katie stuck her head around the door. "Are you all right?"

Brad nodded a little uncertainly. "Hi, Katie. Hi, Matt," he added, spotting Katie's friend. "I left the money in the special place Mr. Gilson fixed for me." He pointed back toward the counter. He was shaking so hard his teeth rattled. He looked at Kevin, then at his sister. "I was scared."

Katie flew across the room and gave him a hug. "You were so brave."

"Yeah," Brad agreed with some pride. He shrugged away from Katie's hug. His eyes caught and held Kevin's once more. "But I was still scared."

Kevin retrieved his purchases, then threw his arm around Brad's shoulder. "So was I, buddy." He laughed. "That Lonnie Bruss is one tough guy." He let Brad lead the way out of the store.

Brad nodded, exhilaration replacing his fear. He jabbed at the air like a boxer, the movie still clutched tightly in his hand. "We beat him this time, though."

"Yeah, but remember, it took four of us to talk him down," the boy whom Brad had called Matt added, with a wisdom beyond his years.

"I would've had to give him the movie if you weren't there." Brad's smooth forehead creased into a frown. "Lisa says never to get in a fight with somebody bigger than me because they'll beat the tar out of me."

"Pretty sound advice," Kevin agreed, hiding a grin. They were walking toward the cars. Matt was driving a green Ford pickup that had definitely seen better days. Kevin noticed his own two-year-old Chevy sedan didn't look much better, with its thick coating of dust and smeary windshield.

"She says never to get into a fight with anyone smaller than me, either, 'cause that's bein' a bully like Lonnie Bruss."

"She's right there, too."

"I think she means it's better not to get in fights at all." Brad looked triumphant, proud of his reasoning.

"Bingo." Kevin gave Brad a thumbs-up.

Katie came alongside her brother and looked him over carefully. "Are you sure you're all right?"

"Sure." Brad grinned, his good humor restored. "My bike's got a flat tire. That's why Kevin gave me a ride."

"We stopped by on the way to my ball game," said Katie, "to get some soda and extra ice for the cooler." She didn't look convinced that her brother had come to no harm. "I don't have to play. I can come home and help you fix your bike." For the first time Kevin noticed she was wearing a uniform of sorts: red shorts, high white socks and shoes and a V-neck T-shirt with red numbers on the back and front.

"You can't do that," Brad said. "You're the best catcher they've got."

"She's the only catcher they've got." Katie's friend came around the front of the pickup and stuck out his hand. "Katie's got lousy manners sometimes. My name's Matt Swensen."

"Kevin Sauder." Kevin held out his hand in turn.

"Pleased to meet you." Matt grinned. His grip was firm and strong.

"Same here."

Katie's face flushed a becoming rosy pink. "Oh, I am sorry. I do have manners, really. I just forgot to introduce you with so much going on."

"There's no need to apologize, Katie." Kevin smiled down at her. "You're right. We had other things on our minds at the time. Thanks for the backup." Katie blushed even harder but managed to smile back.

"Lonnie Bruss and his cousin are..." She paused as if her vocabulary was inadequate to express the boy's villainy.

"Come on, Kate," Matt broke in with the ease of long practice. "We're already late. You don't want the Pike

Lake Lady Eagles to forfeit the game 'cause they don't have a catcher, eh?''

"Of course not." Katie was suddenly full of dignity. "I'll be there in a moment." With a regal wave of her hand, she motioned Matt to go over to his truck.

"This is for helping Brad." She reached up, and to Kevin's surprise pulled him down by the collar of his shirt, put her arms around his neck and gave him a quick light kiss. "I truly am grateful you were here for Brad. Thank you." She spoke so quietly that only Kevin could hear. She released him, and as he straightened he saw a saucy and very feminine little smile curve the corners of her mouth. "And it won't hurt Matt to see me kissing Harrison Ford."

Before Kevin could demand an explanation of that cryptic remark she'd skipped up into the pickup and slammed the passenger-side door. Her smile grew wider and very definitely female when Matt looked over at her with a scowl on his handsome Viking face.

"Women," Kevin marveled, shaking his head.

"Yeah, women," Brad echoed obligingly. He changed the subject. "Let's go home and watch the movie. I'll pop some corn."

"Sounds great, buddy," Kevin said. "Let's go."

LISA TAPPED THE SWITCH that turned off her headlights, twisted the key to kill the engine and rested her chin on her hand, which was still curled around the steering wheel. She sat that way for several moments, savoring the quiet solitude of the summer night. Outside the open car window, night sounds swirled and eddied around her on a warm breeze. In the west, thunder grumbled and lightning flickered above and behind an inky mass of banked clouds. Breathing deeply, Lisa believed she could almost smell rain in the air, but she suspected it was only an illusion born of anxiety.

No rain was forecast for the central Upper Peninsula. She'd been listening to the coast-guard weather frequency on her radio for most of the way home. The storms were there all right, but they were also predicted to move north and east, dropping their precious moisture where it was needed least, over Lake Superior, as they drifted on into Canada. For Marquette and vicinity, there was only a chance of scattered showers in the next forty-eight hours.

With every day that passed, the chance of lightning or a carelessly tended campfire igniting the tinder-dry forest grew more likely. A fire was almost inevitable, given the time of year and the dry conditions. The best that could be hoped for, outside of a week-long soaking rain, were small separated fires in accessible areas that could easily be contained. Lisa shuddered to think of the damage, the death and destruction that would result from a major blaze.

For the time being there was little more she could do than hope and pray and be alert every moment she was in the field.

But sitting here in her car at ten o'clock at night, staring into the darkness and being eaten alive by voracious mosquitoes wasn't being prepared. It was being a coward. It didn't benefit anyone or anything but the bloodthirsty insects swarming in through the open window. She had to go into her house sooner or later.

Would Kevin Sauder still be there?

Lisa had spent the morning at the district office in Marquette doing routine follow-ups and meeting with her immediate superior, Sergeant Jack Harris. She'd spent the afternoon in court, giving testimony in a deer-poaching case. That was why she was wearing civilian clothes—a soft khaki-colored cotton skirt, low-heeled pumps and a pale turquoise, long-sleeved blouse. That was why she'd had time to stop off at the ball field behind the high school to catch the last few innings of Katie's softball game and hear her impassioned account of the incident at Gilson's.

That was why she knew she might find Kevin Sauder sitting in her living room watching a Michael J. Fox movie with her brother.

Lisa felt around on the seat for her purse. Perhaps he'd already returned to his cabin and she wouldn't have to confront him at all. She hadn't spoken to him for almost two days. She really didn't want to see him tonight. It had been a long day. She was tired and keyed up and still embarrassed by the way she'd reacted to his kiss.

"Hi."

Lisa nearly jumped out of her skin at the sound of a voice just outside the open window.

"Sorry. I didn't mean to startle you." Kevin leaned both arms on the car door and bent nearly double to bring his face level with hers.

"You didn't startle me," Lisa said, her hand at her throat.

"No?" Even in the near darkness she could see one dark blond eyebrow quirk upward.

"No. You just about scared me to death! Don't you know it's dangerous to sneak up on people like that?" He was wearing a black sweatshirt and jeans, and except for his blond hair shining in the moonlight, he seemed to be almost part of the night itself.

"I forgot you might be armed." Lisa felt his gaze wander over the soft silky material of her blouse, and lower, to the slender curve of her waist.

"That's not what I meant." She gave him a stern disapproving look. "You very nearly gave me a heart attack."

"Then we're even."

"What?" Blood was still pounding in Lisa's ears. She couldn't make sense of his words.

"Nothing. Here, let me help you out of the car." Before she could protest Kevin had opened the door. He held out his hand. She slid off the seat, forgetting her purse. Lisa wanted very badly to ignore the strong brown hand, but she could not. She placed her fingers on his palm. They closed over her hand. His grasp was warm and hard and gentle all at once.

He drew in his breath on a long low whistle. "You look very nice."

"Thank you." He closed the door but didn't move away from the car. Lisa wasn't touching the car. She wasn't touching Kevin, except for his hand, but still she felt trapped, walled in.

"This outfit isn't standard issue." Kevin's long lean-muscled arm formed a barrier on her left. He'd propped his hand against the roof of the car, resting his weight on the vehicle. Lisa didn't even have to turn her head to see the muscles contract and tighten with every movement he made.

"I've been in court." She fought to keep her voice steady, and won. She ought to resent his invasion of her personal space this way, but surprisingly she did not.

"Did you win the case?"

Lisa smiled, and Kevin felt his breath catch in his throat. There was a world of satisfaction in the generous curve of her mouth, the tilt of her pretty, stubborn chin.

"Yes." Lisa lifted her head proudly and met his gaze. His eyes were almost emerald in the silvery half light of the summer moon.

"This conservation officer always gets her man?" His voice was low and rough, taunting but in a friendly, nonthreatening way as he adopted the famous slogan of the Mounties.

"We did this time. An anonymous call came into the department's poaching hot line. We caught him red-handed with two out-of-season deer. Second offense." Lisa's voice became more animated as she spoke of her triumph. Kevin listened as much to the sound of her voice, to the images of splashing water and summer breezes her lilting speech conjured up, as to the words she spoke. "Willie Gleason was one of my first collars," she went on. "That arrest was pure luck. He ran out of gas trying to make his getaway, but all he got from the judge for that first offense was a slap on the wrist." A tiny sliver of that younger, more idealistic Lisa's disillusionment still lingered in her voice.

"Robin Hood," Kevin said, and Lisa was pleased by his insight.

"Exactly. A lot of people, including judges and juries, still think wildlife belongs to the state, or the federal government. Or they don't want to send a neighbor to jail for spearing fish while they're spawning, or for shooting a deer out of season. They don't understand they hurt all of us by allowing this kind of criminal, these spoilers, to go unpunished. The wilderness, all of the outdoors, belongs to each and every one of us. We all have to be responsible for its welfare—animal, vegetable, mineral." Lisa stopped for breath.

"I know," Kevin said quietly. He smiled at the passion in Lisa's voice. He could imagine it translating into passion of the flesh, of the heart, as well as the soul.

Lisa felt embarrassment color her cheeks, but she didn't look away from the sudden darkness in his green eyes. The pain she'd noticed before, the awareness of his loss was still there, but now there was something else, some other emotion, or need. She wasn't sure how to describe what she saw. She didn't have the words; she didn't have the experience. She sensed heat and longing—and passion—reflected in the bottomless green depths. Passion—not for a cause but the kind that can exist between a man and a woman. She shivered as much from the unbidden, unsettling erotic direction of her thoughts as from the chill of the night air. "I'm sorry." This time she did look away, at his jean-clad legs, his shoes, her shoes, anywhere but into his disturbing knowing gaze. "I don't usually get this carried away about my work."

Her voice was low and soft, hesitant, embarrassed and vastly appealing. "Don't apologize. Finish your story," Kevin ordered as he tipped up her chin with the end of his finger. The touch was fleeting, over in a heartbeat, but her skin was as soft and smooth as he remembered, like cream and honey beneath his fingers, like ivory and gold beneath the moonlight.

"This time the judge agreed. She gave him a hefty fine, three months' probation and loss of hunting privileges." Lisa's voice was stronger. She laughed again as though in delighted remembrance. "She told him if she saw him in her courtroom again she'd throw his butt in jail."

Kevin laughed, too. "Good for her. And good for you."

"Good for me? I was just doing my job."

"Oh, yes. I forgot." Kevin shook his head. He moved from his lounging stance against the car and took her face between his hands. "Then congratulations on a job well done, Officer Emery."

"And I want to thank you, too."

"Thank me?" Kevin guessed what she wanted to say, but he liked playing this game, keeping her off balance with both his words and his touch.

"Thank you for being there to help my brother this afternoon. I talked to Katie a little while ago, after her softball game. I know what happened."

"Brad handled himself very well. You would have been proud of him."

"I would have been scared to death for him," Lisa admitted honestly. Her heart was hammering against her ribs. She really ought to tell him not to touch her this way, as if she belonged to him, as if he belonged to her. It was too intimate, too exciting. She couldn't think straight, couldn't speak intelligently while his hard callused fingers were tangled in her hair, while his thumbs skimmed lightly over her cheeks. She took a deep breath and gathered her scattering wits. "It's getting late. I should be going in."

"Is that what you really want to do?" Kevin asked, his voice taking on a husky challenging tone that sent shivers of longing racing up and down Lisa's spine.

"No." She managed to get the word out despite the sudden constriction in her throat. She marveled at finding the courage to speak at all.

"What do you want?"

No amount of new-minted courage could enable Lisa to answer that question. She just shook her head, apprehension and bewilderment competing with desire in her gold-brown eyes. "I don't know."

"I see." Kevin sighed, his eyes dancing with sparks of devil fire. "Then I guess I should let you go inside." He didn't release her, though, instead let his hands glide over the slope of her shoulders, down her arms, to rest on the slender curve of her waist and the swell of her hips. "Or I could kiss you again, even though I gave you my word I wouldn't."

"I never asked you to give me your word," Lisa said with bravado. "That was your idea." She could handle his sensual banter when he teased her this way. It made it easier somehow, but no less exciting.

"Ahhh, you're releasing me from my sacred pledge?" He put his hand over his heart. The gesture was dramatic, the words drawn out with theatrical flourish.

Lisa's answer was far more prosaic, but the impact of it hit him like a fist in the stomach. "I believe I am," she said in a wondering tone.

Kevin didn't waste any more time or energy on words. He lowered his head and kissed her, gently at first, letting her get used to the feel of his mouth on hers, letting her learn the taste of him, the texture of his skin. Her hands came up around his neck, her fingers touched his hair.

She kissed him back, reluctantly, even a little clumsily at first, but then with more confidence and growing desire. Kevin felt the blood singing through his veins. He was dizzy with the need to hold her close. He pulled her into his arms, angling his body against the car, cradling her against his long hard length. She tasted of mint and passion. She smelled of meadow flowers and spice and desire.

Lisa didn't know where she found the expertise to return his kiss; she'd never tapped that reservoir of instinctive feminine knowledge before this night. He touched the side of her breast with his hand and she felt her nipple tighten, felt herself move and press against the pleasant exploring caress of his hand. His hands slid lower over the curve of her spine to cup her bottom and press her hard against him. Lisa moaned, a soft wordless protest low in her throat.

Kevin felt her stiffen, released her the moment she began to pull away, but he was confused. Her body still molded itself to his, her lips were still soft and pliant against his, but her will had refused to obey its signals.

"I'm sorry." Her whispered words were low and husky. "I don't usually..." He didn't try to stop her as she took a step backward. She had known he would not. It was what she wanted, to put some distance, some cool crisp night air between the heat of their bodies, but still, perversely she felt deserted and bereft outside the circle of his arms.

Kevin didn't let her move far away, but kept her near, his hands on her elbows. He lowered his head, kissed her forehead, her eyelids and then again, softly, sweetly, her mouth. Lisa knew she should step away from that kiss also, but she did not. It helped to quell some of the raging fire inside her body and her mind. The wonder of his kisses, the magic of his touch was a spell almost too strong to break, but for both their sakes she must. From somewhere deep inside her the strength and courage to move completely out of his arms found its way to her consciousness. Lisa put her hand on his chest and stepped away.

"I think I should go now." Thankfully he didn't argue. He looked at her for a long questioning moment, then leaned in through the open window of the car, retrieved her purse and handed it to her.

"Good night, Lisa," was all he said.

"Good night." She hurried toward the house before she could change her mind. She'd never experienced such strong feelings for a man so quickly. In the past, any relationship that threatened to grow beyond friendship had been terminated in the blink of an eye.

With Kevin Sauder she'd had no such option. It had all happened too fast, but she couldn't allow it to go any further. There could be a brief tomorrow, a lovely little affair of the heart, but there couldn't be a real future for them. That was what she had to remember no matter how sharp and hurting the pain it caused.

Kevin watched her go with a puzzled smile on his face and a fierce ache in his body. It didn't surprise him to discover that Lisa Emery had obviously done very little kissing and caressing in the moonlight in her lifetime. Or that beneath her uncertainty and lack of experience there lay much unawakened fire and desire.

What did surprise him a little was his own intense reaction to that passionate being, that hidden Lisa. She was every inch a woman, and loving her—falling in love with her, because he was very much afraid that that was what was happening to him—was an experience he was likely never to forget.

Chapter Six

"Everybody in the junior and senior class is going on thi[s] camping trip. I don't see why I can't." Katie slapped th[e] last of the silverware down on the kitchen table. She glare[d] at Lisa from the doorway, then flounced out of the kitche[n] and headed for the big chair by the fireplace. She droppe[d] into it with a weighty sigh, evidently ready and willing t[o] do battle for as long as it took to get her own way. "[I] should have known you'd start acting like some uptigh[t] old-maid aunt the minute I said anything about it."

Lisa clamped her mouth shut hard to keep from return[n]ing a childish rejoinder. Instead she stirred the spaghett[i] sauce on the stove so hard it sloshed over the edge of th[e] pot. She and Katie were alone in the house. Brad was of[f] somewhere with Kevin Sauder "getting something fro[m] Gilson's." Or at least that's what Lisa thought she'd hear[d] her brother yell through the bathroom door as she'd com[e] out of the shower.

"I can't believe everybody in the junior and senior clas[s] is going to be there." Lisa knew she'd made a mistake a[s] soon as the words left her mouth. It had been a long har[d] day. She'd been on the road at six, driving to Munising t[o] teach a course on hunter safety to a dozen teenage boy[s] and two girls, all eager to qualify for a hunting license i[n]

e fall. On the way back she'd checked out boat licenses
nd registrations at several resorts in the area. She was
red and in no mood to argue with Katie, but it looked as
 she wasn't going to be given any choice.

Katie folded her hands across her chest and scowled even
arder as Lisa walked out of the kitchen. "Okay, I'm ex-
ggerating a little. But there's going to be at least a dozen
f us."

"All couples?" Lisa tried to keep her voice sounding as
en and normal as possible. It wasn't easy. Every time she
ad one of these discussions with Katie she felt herself
ating farther out on untested ice. Her sister turned her
ead and looked her straight in the eye.

"Yes."

"Then I don't think it's wise—" Lisa didn't have a
ance to finish what she'd been going to say. Katie
upted out of her chair in a flurry of peach-tinted nails
d lips. A wave of perfume washed through the air to
velop Lisa in its heavy floral scent, almost overpower-
g the aroma of spaghetti sauce from the kitchen.

"We've got two tents!" Katie exclaimed. "One for the
ys and one for the girls. It isn't going to be some kind of
ld orgy or anything."

"I never said it was."

"You were thinking it," Katie accused.

Lisa pulled her lower lip between her teeth and consid-
ed her options. She'd gladly taken on the responsibility
 raising Katie. She didn't regret it. Still, she worried
out the decisions she was making in discharging that re-
onsibility. It had been far easier to steer a course through
e unknown waters of parenthood when boys and dating
ere not issues.

Of course, she could pick up the phone and call their
other, ask her advice on the camping trip. But that

wouldn't settle the more important question—the painf
reality of telling Katie the truth about Brad's condition an
what it would mean to her future.

Lisa had been sixteen when she'd learned those facts.

Her mother would say that Katie should be told, a
though so far she had remained silent at her eldest daugh
ter's request. Lisa knew that eventually she would have
explain the situation to her sister. But not now. Not ye
She didn't want to spoil this special time in Katie's lif
Being almost sixteen, almost grown-up, was hard enoug
Reality could wait a little longer.

"Let's start this discussion over, okay?" Lisa smile
"The sauce is starting to burn and I don't want the sp
ghetti to boil over on the stove. If we're going to keep a
guing we'll have to do it in the kitchen." She didn't wait fc
Katie's reply but turned and walked back into the co;
pine-paneled kitchen that opened off the far side of the b
main room. Katie didn't return the smile but followed h
sister. She sat down at the table, still ready to do battle f
her cause. Lisa took a deep breath. "Who exactly has bee
invited along?"

Katie named several couples. Lisa recognized some
the names, others she did not. "Aren't most of those kir
seniors?" she asked unwisely. "Nancy Amos is the on
other junior you mentioned. I take it she's still dating th
Metson boy? The one whose parents have a mobile hon
over on Silver Lake?"

"Yes." Katie's voice was still mutinous, but witho
being asked she began buttering the slices of French brea
that Lisa had left lying on the table. When she was fi
ished she wrapped them in foil and handed them to Lisa 1
pop in the oven.

"I thought the Metson boy joined the navy." It was
close as Lisa wanted to come to mentioning that he was

least three years older than Katie and had been in trouble all through high school.

"He's on leave, spending time with his parents before he ships out for California. That's where he's going to be stationed." Katie began to tear lettuce into chunks for salad.

Lisa decided to quit beating around the bush. "Except for Nancy, everyone you mentioned is older than you are."

Katie sat the salad bowl on the table with a great deal more force than necessary. "I can't help it if my birthday's at the end of September. I didn't ask to be the youngest person in the junior class."

"All right, all right," Lisa conceded. She slipped on oven mitts and took the spaghetti over to the sink to rinse. The steam rising from the pot curled wisps of hair around her face, which she pushed away from her cheek with the back of her hand. She still didn't know the best way to voice her reservations about the coed camping trip. She certainly hadn't contemplated doing anything like it when she was sixteen. But that was a long time ago, a lifetime ago, as far as Katie and her friends were concerned.

"I don't care what you say," Katie said. "I'm going."

"Not unless I give my permission, young lady." Lisa could be just as stubborn as her sister when she put her mind to it. She set the spaghetti down on the table with a thump that rivaled the one Katie had given the salad. Hazel eyes clashed with gold. Katie looked away first. Lisa took a deep steadying breath and turned to the cupboard to find a bowl for the sauce. She was determined not to lose her temper. "When is this trip scheduled?"

"A week from Friday. For the whole weekend," Katie added, still with that unsettling hint of defiance she'd adopted at the beginning of the discussion. "I don't know why you're even asking all these questions if you don't intend to let me go."

"I said I'd think about it." Was she being too stuffy and old-fashioned? Katie was almost grown-up. Her hesitation must have come through in her voice.

"Really, Lisa?" Katie dropped her belligerent pose in the blink of an eye. "You're not just saying that to shut me up?"

Lisa laughed and shut off the gas under the bubbling sauce. "No, I'm not just saying that to shut you up."

"Lisa." Katie flew out of her seat. "I knew you'd see it my way." She wrapped her arms around Lisa from behind and squeezed for all she was worth.

"It's still not settled, Katherine Lenore," Lisa reminded her, using her sister's baptismal name to add emphasis to her warning. "I want to check with some of the other parents. You haven't even told me where you're planning to camp." Katie named a lake about twenty miles away that had a small state campground on its northern shore.

"We're hardly going to take any supplies," Katie said, her eyes sparkling. "The guys are going to catch fish. We're going to pick blueberries and raspberries. Very primitive. I wonder if I've got extra batteries for my Walkman? I'd better check." Katie whirled out of the kitchen, suiting actions to words. She seemed totally unaware of the irony of her last couple of statements. Lisa laughed out loud, earning her a puzzled over-the-shoulder look from Katie as she disappeared from sight.

Lisa was still smiling as she finished putting dinner on the table. She was used to eating alone, or to having meals interrupted. She'd called Katie once, reminding her it was time to eat. She had no idea when Brad would return. She liked it when they could all sit down together, but evenings like this one were more the rule than the exception these days. If she waited the food would only get cold. Besides, she was starving. It was after seven and a very long time since her brown-bag lunch.

"Lisa!" The screen door slammed. Brad pounded across the front room and skidded to a halt inside the kitchen doorway. Lisa looked up from her half-filled plate of spaghetti.

"Slow down and sit down," she ordered. "Dinner's ready."

"We ate at McDonald's," Brad said waving aside her offer of food. He was excited but happily so. "Guess what?"

"What?" Lisa wound several strands of pasta around her fork, not looking up.

"Kevin rented a canoe from Gilson's. We brought it home on the top of his car."

"What did he do that for?" Lisa asked. "He paid fifty dollars for a boat and motor here that he's hardly used." *The man must have money to burn*, she found herself thinking irreverently, and a little enviously.

"Ahhh, yes. But don't you think paddling along the shoreline beneath the light of the silvery moon is much more romantic than putt-putting along with the scent of gasoline fumes filling the air?" Kevin's blond head appeared behind Brad's. There was more than a hint of devilry in his jade-green eyes and the beginning of a smile on his lips. "Is that spaghetti sauce homemade?"

"Of course." Lisa pretended she wasn't at all disconcerted by his sudden appearance, or the fact that he'd overheard her last remarks. "I opened the jar myself." She indicated the empty chair at the foot of the table. "Help yourself if you like, but Brad said you had dinner at McDonald's."

"We did," Kevin answered before her brother could reply. "But I never turn down spaghetti, no matter who made the sauce." He began piling his plate with noodles and ladling on the sauce. "When you spend almost a year at a time somewhere miles past the back of beyond, you learn to take spaghetti, and pizza, or a good piece of apple pie anytime or anyplace you can get them." He looked up from his food and gave her a very wide, very sexy grin. "I've been back from Brazil five, no, six months now and I'm just starting to get filled up."

"I'm glad you've passed the critical stage," Lisa said dryly, watching him eat.

"Yes." Kevin reached for a second slice of bread. He sounded perfectly serious. He would have been thoroughly convincing if it weren't for the telltale teasing glint in his eyes. "At this time last month I probably wouldn't even have bothered with a plate."

"That bad?" Lisa tilted her head and let a small smile of her own curve the corners of her mouth. Two could play this game. She felt very much in harmony with him at the moment. She had both feet firmly planted on the ground, or at least firmly planted on the kitchen linoleum. She would be on her guard; she wouldn't allow this bantering to get out of hand, allow it to turn, in the space of a heartbeat, into something darker, more compelling—and ultimately more dangerous.

He nodded with mock seriousness. "I would have gone straight for the platter, believe me."

"Oh, I believe every word you say."

"I'll remember that." Kevin was no longer smiling. He refused to release her unwary gaze. Lisa felt the breath catch in her throat. Her heartbeat sped up. She didn't know whether to run away, or stay and play with the lure of sweet sensual fire.

Brad dropped into his seat and eyed with fascination the inroads Kevin was making into the spaghetti. "What's for dessert?"

"Fruit." Lisa indicated a bowl of apples, grapes and bananas on the counter. "Help yourself." As far as mystical chants went, "help yourself" didn't rate very high on Lisa's list, but coupled with Katie's entrance into the kitchen at the same moment, it seemed to possess enough power to break the spell of Kevin's jade-green eyes.

"I didn't know you'd invited Kevin for dinner," Katie said with just enough accusation in her voice for Lisa to pick up on. She sat down in another almost overpowering wave of perfume, giving Kevin her most dazzling smile. "I'm sorry I'm late."

"We started without you," Kevin said, as though he'd been eating in their kitchen every night of his life.

Katie turned her smile on Lisa, backing off on the wattage considerably. "This stupid thing has something wrong with it." She placed a small, inexpensive camera on the table beside the bowl of fruit Brad had just passed to Lisa.

"Katie, I don't know a thing about cameras."

"Maybe Kevin can look at it," Brad said, peeling a banana.

Katie looked at Lisa, her face stricken. Lisa saw the movement only from the corner of her eye. Kevin was holding out his hand for the camera, a slight frown between his strongly arched brows, nothing more. The angry bewildered look she'd encountered so often the first day or so he'd come into their lives wasn't there. Did this casual acceptance of one of the instruments of his craft mean Kevin was coming to accept his handicap?

"Sure, I'll look at it, but I have to warn you in advance, it usually costs more to fix these things than it would to buy a new one."

Lisa realized she was holding her breath and let it sift out between her lips. It wasn't acceptance she detected in his actions and his words. It was dismissal. He didn't consider the item a camera, but a toy.

"I like taking pictures," Brad said into the sudden silence as Katie passed Kevin the camera. He didn't say anything about Kevin's book. Lisa couldn't be certain he remembered it from the store in Marquette. She'd bought a copy for Katie as she'd promised. Last night she'd looked at it for the first time herself. If Kevin Sauder didn't regain his sight, wasn't able to continue his work, it would be everyone's loss.

"I sure hope you can fix it." Katie sounded certain he could.

I hope the doctors can make you well. Lisa's silent prayer was from the heart.

"I'll do my best." Kevin tucked the little camera into the breast pocket of his blue-and-gray plaid shirt, then took an apple and a banana from the fruit bowl.

"Want to see some of the pictures I took of Katie and Lisa?" asked Brad.

"Sure." Kevin smiled at him before taking a big bite of his apple.

"Tonight," Brad decreed with his usual enthusiasm.

Kevin took the exuberance in stride. "Not tonight, buddy. I'm going to take your big sister for a canoe ride in the moonlight." He looked straight into Lisa's startled eyes, daring her to say no. Lisa obliged him.

"I'm sorry. I have laundry to do this evening."

"At least you didn't say you have to wash your hair." Kevin's left eyebrow climbed toward his hairline, expressing his disdain for her unimaginative excuse far more forcefully than his offhand words.

"Brad and I will do the dishes and start the laundry."
The look Katie gave her brother across the table silenced
any protest he might have wanted to make. "Go ahead,
Lisa," she urged, sounding more like sixty than sixteen.
"It's great out. There's barely a ripple on the lake." Katie
smiled benignly at Lisa, but there was a far more worldly,
timelessly feminine sparkle in her eyes. "It'll be fun."

Lisa wasn't so sure of that. Stimulating, provocative and
dangerously appealing, yes. But fun, no, she didn't think
it would be fun.

Kevin stood up, ignoring her frown of uncertainty.
"That's settled then. I'll meet you at the dock in half an
hour. Don't be late. And don't forget the bug spray."

THE SUN WAS LOW on the horizon, a huge orange ball balanced precariously, it seemed, on the serrated tops of the
pine trees along the far side of the lake. Already darkness
was spreading outward from the eastern shoreline, held
back only by the long splayed fingers of sunlight floating
on the still dark water. Kevin pushed his sunglasses onto
the top of his head, no longer needing them as the sun
slipped below the horizon.

The motor of a fishing boat roared to life, loud in the
silence that surrounded them. Kevin watched as its wake
arrowed through the water, disturbing the fingers of light,
changing them from gold to silver and finally to a luminous pearly gray as the surface of the lake smoothed to
satin once again.

A loon called from somewhere nearby. Kevin twisted in
his seat, his paddle dripping copper-bright droplets into the
dark water like sparks of fire being swallowed by the night.
Lisa stopped paddling also, as her eyes searched the dark
shoreline.

"There." She pointed with her free hand, her voice a soft low whisper. "Can you see it?"

"Yes." Kevin willed himself not to strain to see into the distant line of rushes growing out of the shallows at the lake's edge. Instead he picked up the field glasses from the floor of the canoe and focused on the big dark bird floating serenely above its reflection.

The loon called again, its wavering melancholy cry pulsing through the gathering dusk. The short hairs at the nape of Kevin's neck stood on end, for the haunting sound spoke to something deeply buried and completely primitive in his heart and soul. In the distance, somewhere behind them, the loon's mate answered.

"She has a baby on her back." Kevin watched the big black-and-white bird as it floated low and sleek in the water. Its head was covered with iridescent green feathers, its beak long and razor sharp, its eyes a wild, other-worldly shade of red. But it was the small ball of gray fluff nestled on its back that drew and held Kevin's attention. Riding safely above the waterline, protected from marauding pike and hunting turtles, the baby was warm and dry and safe from harm.

He passed the glasses to Lisa. She watched the bird as the canoe rocked gently in the slight rippling of waves stirred by a passing breeze. While Lisa concentrated on the loon, Kevin watched her. Her hair was clipped on top of her head in a spill of cinnamon curls. A few wispy strands had escaped confinement to lay against her cheeks and the back of her neck. Her jeans were old and soft and clung to her body in ways that made him itch to touch her. Her sweatshirt was the same coppery orange as the fading sunset. She smelled of sunshine and wildflowers and insect repellent, just as he did himself. Kevin smiled, wondering for a moment how she could have come to be so important to him in only the space of a handful of days.

Lisa was such a contradiction: strong, intelligent, successful in her work and in her relationships with others. Yet at the same time she was soft and vulnerable, innocent, really. Kevin knew she wouldn't appreciate his using that homey and old-fashioned adjective to describe her, but it was accurate nonetheless.

Still, beneath her outward calm and down-to-earth attitude, he could detect a hint of wildness, like this half-tamed place that meant so much to her. It was that wild and sensual Lisa he wanted to know, that Lisa he wanted to possess, to love as he'd loved no other woman in his life.

"Enoch has a loon and chick that he carved two winters ago. I wish you could see it." She was whispering, the sound of her voice still, like the twilight surrounding them. "It's so beautiful . . . so real."

Kevin nodded his understanding of her halting explanation. They had come across her eccentric neighbor an hour ago, hip deep in water, making last-minute adjustments to the weighting of a "rig" of Canada goose decoys. A rig, the sixtyish, ginger-bearded bear of a man had explained to Kevin, as he steadied the canoe with one hand and tugged at the drooping strap of his chest-high waders with the other, is what hunters called the decoys they set out to lure ducks and geese into range of their guns.

He plucked one of the decoys out of the water and passed it, still dripping, into Kevin's hands. The carving was about two feet long and surprisingly light. He couldn't identify the wood that had been used, but the only seams he could detect were at the base of the carved neck and where the beak was connected to the head. It was stylistically painted in shades of black and white and gray. A minimum of brush strokes and detail, barely more than a suggestion of feathering, coupled with the clean flowing lines of the body worked some magic, some alchemy that almost brought the bird to life.

"If the loon and chick are anything like the geese we just saw, it must be magnificent." Kevin wasn't just mouthing polite phrases. He considered the sample of Enoch Spangler's work he'd just seen to be a masterpiece of its kind.

"Enoch's decoys are stylized, of course. They're made to perform a specific function just as they have for hundreds of years. But the loon . . ." Lisa shook her head, at a loss for adequate words to describe it. "He captures something in his best work, some magic in the wood. The same magic I've seen in your photographs."

"Where have you seen my work?" It startled Kevin that she should choose almost the same words to describe his work that he'd applied to Enoch's carving. He knew he was good, his technique excellent, but no one had ever told him his work was magic.

Lisa glanced back over her shoulder as they glided into shore. His face looked dark and hard, but that may only have been a trick of the shadows cast by the birch trees overhanging the small crescent of sand where Kevin had indicated he wanted to beach the canoe. "I bought a copy of one of your books for Katie after she saw it in the bookstore in Marquette."

Kevin dropped down to shove the paddles under the low seat of the canoe. He balanced on the balls of his feet, his upper body half turned to face her. His hair was almost silver in the near darkness, his eyes shadowed, making it impossible to read his expression. "You didn't have to do that. If you'd only asked, I would have given you a copy for her."

He rested his hand on his thigh and watched her. Lisa noticed the taut muscled curve of his leg beneath the new dark blue denim of his jeans. She noticed the strength and beauty of his hand and wrist as he flexed his long fingers against his knee.

"Thank you for offering, but it isn't necessary."

"Of course it isn't necessary." Kevin stood up in one quick fluid movement that left Lisa staring at the ground. His voice cracked like a whip, but softened almost at once. "It's something I want to do for you."

The moon had risen, its light gaining intensity as the night deepened around them. Its silvery shards filtered through the birch leaves. Diamond chips of moonshine danced on the water, caught on Lisa's eyelashes, glittered in her hair. He couldn't stop himself from reaching out to brush a stray curling wisp off her cheek.

"She would like an autograph." Lisa turned her head a fraction of an inch, seeking more of him. She'd never known the mere touch of a man's hand could mean so much, be so desirable, so... necessary. She wanted him to take her in his arms. She wanted to attach herself to the lean hard strength of his body, stay with him night and day, day and night, forever.

"It would be my pleasure." Lisa lifted bemused golden eyes to his. She smiled and the earth tilted on its axis. Lord, how he wanted her, needed her, desired her. "My very great pleasure." Something of what he was experiencing must have escaped into his voice, because the smile faded from her eyes. She took a tiny step backward. Kevin let her go.

"Thank you." Lisa couldn't think of another coherent word to say. She turned to start up the path leading to the house. She couldn't just throw herself into his arms and start kissing him. He'd think she'd lost her mind, but heaven help her, kissing him was what she wanted more than anything else in the world. The loon called again and

close by, its mate answered. "They've found each other,"
Lisa said.

"I'm glad." Kevin didn't move closer, but the heat and
shape and scent of him filled the air around her. At thi
distance she didn't need to tilt her head to meet his eyes
She had only to raise her eyes to meet his, but she kept her
gaze lowered, fixed on the slow steady beat of the pulse in
his throat. The collar of his shirt was open and a shaft of
moonlight lay like a silver band across his neck and chest

"Lisa."

"Yes?"

She was only two steps away, a distance he could cover
in the blink of an eye. Yet Kevin made himself stay where
he was. The next move was up to her. The next time he
took her in his arms, kissed her, made love to her, it would
be because she had invited his caress, not because he had
overcome her reluctance by the sheer force of his own de
sire. "Is the cottage available after this week?"

"Yes, it is." Whatever she'd thought he might be going
to say, it wasn't that. He made no move to come closer
Lisa couldn't find the courage to close the small gap
either. She had hoped he would kiss her again, make her
forget all the reasons she shouldn't let him, take her fur
ther out of herself than she'd ever before dared. But he did
not. Her disappointment was so intense it was almost pain

"I'd like to stay on, then, at least for a week or two."

"Of course. I'd . . . we all would like to have you stay a
long as you wish." Lisa's heartbeat had accelerated pas
the speed of light.

"Good. It's settled. I'll walk you home."

"You don't have to bother." It was an automatic re
sponse, a polite disclaimer, not really what she wanted t
say at all, but Kevin took the denial at face value.

"All right. I'll see you tomorrow, then." Kevin started up the path in the opposite direction, leaving Lisa feeling very much alone.

This man had come to mean a great deal to her in a very short time. Was she falling in love with him? Lisa started walking toward the house very slowly, her thoughts rushing around in her brain at a far quicker pace than her feet were moving along the sandy path. She'd never been in love, so she couldn't know for certain if this strange malaise she was experiencing heralded the onset of the disease. She didn't want to know, because she was afraid there wasn't a cure.

Kevin would be staying with them for a little longer, but someday soon he would fade out of her life as quickly as he'd just disappeared into the darkness beneath the trees. She would be alone again as she'd always been. But this time it would be different. The knowledge bloomed like a small aching flower inside her. Alone. Somehow Lisa knew that tiny lump of misery might never go away, might be her constant companion from this day forward. Without Kevin Sauder in her life, a part of her would always be alone—and lonely.

Chapter Seven

"Okay Brad, what does a red sign like this one with eigh
sides always mean?" Katie pointed to an illustration in the
pamphlet on Michigan's driving laws. She'd been quiz
zing Brad on the subject for the past twenty minutes.

"Stop." Brad sounded immensely pleased with himself
Kevin didn't open his eyes. He didn't need to see Brad'
face to recognize the young man's satisfaction.

"Good." Katie shifted position on the seat, and the bi
old wooden fishing boat, an Arkansas Traveler, rocke
with the movement. It was the tag end of a hot lazy Fri
day afternoon. Lisa was out on patrol and the two youn
ger Emerys had decided to go fishing, dragging a not-too
reluctant Kevin along with them.

The only trouble was that no one had told the fish the
were coming. After half an hour with only one or tw
desultory bites and not a fish on the stringer, Brad ha
begun to get restless. Always resourceful, Katie had pulle
the pamphlet out of her tackle box and started the lesso
while Kevin continued to fish.

As he listened with only half his attention, Katie went o
with her drill, her voice mixing pleasantly with the lap o
waves against the hull, the call of gulls circling high in th
cloudless blue sky, the murmur of a light breeze skim

...ing through pine branches along the shore. The signs
...enoting curves and intersections, hills and road hazards
...eemed to be giving Brad some trouble, but he kept on
...ying. Katie was patient, explaining each in relation to
...rad's recent driving experience.

Kevin stretched out one long arm along the gunwale to
...eady himself against the slight motion of the boat and
...ondered, briefly, if he was doing the right thing, aiding
...nd abetting this conspiracy of Brad's and Katie's. The
...ought gave him a momentary pang of uncertainty. Nar-
...owing his eyes behind the protective lenses of his sun-
...asses, Kevin considered his actions as he watched the two
...oungsters at work.

Brad ran his hand through his hair, making it stand up
...tousled spikes. His brow was furrowed in concentra-
...on, his head bent close to Katie's. Or at least as close as
...e could get. His sister was wearing a big straw hat with a
...oppy brim that looked like something out of *Gone with
...e Wind*. The brim fluttered in the breeze, nearly hitting
...rad in the eye. The lesson threatened to degenerate into
...squabble.

"Hey, guys," Kevin complained, shoving his brand-new
...etroit Tigers baseball cap back on his head. "Give me a
...eak, or I'll spill the beans to your sister."

"You wouldn't dare." Katie looked ready to do battle.
...rad looked stricken. Kevin held up his hand in mock
...rrender.

"Besides," Katie added, eager as always to have the last
...ord, "if Lisa finds out you're in on this she'll skin you
...ive."

"That's what I'm afraid of." The truth was that he'd not
...ly been aiding and condoning the clandestine activities,
...r the past three days he'd been actively involved.

When he first found out, purely by accident, what th
scheme involved, he'd never intended to volunteer the us
of his car. But he already knew how much obtaining
driver's license meant to Brad. And he didn't particularl
like the idea of him learning to drive in Matt Swensen'
beat-up old Ford pickup.

Katie had already learned that her brother could take a
oral test to qualify for a learner's permit, and because h
was eighteen he didn't need Lisa's signature to do so. "Bu
Brad needs hands-on instruction," Katie had explained t
Kevin. "It's so much easier for him to understand thing
if he can put them into a familiar frame of reference."

"I can do it," Brad had told him, his eyes shining wit
determination. "I know I can." Kevin couldn't have re
fused then if his life depended on it. So even though a
lowing Brad to drive without a learner's permit was agains
the law, each afternoon Kevin found himself in the pa
senger seat of his car, driving on one of the rarely use
gravel roads in the area, explaining the basics of drive
education to a fiercely concentrating Brad while Kati
chattered in the backseat.

Once again Kevin appeased his uneasy inner voice b
rationalizing that he wasn't doing anything injurious t
Brad's health or welfare, or anyone else's, for that ma
ter. He was simply helping him to achieve a goal.

Besides, he thought Lisa was too protective of he
handicapped brother. She would probably be the first t
admit it if the fact was pointed out to her. There was n
question that both she and Katie loved Brad very muc
They both wanted what was best for him, to help him reac
his potential. They just went about it in different way
And this time Kevin found himself favoring Katie's poi
of view.

He hoped Lisa didn't find out just how much he was involved in her sister's scheme. He had no doubt she would want to skin him alive.

Kevin readjusted his cap to block out the sun and settled back against the boat cushion he'd shoved behind his back. The boat was almost wide enough for him to stretch out comfortably along the seat. Almost, but not quite.

He looked ruefully down the length of his body to his feet, in their size-twelve running shoes, propped up on the opposite gunwale. Crossed at the ankles, they provided the perfect place to rest the tip of his fishing rod. He couldn't see his red-and-white bobber from that angle, of course. Or much of anything else, really, since he'd pulled the bill of his hat down over his eyes, as much to facilitate a catnap as to diminish the glare of the sunlight reflecting off the choppy surface of the lake.

The sun felt good on his bare arms and the skin of his legs below his denim cutoffs. The gentle rocking of the boat began to lull him toward the edge of sleep. The give and take of Brad and Katie's conversation retreated to a buzz of sound just below the level of his consciousness. His thoughts faded away into hazy daydreams. He hadn't been this contented and at peace with the world for many months.

Lisa's home was a far cry from the flat, grain-rich farmland of his childhood. For that matter, it was also a long way from the rain forests of Brazil, or the icy vastness of Antarctica, or the sweeping plains of Africa. Those were all places he'd lived in, worked in, grown to love over the past dozen years. But they were part of the far away and long ago. The Upper Peninsula was here and now. In its own way it was as rugged and beautiful as all those other places, even if it lacked exotic allure. Still, there was something about this wild land that called to him.

Maybe it was being able to sit on the dock in the evening, listening to the loons in the distance and watching a bald eagle swoop out of the sky to grab a fish. Or perhaps it was the serenity of waking early in the morning to see a white-tailed deer and her fawns picking their way daintily through the trees to drink at the water's edge. Or was it the small thrill of danger he experienced stepping out of his back door to find the fresh tracks of a black bear in the sandy earth?

Small adventures, it was true, compared to some he had experienced in the past, but satisfying, nonetheless. Ever since he'd left his parents' home in Bartlow to join the navy when he was nineteen, he'd always thought he couldn't be happy anywhere so close to his own backyard. Now he was beginning to wonder if he was wrong. There was something about this place, a feeling that was hard to pin down, even harder to describe in words—except to say that it was beginning to feel very much like home.

"Kevin! Wake up, you've got a bite!" Katie's yell jerked him upright just as there was a tremendous yank on his line. "It must be a pike," she went on, hanging precariously over the side of the boat, one hand anchoring the ridiculous hat on top of her head. "He was probably laying up in those weeds, staying out of the sun, and just couldn't take your poor little minnow bouncing up and down in front of his nose any longer. Keep your rod up! Keep it up! Brad," she ordered in the same breath, "get my pole out of the way. I'll get the net."

"You've got the makings of a great drill sergeant, you know that?" Kevin said through clenched teeth. He hadn't been fishing in years. The pike, or whatever it was on the end of his line, wasn't perhaps enormous, but it was big enough to give him a battle on the lightweight line and small hook he'd been using.

Katie shoved her pole into Brad's hands and he dutifully began to reel in the line. "Cheez it, the cops," Brad hissed from his seat in the prow of the boat. Kevin smiled, aware that old Cagney movies were some of Brad's favorites. Out of the corner of his eye he saw Katie scoot around to look over her shoulder in the direction Brad indicated.

"Good grief, it's Lisa. Where'd she come from? She told me she'd be spending most of the day on Pike Lake."

Kevin risked a glance over his shoulder. It was Lisa in a small green runabout with the Department of Natural Resources insignia. She waved. Brad picked that moment to lunge for the pamphlet on driving laws, sticking it inside a comic book he'd brought along. He dropped back down on the seat, unbalancing Kevin, who made a grab for the side of the boat to keep from being flipped into the water.

"Keep your rod up," Katie said again, shaking her head in dismay at his ineptitude. "Don't give him any slack. If he wraps himself up in your line he'll bite through that wimpy little plastic leader in a second."

"I'm doing my best," Kevin assured her, shoving his sunglasses back on his nose. He forgot the painful glare of sunlight glancing off the surface of the lake. He forgot the ever-present haziness of his vision, the ache of loss buried deep in his heart. Instead he felt the same quick spurt of pleasure he'd experienced so often lately. He felt great. He was having a hell of a good time.

On her third try, Katie finally managed to scoop the thrashing and uncooperative fish into the net while Brad offered encouragement from the front of the boat. Unfortunately she managed to lose her floppy-brimmed hat in the attempt.

"My hat!" Katie screeched, as her headgear floated away. "It'll be ruined."

"No big loss." A distinctly unsympathetic look on his face, Brad watched the hat slide over the wave tops.

"It cost ten dollars," Katie wailed, "and I'll end up with a batch of freckles on my nose that you won't believe if I'm out in the sun without it."

"M'lady," Kevin said, flipping the pike out of the net and into the boat, "I will attempt to rescue yon hat the nonce I unspit this wily varlet from my trusty hook."

"Forget the Ivanhoe spiel," Katie said, eyeing the up-ended and still-combatant pike darkly. "By the time you get that slimy thing unhooked my hat will have drowned."

"I think you're right."

Kevin had to agree with Katie. The pike was indeed slimy and in no hurry to throw in the towel and admit defeat. It was beginning to look like a fight to the finish, and Kevin wasn't altogether sure the fish might not win. Twice it had made leaps high enough to bring it within inches of going over the side of the boat.

Deciding results were preferable to technique at this juncture, Kevin rested his foot lightly on the fish's middle, reached for a pair of needle-nose pliers from the tackle box and proceeded to remove the hook. He had no intention of sticking his hand in a mouth filled with razor-sharp teeth to retrieve a single small hook.

The sound of a motor idling nearby caught the edge of his attention as he struggled to put the pike on a stringer, and it wasn't until much later that he realized he hadn't hesitated at all to attempt the procedure, a task that involved hand-and-eye coordination of a type he hadn't felt equal to performing for weeks. When he was finished he looked over at the woman in the other boat and smiled. He held up his catch for Lisa to admire, and his heart started to beat slow and hard against the wall of his chest when she smiled back.

"Nice catch."

It really was a good-looking fish. About two feet long, he estimated, and weighing three or four pounds. A long way from a trophy winner in anybody's book, it was still the biggest fish he'd caught in years. Kevin looked up from admiring his prize and smiled again. "Thanks."

Lisa's hand tightened on the steering wheel. His smile did such incredible things to her. She hadn't seen him for more than a few moments at a time for several days, and if she'd hoped that abstinence might help lessen his appeal, she'd been wrong.

"I was fishing for bluegill," Kevin explained.

She couldn't see much of his expression beneath the shadow of his dark blue baseball cap. But what she could see, she liked. The tension lines that had carved deep grooves from his nose to his chin had smoothed out. His broad shoulders, beneath the thin cotton knit of his burgundy-colored tank top, were relaxed, the rigidity of his posture replaced by a slow lazy grace that brought her heart into her throat.

Unnerved, Lisa fell back on routine. "All the more impressive," she said. "May I see your license, please?"

"Lisa, not now," Katie said, exasperated by her sister's inattention to matters of greater urgency. She pointed to the hat now listing badly and already partly submerged beneath the waves, brave coral-colored ties trailing like banners. "Save it. We still have the anchors out. It'll sink before we can get to it."

"All right." Lisa laughed and shifted gears, sending the runabout forward in a slow smooth glide. "I'll see what I can do. I trust you'll be here when I get back." The words were a sugar-coated order. Kevin didn't have any trouble imagining the flash of devilry in her golden eyes, even though they were hidden behind sunglasses.

"Yes, ma'am," said Kevin.

One hand on the steering wheel to guide her, Lisa nosed the runabout alongside the fast-disappearing hat and scooped it up. Flipping the bedraggled, nearly shapeless millinery onto the seat beside her, she made a wide circle, returning to the lee side of the fishing boat. Both Brad and Kevin reached out to hold the boat steady beside their own.

"What a mess." Brad's comment pretty well said it all.

Kevin shook his head. "You lost it netting my fish. I'll get you a new one."

"There's no need." Lisa's voice was sharper than she'd intended. "I mean, it wasn't your fault. It was an accident. Katie, maybe if you shape it over a bowl while it's drying..."

Kevin noticed a smile fighting to gain freedom at the corners of Lisa's mouth. She was wearing the same dark green fatigues he'd seen her in that first night. The color suited her creamy complexion, and her breasts pushed against the cotton fabric with each move she made....

"It's ruined." Katie inspected her hat, shaking her head mournfully.

Lisa smiled at her sister. "We might be able to save it."

Katie scowled back. "I doubt it."

"Well, it can't hurt to try." Lisa smiled again. Kevin didn't say anything further about replacing the hat. He'd take that up with Lisa later.

"No, it won't hurt to try," Katie said with a distinct lack of enthusiasm. She began smoothing the hat into shape on the seat beside her.

Lisa wanted to change the subject. She knew that Kevin would end up replacing the hat, but she didn't want him doing nice things like that for Katie and Brad. It would only hurt them more when he left, as he inevitably would.

"Nice pike," she said at last.

"Thanks." Kevin leaned over the side and grinned down at his catch swimming at the far length of the metal stringer, bent on escape.

"I'm afraid I still have to ask to see your fishing license."

"Not that again," Katie moaned.

"He's our friend," Brad said accusingly.

"Brad, it's my job," Lisa reminded him, her voice gentle but slightly bewildered, as if she weren't used to being censured by her sibling.

"No problem, Officer." Kevin stood up and reached into the back pocket of his shorts. Lisa looked out over the water toward the opposite shore. The last thing she wanted to see right now was the sleek, muscled curve of his backside outlined beneath the tight denim. His hand came away empty. Kevin cleared his throat. "Um, I seem to have forgotten my wallet." Lisa risked looking at him again. There was a sheepish, infectious grin on his face.

She grinned back, despite her resolve not to. The tension she felt radiating from her unusually quiet brother and sister dissipated. "Would you believe this is the first time I've heard that excuse?"

"Really?" said Kevin in mock surprise. Lisa hadn't exactly been avoiding him the past three days, but she hadn't sought his company, either, so he wasn't in any hurry to end the lighthearted conversation. "It's the truth, Officer Emery."

"I'm sure it is." She waved off their hold on her boat. "Nevertheless, I'll be over this evening to check it out."

Lisa could have bitten off her tongue when she heard herself say those words, but it was too late. It was procedure to follow up on an angler who wasn't in possession of his license. It was up to Lisa whether she took the offender into shore then and there or extended him the courtesy of meeting him at his lodging at a later time. Since all licenses carried the date and the hour in which they were issued, the violator couldn't sneak into town and purchase one in the interim.

"Can't you take his word for it?" Katie's protest sounded less impassioned than before. Kevin glanced in her direction and found her watching him with a speculative look in her eye. She turned her attention to her older sister, watching Lisa just as closely. Kevin began to feel distinctly uneasy.

"No, I can't take his word for it," Lisa explained with what little patience she had left.

"I'll be at my cottage all evening, Officer Emery." Kevin gave her a half-challenging salute. Lisa didn't answer. She wished she'd never even brought the subject up. Wondering why on earth she hadn't learned to keep her mouth shut, she backed off a safe distance from the smaller boat, gunned the motor and roared away in a rainbow arc of drifting spray.

"Let's go in," Katie suggested, still with that knowing feminine look in her eye. "I'm getting a headache." Kevin wouldn't have minded trying to catch another pike, and though the tone of Katie's request seemed to brook no argument, he stated his desire.

Katie pointed at the captive pike. "That stringer is a thousand years old. It's probably got terminal metal fatigue. In another fifteen minutes your precious fish will be back in the lily pads watching us sitting here with our mouths hanging open wondering how he got away. Besides, it's getting late."

Kevin couldn't think of anything to say after that. He looked at Brad, a fellow male trapped in a steely web of convoluted feminine logic, for support. Brad shrugged, shaking his head in silent defeat.

"A couple of nice perch to go along with the pike would make a great dinner." Kevin gave it one more try.

"We have plenty of fish in the freezer."

In some cases discretion was still the better part of valor. Noting the set look on Katie's face, Kevin decided this was one of those cases. Without another word he hauled up the anchor and they headed into shore.

"HE'S A GOOD-LOOKIN' FISH." Brad propped one foot on the edge of the low concrete holding tank just as Kevin was doing.

"He sure is, eh?" Kevin replied, trying out his north-country twang. He watched the sleek, golden torpedo-shaped predator glide along the edge of the tank.

"We should take your picture," Brad decided, slapping his thigh. "I'll go get the camera."

"Okay," said Kevin. "My dad would like to see a shot of this beauty."

"I'm sure glad you fixed our camera. Otherwise we couldn't get the shot." Brad chuckled and took off for the house at a trot.

Kevin grinned at Brad's retreating figure and closed the tank's cover, a heavy wooden barrier designed to keep marauding raccoons and the occasional curious black bear away from the catch. Then he sat down with his back against the small white-painted fish shack. Even though the area was scrupulously clean inside and out, now and then a fly went buzzing past his head. A faint odor of fish lingered in the air.

The sun had slipped behind the trees. Already the air was cooler, the heat of the afternoon dissipating quickly in the clear air. Kevin removed his sunglasses and watched the shadow of the big two-story garage directly in front of him creep steadily closer to his outstretched feet.

He closed his eyes and listened to the sounds of the dying day. He could hear the distant coughing stutter of a boat's motor roar to life as a homeward-bound fisherman prepared to call it a day, and from down the road, he could hear one of Lisa's neighbors calling to her children to come inside before it got dark. Close by, high up among the branches of a huge cedar, two gray squirrels argued over a pinecone, sending a shower of needles and twigs onto the grass.

He could smell the tang of wild raspberries ripening on a cane just a foot or two away from his shoulder, and the dusky scent of wood ferns growing in the moist soil near the fish tank's overflow.

Kevin rested his head and shoulders against the side of the building, folded his arms across his chest and let the peace and tranquility of the waning day seep into his mind and his soul. He was content, and the feeling was novel enough to engage his attention to the exclusion of everything else.

"Kevin?" Brad's voice snapped him out of his contemplative mood. He opened one eye and saw Brad, frowning and agitated, running his hand through his hair, standing it up in short spikes.

"What's wrong, buddy?"

"Katie used up all the film in the camera after you fixed it. I'm sorry. I can't take your picture." He scuffed the toe of his shoe in the sandy ground. "I could ride my bike to Gilson's if you'd lend me the money for some film. I don't get my allowance until Tuesday. Will it be dark by the time I get back?" Brad looked at the already-darkening sky above them.

"It'll be dark." Kevin answered, rising to his feet. "Hey, don't worry about it." Then an idea popped into his head, and he spoke before he could give himself time for second thoughts. "Listen, I've got a camera back at the cabin I think you might like to try. Want to?"

Brad looked uncertain. His brow wrinkled, and he pulled his lower lip between his teeth. "I don't know. I don't like new things very much."

Kevin, recalling the way Katie and Lisa handled Brad's reluctance to try some new skill, said quietly, "I think you'll like this camera. It's nowhere near as complicated as driving a car."

"Really?" Brad didn't look convinced.

"It has a brain."

"A brain!" Kevin had forgotten Brad was likely to take every word he said literally.

"Well, not a brain exactly," he backtracked hastily, "but it's pretty smart for a camera. All you have to do is frame up the picture you want to take and press the button. It does all the rest."

"I've seen that kind on TV." Brad looked awed. "You must be rich like Katie says. Those things cost a bundle."

Kevin laughed; he couldn't help himself. Brad looked very much like Katie when he talked about money. "No, I'm not rich. But remember, I'm a photographer. Cameras are how I earn my living." There was no reason for Brad to know he'd purchased the fully automatic 35 mm camera as a kind of control when he'd first started to realize something was wrong with his vision. He hadn't touched it since, just put it away with the rest of his equipment.

"A tax deduction," Brad said wisely. Kevin wondered where on earth he'd picked up that concept. The young man beside him, as limited as his prospects were in many respects, never failed to amaze him with some of the things he did know.

"Close enough. Come on, let's get the camera. Then I'm going to fillet that pike and dine in splendor."

"Okay, Lisa. Smile." Lisa turned from hanging her jacket on a hook by the back door to be assaulted by the sudden glare of a flashbulb. The motorized whir of an automatic camera sounded loud in the twilight shadows of the utility room. "Got it." Her brother sounded immensely pleased with himself.

Lisa blinked away colored sparkles of light as she hung her hat on top of the jacket. What in heaven's name was going on? Brad liked to take photographs, it was true, but she also knew Katie had taken the last two photos on the roll just after Kevin had fixed the stuck shutter on their own little camera. Film was on her shopping list for her next day off.

Brad had already retreated into the living room and was sitting cross-legged in front of the TV when she joined him a few minutes later. In his hand was an expensive-looking automatic-focus camera. "Where did you get that?"

Brad looked up, surprised at the sharp tone of her voice. "What's wrong, Lisa?"

"Nothing." She softened her words with a smile. "I'm just tired, I guess."

"Long day, huh?"

"Very long." It had been a long day of jockeying the boat and trailer from one small lake to the next, checking licenses and catches, life jackets and other items major and minor that were part of the job. She felt dirty and gritty. She smelled of gasoline fumes and fish. Her head hurt from being out in the sun all afternoon and her equilibrium was still out of balance after her unexpected meeting with Kevin just a couple of hours ago. "Tell me about the camera, okay?"

"It was Kevin's. But now it's mine." Brad held up the compact camera for her inspection once again. "It's great, Lisa. He showed me how to work the tele . . . the tele . . ." Brad drifted off, unable to recall the unfamiliar word.

"Telephoto?" Lisa guessed.

"That's it, Lisa. Telephoto. Telephoto lens and the flash, too. I'm pretty good at it already." He stopped talking long enough to demonstrate his newfound abilities. It took a moment for him to locate the small button on the front of the camera that controlled the flash mechanism, but once that obstacle was overcome, he lifted the camera confidently to his eye and snapped a shot of Lisa with a frown on her face.

"You're supposed to smile." Brad carefully retracted the telephoto lens and turned off the camera. "The picture won't be as good if you frown, but it still won't turn out bad. This camera has a brain." He grinned infectiously. Lisa grinned back.

"That's not the problem," she said. "I'm used to taking bad pictures. But you can't keep the camera, Brad. It's much too expensive a gift." She held out her hand. "It's best to take it back to Kevin right now."

"N-no." Brad stuttered in his haste to get the word out. "It's mine. We made—"

"Give it to me." Lisa was too tired to argue. Brad could be stubborn as a mule when he made up his mind about something.

"No." Brad clutched the camera with both hands. He spread his legs and stood his ground. "I have his address."

"What?" Lisa was confused by the sudden shift in the conversation.

"I have his address." Brad took a deep breath. He ran his tongue over his lips but spoke slowly and clearly. "I'm going to pay him ten dollars every month for a year. I'm buying the camera on the—" he searched his memory for just the right word "—installment plan," he burst out triumphantly.

"You're buying the camera on the installment plan?"

"Yes." Brad grinned, nodding his head, satisfied that he'd presented his case well. "I'm buying it with my own money. One hundred and twenty-five dollars. I'm giving him a five-dollar down payment." Brad paused, scrupulously honest as always. "At least I will when I get my allowance on Tuesday. It has a real neat case, too."

"I'm sure it does." Lisa rested one hip on the back of the couch. She couldn't allow Brad to keep the camera. It must have cost three times the amount he'd just mentioned. "Why are you paying Kevin that much money for the camera?"

"He said that much. He knows everything about cameras. He wouldn't try to cheat me." Brad was adamant in his support of his new friend.

She'd warned her brother so many times about people who might try to take advantage of his good nature and the difficulties he had determining the value of things that he must have thought that was what she suspected Kevin of, also. As angry as she was becoming with the man, she would never undermine Brad's trust in him. "Of course he wouldn't do anything like that, but I'd better talk to him about the camera, anyway." First he'd offered to replace Katie's hat. Now he was practically giving Brad an expensive camera. She didn't like it.

Brad looked troubled, but answered readily enough. "Kevin's out in the fish house cleaning his pike so he can have fish for supper. Are you going to check his license now, too?"

"What?" Lisa felt a small wash of color rise into her cheeks. Her thoughts flew back to the incident that afternoon. She wished she could get the image of Kevin's bronzed skin and wheat-blond hair out of her mind. He'd looked fit and tanned and exceedingly handsome in that burgundy tank top and denim cutoffs. "Yes, I guess I may as well get it over with."

"Okay." Brad relaxed a little. He grinned from ear to ear as he carefully placed his new camera on the mantel. Lisa guessed he wanted it close at hand to show Katie and Matt when they returned from her softball game.

"Would you fix me a sandwich and some iced tea while I'm gone? I'm starved."

"Sure. What kind of sandwich?"

"Peanut butter will be fine."

"Do you want some soup?"

Lisa smiled and put her arm around his shoulder. "That would be nice, Brad. I'm glad you thought of it."

"Tomato? That's your favorite." Brad hugged her back. "Tomato's fine."

Lisa thought about taking the time to freshen up, maybe do something with the windblown mop of curls on top of her head, but decided against it. For all she knew Kevin was out there right now in her fish house filleting an illegally taken northern pike. This was business, not pleasure.

Kevin Sauder had turned her life topsy-turvy in a matter of days. Now he was doing the same to Brad and Katie. They were going to be hurt when he left. She didn't want that to happen to her brother and sister.

And most of all she didn't want it to happen to herself.

Chapter Eight

As she crossed the backyard Kevin was whistling a spirited and off-key rendition of a Beatles song. Lisa stopped for a moment, hidden in the shadows just beyond the rectangle of light coming from the screened openings that formed the top half of the small building, and watched him work.

He'd just finished cleaning his pike and was rinsing the large pale yellow fillets under the hose, inspecting them with obvious pride. Lisa smiled. Men and fish—something seemed to just naturally draw them together; she'd seen it countless times. Kevin laid the fillets on a large glass platter, carefully setting it to one side as he quickly and efficiently dealt with the entrails and began scrubbing down the wooden filleting table.

Golden light from the overhead bulb glinted in his blond hair. Lisa watched the play of light and shadow across the sleek muscles of his arms, the movement of his hands and wrists below the rolled-up sleeves of his gray flannel shirt. She found herself longing to run her palm over the curling dark blond hair covering the skin of his arms. She wanted to feel those same arms gather her close once again, hold her, caress her....

He'd stopped whistling, but when he spoke it was still a surprise.

"You don't have to stand out there in the dark. I'm all finished. I won't ask you to help clean up. One of us smelling like fish is enough." Kevin didn't look up from his task. He wasn't absolutely certain she was out there. It was more a hunch than anything else.

Lisa stiffened for a moment as he spoke, then she walked forward. She didn't think he'd heard her approach. The wind had risen since sundown. It was sighing through the birch trees like a lost soul, fracturing sounds, sending them scurrying off into the night like leaves before a storm. Crickets made scratchy music around the foundation of the building. In the swampy ground behind the garage, a chorus of frogs added to the symphony. "You have excellent hearing." She halted just beyond the screen door.

"Have you come to check my license, Officer?" Lisa wondered if she'd ever grow tired of seeing that wicked teasing glint in his eyes.

"Uh, yes, I did." She reached out one long honey-gold hand and opened the door, determined not to let herself be disturbed by his proximity.

"Right here in my back pocket." He had reached for a bottle of lemon-scented dishwashing liquid to clean his hands as she stepped inside the small building. Now he held up both soapy arms, like a surgeon scrubbing before an operation. He half turned away from her, presenting his backside, daring her to reach into the pocket of his jeans to remove his wallet.

"I'll wait until you're finished," she said.

She lifted her eyes to his and Kevin saw anger and anxiety reflected there. He suddenly felt uncomfortable teasing her in such a suggestive way. If he were honest with himself, he'd have admitted he was trying to intimidate her a little, throw her off balance, get her into his arms so that he could stake a claim on her.

"Sorry." He bent to rinse his hands under the hose attached to a hook above an old iron sink. "It'll only take me a minute."

"Never mind." Lisa risked another glance into his eyes. The jade-green irises had held a definite warmth just moments before. Now they were dark and shuttered. She'd overreacted to his teasing, pushed him away yet again. Deep in her heart she was sorry she'd done so. "Turn around." He did as he was told.

Lisa reached out two fingers and pulled the slim leather wallet from his pocket. She hadn't touched him in days, not since the night he'd kissed her beside her car. She ought to have been able to handle this. She ought to have built up an immunity to the fire he ignited in her blood. But she had not. The tips of her fingers barely grazed the denim of his jeans, yet she felt the heat of his body through the fabric, the firmness of muscle. She almost dropped the wallet in her haste to step away.

"It's in the middle section."

Lisa opened the wallet, feeling as though she were attempting something far more intimate than merely checking for evidence of his compliance with the fish-and-game laws of the state of Michigan. There were a couple of credit cards, a voter-registration card, a library card and his driver's license in plastic sleeves. She glanced at his birthday, unable to help herself. He was thirty-five, but only by a few weeks. His birthday was the last day of June. He was six foot four, weighed 185 pounds. She'd been very close in her estimation on both counts. Hair: blond. Eyes: green. Understatements, to say the least. Hair like a strand of summer wheat in the sunshine. Eyes like jade pools filled with silver sparks of cool fire. Lisa bit her lip and pulled her mind back to the business at hand. Inside the middle section, just as he'd indicated, she found a familiar green envelope from Gilson's that held a duly authorized non-resident fishing license. She noted the date. It had been issued several days before.

"Satisfied, Officer?" Kevin asked as he dried his hands with a wad of paper toweling.

"You should carry this with you at all times when you're fishing. Many people place them in waterproof bags and keep them in their tackle boxes." It was the standard opening of her "negligent fisherman" lecture.

"Yes, ma'am." He sounded both impatient and disappointed with her response. Kevin threw the paper towel into the trash basket. "It won't happen again." His face was stern and set in the harsh light cast by the single overhead bulb. He was standing very close, but he seemed at the same time very far away. He turned away from her to pick up the knife and the platter of fish.

"Kevin, I..." Lisa didn't know where to start. She just couldn't blurt out the truth. *I find you fascinating, appealing, intelligent. I'm falling in love with you, and oh, by the way, I have a genetic quirk that means my sons might be handicapped like Brad. And my daughters might be carriers like me.* The agony of saying those words out loud and seeing his horror made her weak in the knees. She leaned against the edge of the wet wooden table for support. When she did speak her voice was harsh and stilted with the effort she made to keep it steady. "I want to speak to you about something."

"Lisa, I'm sorry I made you uncomfortable with that wallet shenanigan." He hadn't touched her in days. He'd had no idea she'd react so strongly to the sexual game-playing he'd fallen to the temptation of indulging in. He felt like a jackass. He wanted to reach out and pull her into his arms, tell her he was falling in love with her. Hell, tell her the truth. He *was* in love with her. He wanted to watch her honey-gold eyes darken with passion and joy, hear her say she loved him, too.

"It's not that." Again she spoke too sharply, too fast. Darkness, deep and shuttered, changed the jade of his eyes to the color of pines in the twilight.

"Then what is it?" He put the platter of fish back down on the table. Kevin stood before her, towering over her, both legs planted firmly on the sand-and-gravel floor beneath them. "What's wrong?"

"The hat. And the camera." The words tumbled out.

"What?" His dark gold brows drew together in a puzzled frown. "What are you talking about?"

"I'm talking about your giving things to my brother and sister." Lisa stood her ground. Maybe indignation would blot out the need she felt to be close to him, to smooth away the deep furrows between his eyes, to stop thinking so much and just let herself feel.

"I'm not giving things to Brad and Katie."

"Yes, you are."

Kevin took a deep breath. He wasn't going to have this discussion degenerate into a shouting match. "Be specific." She was, next to his sister Laurel possibly, the most aggravating woman he'd ever met. But still he couldn't help notice the rise and fall of her breasts beneath her shirt, the stubborn tilt of her chin, the kissable curve of her lips.

"I don't want you to buy Katie a new hat to replace the one that fell in the lake."

"Why not? It was my fault it happened. She was helping me net that damn pike." He gestured with a flick of his hand at the platter of fillets. "I owe her a replacement."

He crossed his arms over his chest and glared back at her. "How old was the thing?"

"What?" The question startled her. She couldn't understand what he was getting at.

"When did she buy the hat?" Kevin spoke with exaggerated clarity, as though she were somewhat deaf.

"This spring." Lisa was totally off balance and Kevin knew it. He pressed his advantage. "Then I'll prorate the price. I'll offer her seven dollars and fifty cents. Maybe she can find one on sale. I'll also explain to her that you wouldn't allow me to fully compensate her for her loss like the gentleman my mother raised me to be." He scowled down at her from his great height.

"I..." Lisa couldn't be sure any longer if he was serious or not. He still looked angry, but the sparks of amusement had returned to his eyes. "I...see your point," she conceded as graciously as she could manage. "If that's the way you feel about it, of course you may replace Katie's hat."

"Thank you." Kevin smiled and Lisa felt the heat of it all the way to the base of her spine. She spoke quickly before she lost her train of thought and began to think too closely about how, exactly, it felt to be kissed by that mouth.

"But that doesn't solve the problem of your selling Brad the camera."

"Do you think I took advantage of him?" It saddened him that she might think that.

"Exactly the opposite." He frowned harder. The amusement left his eyes. Lisa hated to see it go, but she couldn't back down now. "That camera is worth far more than the price the two of you agreed on."

"I think that's the operative phrase here, Lisa. The price we agreed on." Had he been reading her all wrong? The thought was as painful as a knife wound. Were the feelings he was experiencing all one-sided? He looked deep into her golden brown eyes and saw only confusion and distress.

"You're practically giving it away."

Kevin laughed, and it was a hard rough sound that grated on her nerves, made gooseflesh pop out on the skin of her arms. Why was she arguing with him like this? What made her feel so antagonistic, so defensive?

"I certainly wouldn't want to make the mistake of offering a deal to a member of the Emery clan again." He leaned one hand flat on the wooden table. "Listen. I'll try to explain my reasoning, okay?" He wasn't smiling now. He was deadly serious. Lisa nodded. "Brad enjoys that camera. He can take snapshots just as well as you or I. It will give him pleasure and satisfaction. But to me that camera is nothing but a toy."

"Why do you have it with you?" Lisa couldn't stop herself from asking. She already knew his answer; he would call it a toy, just as she imagined he viewed the camera he'd fixed for Katie.

"I bought it as a control. I thought, maybe, please God just maybe, there was something wrong with my cameras, my lenses, anything but what it really was."

"Your vision." Lisa felt her breath come quick and hard, fighting its way past the lump of emotion that blocked her throat.

"My vision." Kevin's voice was low and quiet, almost devoid of emotion. "I must have shot half a dozen rolls of film in the next few hours. I took photos of everything I could get in my viewfinder. I developed them myself so there'd be no question of negligence there. Every damn exposure was perfectly in focus. Every one. Even though some of the shots had been so blurry when I composed them that I wasn't even sure I'd gotten the subject I intended to shoot. God, I hated that camera."

"Why did you keep it?"

Kevin shrugged. He smiled down at her, but it was really a grimace, completely lacking the easy grace and charm she so loved to see. "Do you mean why didn't I make some extravagant, useless gesture like throwing it into the trash, or smashing it into a thousand pieces with a hammer?"

"Yes." Lisa spoke so softly he had to bend his head to hear. Was the emotion he saw in her eyes compassion for his pain, or merely pity? He couldn't be sure, and the uncertainty haunted him.

"I guess I just wasn't raised that way. Besides, it's a perfectly good camera. I put it in a big case with twenty thousand dollars worth of lenses and cameras, stuck the whole thing in my trunk and drove around Bartlow for six weeks without ever looking at any of it again." His tone was ironic. He shook his head as if he couldn't quite believe he'd done such a thing.

"Until today." Lisa felt more and more distress. She could almost feel his agony, the pain that had come near to shattering his soul, and she wished to heaven she could not. It frightened her to be so attuned to another human being. So attuned to a man—this man in particular.

"Until today." Kevin raised his hand to touch a curling wisp of her hair. She turned her head slightly. Her breath grazed the inside of his wrist. Sensation shot through him like a live current.

"You did this for my brother." Kevin cupped her face with his hands, and Lisa didn't back away although her logical mind warned her to. Would it have been so wrong to give in to this feeling of oneness? Would it have been so wrong to let someone else direct her life, to follow her heart, even if only for a short time?

"I know he can't handle light meters and f-stops yet—maybe he never will. But he'll enjoy this camera. Let him broaden his horizons, Lisa. Let him accomplish all he can on his own. He'll try his damnedest to succeed, just like he's doing with the driving lessons."

"Driving lessons?" Lisa had nestled her cheek into the curve of his palm. Now she straightened abruptly, leaving him standing with his hand in midair. She stepped back, her golden eyes shooting sparks of amber flame. "What driving lessons?"

"Damn." He'd been thinking with his heart, not with his brain. He'd given his word to Brad and Katie to keep quiet about the driving lessons. Now he had spoken out of turn, betrayed by his own physical responses to the woman standing stiff and unbelieving before him.

"Katie's helping Brad work toward getting his learner's permit. I volunteered to help."

For a moment he thought she might burst into tears. She shook her head, denying his words. "He can't drive. It's too dangerous, too complicated. He'll get flustered. He'll get lost, have an accident..." Lisa's words rushed out in her haste to vocalize her fears. "You have no right," she said, the edges of her words as sharp as splinters of glass.

"Wait a minute." Kevin wanted to take her by the arms and shake her until she saw reason. He might have if he hadn't known he was in the wrong. "I didn't say we had him out there practicing in an Indy car on the interstate, did I? Give us some credit. Give Brad some credit."

"He's my responsibility, not yours." Lisa put her hands on her hips; she had to do something with them or she was afraid she might slap him. He had no right! He had no right to offer his help and his strength and his caring. She was responsible for Brad's safety and well-being. No one else. Not her mother or Katie. Certainly not this stranger who was only passing through.

"His happiness is the responsibility of everyone who cares for him." Kevin astounded himself with the forcefulness of his declaration. His life was so screwed up at the moment he could barely take care of himself. What was he doing claiming to know what was best for another, more fragile, human being?

"How can you say that? You've barely known him, known any of us, for more than a few days." He'd never seen Brad in one of his rare rages, or the bad weeks when even the simplest tasks seemed too much for him.

"Sometimes a few days is all it takes to learn how much you care for another." His words held several meanings. He did care for Brad, his welfare, his success in stretching the boundaries of his limited world. But he also found himself wanting to take some of the burden for ensuring Brad's happiness from Lisa's shoulders. But she wasn't ready to listen to what he was saying. Maybe she never would be.

"No, that isn't all it takes," Lisa said. "You have to know when to pull back, when to say no. Everything Brad does is a struggle, from picking out the clothes he wears to making change for a dollar bill. Each skill he masters is a task so difficult most people would give up in despair almost as soon as they started—normal people, like you and me." She laughed, and the sound was sad and filled with sorrow and tore at Kevin's heart. "But not Brad. He works and he works, but he has limits. There are things he just can't do."

"You shouldn't be so afraid for him, so afraid he'll fail and be hurt that you don't let him try at all." He hadn't meant to speak so harshly, sound so judgmental, but he could feel her drawing away, retreating within herself, and it scared him. He couldn't force her to acknowledge what he said, acknowledge what was growing between them, offer him a place in her life. She was throwing up barricades around her feelings faster than he could tear them down. She was as much a stranger to him now, this moment, as she'd been the first night they met.

"I hate you." This time she didn't suppress the urge to strike him. She raised her hand and slapped him full across the face, releasing a tidal wave of pent-up rage and agony that had been festering inside her for almost ten years. Kevin never flinched.

"I hate you," she repeated in a tight ragged voice, and for a brief moment she did. He'd come into her quiet serene life and spun her world off its axis. Now it seemed he was threatening her relationship with her brother and sister. Worse yet, he was making her see herself as a woman, desirable and desirous, and that was even more unforgivable. Lisa looked down at her hand as if it belonged to somebody else. Her palm stung. Tears blurred her eyes. She looked up, horrified to see the print of her hand, first white, then red, appear on his cheek. "Don't tell me how to love my brother." *Don't tell me I have to love you.*

She turned on her heel before he could say another word and marched out into the night, leaving Kevin standing alone, as angry and bewildered as she was.

"KATIE, IF I'VE TOLD YOU ONCE I've told you a thousand times. Keep your shoes off the furniture." Lisa pushed her fingers through her hair, lifting it off her neck to catch the cooling stir of air from the ceiling fan. It was hot and muggy with more than a hint of summer thunder in the air. Outside the window above her desk, heavy gray storm clouds hung in a brassy sky. She almost wished it would storm, clear the air, even though lightning strikes would almost inevitably lead to a fire somewhere close by.

"It's more like a million," Katie replied under her breath.

"I don't care how many times it's been. Get your shoes off the coffee table." A small annoying beat of pain stabbed at her left temple. Lisa reached up two fingers and tried in vain to smooth it away.

"I'm not wearing shoes," Katie pointed out with maddening logic, as she inspected the incredibly long fingernails she'd just applied the third coat of Passionate Plum nail gloss to. "My stocking feet—" she kicked one bare leg in the air, motioning to the pink cotton sock folded around her slender ankle "—are resting on a magazine, which in turn is resting on the surface of the coffee table. Therefore, technically, I do not have either my shoes or my feet on the coffee table."

"I said get them off." A meaningful dialogue with an almost-sixteen-year-old on a hot humid July day was almost out of the question.

Katie sighed, a long-suffering kind of sigh that set Lisa's teeth on edge. She waved her hands in the air, stirring wispy cinnamon curls around her cheeks. She turned her head to regard Lisa from narrowed hazel eyes. "I was reading this article on PMS the other day. Frankly, you've got a lot of the symptoms—"

"Enough." Lisa was just about out of patience. She had a week's worth of reports and requisitions to finish before she was due at district headquarters the next morning at eight. She'd been sitting at her desk for more than an hour and hadn't even made it through her mileage log.

"—except that Kevin is acting the same way and I know he can't have it, too," Katie continued, ignoring her older sister's directive. "I asked him if he'd like to come to supper yesterday afternoon when I took my book over for him to autograph, and he nearly bit my head off.'' She was swinging both feet now, her arms folded over the back of the couch, her chin balanced on her hands. ''Then he apologized and smiled at me in that kind of sad sexy way he has.'' She sighed again, remembering the moment. Lisa gritted her teeth, putting a decimal point in her mileage total with so much force that the lead in her pencil snapped.

''I don't want to hear this.''

''I know you don't.'' Katie nodded her head in feigned sympathy. ''He said he didn't think he'd be welcome to dinner in this house. He said that you'd had a misunderstanding. What in the world could you find to argue about with a hunk like that?''

''He's opinionated and manipulative.'' Lisa shut her mouth with a snap. The next thing she knew she'd be asking her baby sister the best way to apologize to the ''hunk.''

''You didn't answer my question,'' Katie pointed out.

''I don't intend to.'' Lisa didn't know why, but she hadn't said anything to Brad and Katie about her knowledge of the clandestine driving lessons. She'd had a lot of time to think about it. Three long miserable, virtually sleepless nights had passed since her argument with Kevin. She still felt betrayed by his going behind her back to work with Katie teaching Brad to drive. Her feelings were hurt and her heart ached, but now it was more because she felt left out, saddened by her sister's lack of trust in her judgment of Brad's abilities than because she was adamantly opposed to the scheme. And because she'd behaved so abominably to Kevin.

Katie wasn't going to let the subject drop if she could help it. ''Well, if you ask me—''

"I specifically didn't ask you." Lisa refused to meet her sister's surprisingly knowing eyes. Katie continued as if she hadn't heard a word Lisa said.

"It isn't PMS, it's l-o-v-e."

"Katherine Lenore, that is more than enough silliness."

Katie laughed and surged up off the sofa. "Of course, that's only my humble opinion."

"Go start the dishes." Lisa stuck the end of her pencil in the sharpener. *Love.* Her mind was a whirl of heated images, her cheeks dark with chagrin that Katie should have guessed the truth so easily.

"I'll do them later." Katie grinned mischievously at her sister's obvious discomfort. "Matt's coming by in about ten minutes to pick me up. We're going over to Nancy's house to make the final plans for the camping trip."

The dull measured pain in her temple intensified. Lisa quit grinding her pencil into sawdust and turned to face her sister. "I'm still not sure..." The camping trip was less than a week away and she hadn't yet given Katie her final decision. The phone rang at her elbow, causing her to nearly jump off her seat. The beat of pain quickened and moved behind her eyes. Lisa picked up the receiver. "Officer Emery. May I help you?"

"Officer Emery?" It was a woman's voice, light and quick and slightly puzzled. It was a long-distance connection. Lisa could hear static, ghostly voices, clicks and whirs, faint but audible in the background. She was also aware that Katie hadn't left the room, but was waiting to continue to press for unqualified permission to participate in the coed camping trip.

There was silence at the other end of the connection. Lisa waited a moment, then spoke again. "May I help you?"

"Yes. My name is Laurel Norris. I'm trying to reach Kevin Sauder. Do I have the correct number?" She didn't sound as if she believed she did.

"I can give Mr. Sauder your message." Lisa pulled her thoughts into order and spoke with formal politeness.

"I want to speak to my brother now, if that's possible. I'll hold the line if you'd be so kind as to tell him I'm calling." Laurel Norris sounded happy, excited and breathless.

"He's out on the lake, fishing." Lisa had seen him walk across the yard an hour ago, fishing gear in hand. She'd heard the boat motor roar to life and move onto the lake. It was just about the same time her headache had appeared.

"Oh." Kevin's sister sounded very disappointed. Lisa caught herself wondering how the other woman looked. Was she as tall and slim as her brother? Were her eyes the same deep shade of green?

"I'll let him know you called as soon as he returns." Lisa let her tone of voice warm and soften. There was no reason to take out her bad temper on a stranger.

"Would you, please? I have the most wonderful news to tell him. It's about the baby. Kevin's his godfather." Kevin's sister broke off laughing. "I'm sorry, Officer Emery. I don't mean to bore you with news that's only important to another Sauder."

"It's no trouble, really. And please, call me Lisa." She had no idea why she'd offered the use of her name except that Laurel Norris's voice was bright and friendly and her laughter infectious.

"Thank you. And please call me Laurel. You see, it's just that my son—his name's Samuel Kevin, by the way," Kevin's sister went on, unable to hide her pride, "smiled today. Laughed out loud actually and he's only twelve days old."

"Remarkable." Lisa spoke with complete sincerity, but her smile was bittersweet. "He must be very advanced for his age."

"Oh, he is. He sleeps through the night already. Well, until six anyway. And when you live on a farm, that is morning."

"You're very lucky." It seemed strange to be speaking so comfortably with a woman she'd never even seen.

"Yes, I am. Very lucky.... Uh, Lisa..." Laurel Norris hesitated so long, Lisa began to wonder if the connection had been broken. "Is Kevin...enjoying himself?" The fleeting moment of intimacy she'd experienced with Kevin's sister faded away. Laurel's voice was still pleasant, polite but distant, as though she, too, had suddenly remembered she was speaking to a stranger. A stranger who wouldn't know anything about her brother or his problems.

Lisa responded in a like manner. "He seems to be."

"I'm glad to hear that." Relief was evident in Laurel's tone. "We've been worried about him. You will have him call me as soon as he can?"

"Certainly."

"Good. Oh yes, one last favor."

"Of course." Lisa pushed the stub of her pencil behind her ear and stared out at the setting sun. A boat containing a single fisherman was silhouetted against the orange and pink of the western sky. Was it Kevin? How could she face him? She wanted to apologize, but what could she say?

"Tell Kevin I'll be at Mom and Dad's until eight. Then Seth and I will be at home."

"No problem." The boat was moving slowly across her line of vision. She turned away from the window.

"Thanks again. And, Lisa, it's been nice talking with you."

"Thank you." Lisa couldn't think of anything else to say.

When Lisa replaced the receiver, she wore a thoughtful frown. Kevin's sister had a new baby. A son. A shaft of painful envy streaked through her heart, nearly cutting off her breath. How she envied Laurel Norris. A baby, a child of her own, was something she, Lisa, could never have.

The sound of Matt's old pickup pulling into the yard disturbed the quiet, broke up the heavy pattern of her thoughts. "Got to go," Katie exclaimed, grabbing her purse and a jacket and heading for the back door.

"Katie, will you run over to the cabin and leave a note for Kevin about returning his sister's call. I...I might have to go check on some things...." Lisa let her voice trail off into silence.

Katie was already shaking her head. "No, I won't. And Brad won't be back until late this evening. It's his bowling night, remember? Looks like you're going to have to deliver the message yourself, whether you're speaking to the man or not." With a saucy shake of her auburn curls, Katie was gone, letting the screen door slam behind her with a satisfying bang.

Chapter Nine

"I'd like to use your phone." Kevin stood just outside the back door, the glow from the porch light giving his hair the texture and color of burnished gold. He was wearing jeans and the long-sleeved gray flannel shirt and black sweatshirt she'd seen him in once or twice before. In his hand he clutched the note she'd taped to his back door informing him of his sister's phone call.

Lisa hesitated a fraction of a second, her hand on the latch. It was getting late. Katie and Brad weren't home yet. They would be alone for at least a few minutes. She still hadn't decided how best to apologize to him. She'd been hoping he'd read her note and go to Gilson's to use the pay phone. Now, instead, he was just a few feet away and she couldn't think of a thing to say, or a reasonable excuse to deny his request.

"I know it's late." Kevin spoke as if reading her mind. "I'd make the call from Gilson's but I have exactly twenty-two cents in change. My sister will worry if I wait until morning."

"She was much too excited for you to make her wait to tell you her news." Lisa smiled, but there was no humor or lightness in her expression. Her voice was soft, slightly husky, as though filled with loss, of wanting, long and deeply hidden.

"I take it this call has something to do with my new nephew?"

Lisa continued to look at him, or maybe "through him" was a better way to describe it. He didn't know if he felt more anger or pain at her continued cool behavior. She opened the door and stepped aside, motioning toward the telephone on her desk.

"Just dial one, the area code and your sister's number. I'll be out on the porch if you have any trouble getting through."

"Thanks." He smiled, just to see if he could get her to smile back. She was wearing a bright coral-colored pull over blouse and shorts. Her legs, tanned the same shade of creamy gold as the rest of her skin, seemed to go on for ever. Lisa wasn't looking at him, didn't see him watching her.

She hadn't realized it would hurt so much to have him so close physically, and yet so distant emotionally. But what could she expect? She'd slapped his face, told him she hated him and to stay out of her life, to stay out of Brad's and Katie's lives. A rift like that wasn't going to heal it self. One of them would have to take the first step. "Kevin, I..."

"Yes?" He'd already started to dial.

"Nothing." Lisa let cowardice win. "I'll be on the porch." She walked stiffly across the room and into the enclosed porch to drop into a big pine rocker her grand father had made seventy years before. She curled her legs up under her and looked out through the screen window at the twinkling lights of other homes and cottages on the far side of the lake. The sky was ebony velvet, dark and overcast. The threat of a storm that had made the after noon so oppressive had never materialized. The night was cool and still. Sound carried clearly through the soft darkness. Kevin's voice carried clearly to the porch.

Lisa was aware she should get up, close the connecting door between the porch and the main room of the house, but she could not. The sound of his voice, low and husky, a little rough around the edges, was too dear, too intriguing to shut out. Instead she tried not to eavesdrop. It was impossible. Every word he spoke came to her ears whole and complete.

Kevin had paused in his dialing, and watched Lisa leave the room, and as he completed dialing his sister's number, he wondered what Lisa had been going to say. But when Laurel answered the phone, his attention was instantly focussed on her and her news.

"Hi, squirt." Kevin propped one hip against the corner of Lisa's desk as he responded to his sister's greeting.

"Kevin. It's good to hear your voice." Laurel didn't even bother to scold him for his use of her detested childhood nickname.

"How's my favorite nephew?" Kevin deliberately kept his tone light and easy. He knew how much his abrupt departure from the hospital that day must have upset Laurel and Seth. He'd talked to his father and mother twice since coming to Michigan, assuring them he was fine and working things out. They had taken his words at face value. Laurel was going to be a lot harder to convince.

"Your nephew is fine. Guess what he did today?"

"Signed a letter of intent to play football at Ohio State?"

"Kevin, be serious."

"Okay, what marvelous feat has Sam-the-Man mastered?"

"He smiled."

"No kidding?" Kevin fought to keep the laughter from his voice. Laurel sounded so triumphant, so proudly maternal.

"This morning when I gave him his bath. And it wasn't just gas, either," she added with a hint of defiance, her voice becoming slightly muffled as though she'd turned her head away from the mouthpiece. Kevin could picture her in the living room of the big old white frame farmhouse she and Seth had moved into after their marriage. His sister, his oldest friend and their son were a unit, a family, each giving and receiving of one another's love. Kevin had been away from home and family, on his own for so many years, that he'd forgotten how caring and supportive that loving circle could be. "Seth thinks it was just gas. But it wasn't." Laurel was adamant. "He smiled at Seth at lunch and at Mom and Dad when we were over there earlier this evening."

"Definitely sounds like the genuine article to me."

Laurel giggled. "I knew you'd believe me, big brother." She paused and when she spoke again there was a slight catch in her light musical voice. "Oh, Kev. When are you coming home? Sam's growing so fast. You're going to miss seeing it."

"Take lots of pictures." Kevin could see his reflection in the dark glass of the window above Lisa's desk. His image was smiling. The smile faded away as he spoke, but the familiar emptiness, the sense of bewildered loss he usually experienced when talking about anything that pertained to photography failed to materialize. It simply wasn't there.

"Kevin?" Laurel was serious at once, possibly picking up on the confusion in his mind and emotions, possibly experiencing some of her own. "Are you...happy there?"

"I'm doing fine, squirt. I like it here. It's quiet, peaceful. I'm working things out."

Working things out. When Lisa heard Kevin say these words, she got up from the rocking chair and moved to the far end of the porch. She stepped close to the window, letting the night sounds—the grating chorus of cricket song, the splash of waves against the concrete retaining wall that protected the front yard from the fury of spring storms— fill her ears and her senses. Mentally she blocked out the sound of Kevin's voice and what he would say next. For logically, after *working things out*, came *I'll be home soon.* When he'd made peace with himself and the limitations to his sight, he'd be gone from her life.

"Lisa?" He was very near. Lisa caught her breath. Startled, she lifted her hand to her throat. He was standing just inside the doorway to the porch, a tall dark figure silhouetted against the light.

"Over here." She tried to hide her emotions, all of them. She stepped forward until she, too, stood in the small pool of light from the doorway, a polite noncommittal smile on her face.

"I couldn't see you in the shadows." He closed his eyes, willing himself not to strain his sight to see her better.

"Kevin ..." She had to apologize, get it over with or she'd lose her nerve.

"Lisa..." Her face came into focus. She looked uncertain yet determined at the same time. They spoke in unison, then broke off. Kevin waited.

"Yes?" she said with reluctance.

He slid one hand into the pocket of his jeans, leaning against the doorjamb with lazy negligent grace. He watched her closely, wanting more than anything else to reach out and take her in his arms, kiss away the uncertainty in her glorious golden brown eyes. He was moving too fast for her again; he could sense it in the tenseness of her gaze, the stiffness in her arms and shoulders. She reminded him of the wary and beautiful animals he'd captured on film for so many years. She had to be handled very gently, with infinite tenderness and understanding, or she would bolt into the night, never to be seen again. "I just want to be sure you include the charge for my phone call on my bill."

It was the last thing Lisa expected him to say. There was something in the way he held his body, the curve of his mouth, the tilt of his head, that made her think he meant to speak...of what? Of things that pass between men and women? Of love? Lisa straightened to her full height. Distance was what she wanted between them, not dreams of coming together, of a sharing of heart and soul, of oneness. Distance was what she was getting. His voice was cool and detached. So was hers. "Don't be ridiculous."

"I insist." Again the reply was clipped and formal. Lisa wanted to cry and didn't quite know why.

"It isn't necessary."

"Oh, but it is, Officer Emery." Lisa opened her mouth to refute him once again, then closed it with a snap. She couldn't see his expression, couldn't make out the dancing silver sparks in his eyes in the half light, but she could hear the amusement in his words, feel the warmth of his low rough voice caress her skin like sunlight, like the touch of his hands.

He wasn't distant. He wasn't angry. He was teasing her again.

"Whatever you wish." She didn't feel like being teased. Had he forgotten what had passed between them Sunday night? "I'll send a copy of the toll charge to your home address if you give it to me when you leave. The phone bill doesn't come for another ten days or so."

"What makes you think I'll be leaving before then?"

"I...I assumed."

"That I'd be leaving just because my nephew smiled at his mother?"

"Your family misses you. I could tell that when I spoke to Laurel this afternoon."

"Laurel?" She sensed rather than saw the upward movement of his eyebrow.

"She asked me to call her Laurel," Lisa replied a bit defensively. "And she's so excited about the new baby...."

"She liked you, too."

"What?"

"My sister liked you, too."

"I'm glad." Lisa spoke before she could stop herself. Yet what difference did it make if Laurel Norris liked her or not? She'd probably never speak to the woman again in her life.

"She asked me what kind of 'Officer Emery' you were. She said you're the first female game warden she's ever talked to." He straightened from his lounging position against the door, stepping closer so that she had to tilt her head back a little to keep him in view. "She's a pharmacist, just like my dad. And Seth, her husband, is a farmer now. Up until last year he was a Secret Service agent. They're all well and happy and getting along perfectly well without me. Does that convince you that it isn't necessary for me to go rushing back home?"

"Don't be silly." Lisa felt as if she were quickly being towed beyond her depth. She wanted to ask him so many more questions about his family, his hometown, his life before he'd made contact with hers. "It isn't any of my business." She said it as much to convince herself as him. He wasn't giving her an opening to apologize for slapping him. If he didn't quit twisting her words around and throwing them back at her, she'd forget her good intentions and slap him again.

"I want to make it your business." Kevin was suddenly serious. He jammed both hands into the pockets of his jeans, stretching the material tight across his slim hips. "The truth is I'm not ready to go back to Bartlow." He paused for the space of several heartbeats. His voice came out husky and strained. So much depended on how she reacted to what he said next. "I want to stay here."

"Stay here?" Lisa repeated, her voice no more than a whisper of sound in the near darkness of the porch.

"Stay here." There was so much more he wanted to add to that simple statement, but he couldn't, not yet. "Are you still so angry about the other night that you want me to leave?"

"No." The word burst from her of its own volition. Lisa reached out her hand, laying her fingers on his arm, feeling the sleek hardness of bone and muscle beneath the soft flannel shirt.

Kevin's pulse began to accelerate. "No, you don't want me to leave? Or no, you aren't angry with me anymore?" He made himself stand quietly, waiting for her answer.

"Both." Lisa took a deep steadying breath. "I want to apologize..." That was as far as she got. He moved so quickly she didn't have time to back away. He took her into his arms and held her close.

"Don't you apologize. I was wrong. I shouldn't have gone along with Brad and Katie's scheme."

Lisa put her hand on his shoulders, pushing him a little away so that they could talk without the overwhelming distraction of his body touching hers. It was important to tell him what was on her mind, what was in her heart. "No. I overreacted. I always do where Brad's well-being is concerned. Driving a car..." She shook her head, trying to word her misgivings so that he would understand her behavior that night. "I'm not sure he can manage that."

She looked up into the dark reflecting pools of his eyes. They appeared almost black now, shadowed by the night. "I'm afraid for him."

Kevin's voice was low, soothing. He touched his lips to her forehead lightly, gently. Lisa closed her eyes and let herself be lulled by the quiet assurance of his words. "We can't let love make us afraid." They were having the same discussion they'd had on Friday night. They were even using some of the same words. But this was different, very different from that painful antagonistic encounter.

Kevin lifted his head. He smoothed curling wisps of cinnamon-brown hair from her cheek with one hand, and held her close with the other. She looked up into his face. She let her fingers curve into the soft flannel of his shirt. "I wish I could make you understand. Brad tries so hard, it's easy sometimes for other people to overestimate his abilities." Here, she realized, was an opportunity to tell him that Brad was less severely handicapped than other individuals with Down syndrome because the abnormality in the chromosomes that caused his particular form of the condition was rare—and hereditary. But for some reason the words wouldn't come. The moment passed.

"Brad deserves the chance to be as independent as possible. Let him try." Kevin had spent little time with the mentally handicapped, but he sensed that what Lisa said was true. Her brother was more advanced in his physical and social skills than others with Down syndrome he'd come in contact with. "I'll help all I can."

Lisa stepped out of his embrace so quickly that Kevin was taken off guard. He lifted his hand as if to stop her then let it fall to his side. She walked past him into the living room, stopping before the fieldstone fireplace. She stared straight ahead. The soft lamplight in the big room brought out golden highlights in her auburn hair, muted the vibrant coral shade of her blouse, made her skin glow like warm honey.

"Lisa, did I say something wrong?" Kevin was genuinely confused. She shook her head.

"You'll help for as long as you're here." She turned to face him. Tears sparkled on her long spiky lashes. She frowned, the dark brown of her eyebrows and eyelashes contrasting vividly with her pale golden skin. "But you're only passing through our lives, Kevin. We both know that."

Kevin made a leap of faith. In the space of a moment he knew the truth. He loved Lisa Emery as he'd loved no other woman. He didn't want to leave her, to take up his solitary wandering life again. Yet he wasn't sure what his future held. What if he had nothing more to offer her than what he was now—a man with no direction, no way of knowing what tomorrow would bring. He hadn't thought much past opening the detested portrait studio on Main Street. He'd made no plans to get on with his life. Lisa came complete with a ready-made family, with responsibilities and obligations he'd never encountered in his footloose existence.

"I don't want to just pass through your life, Lisa. I want to be part of it." He held out his hands. Caution and his own unsettled thoughts had tempered the words he wished to speak, made them less than the total commitment he wanted to offer her. He'd never thought about how he would tell a woman he loved her, what words he would use, and now it was too late.

"Kevin, don't..." She felt like crying. It would be so easy to love this man. He would be everything she wanted and needed in a life partner. She lifted her hands and folded them within the strong hard confines of his own. What was he saying? He was offering her some part of himself, but how much? For how long? She simply didn't know how to respond.

The frightened forest creature he often glimpsed staring back at him from her golden-brown eyes had returned. Had she misunderstood his halting words? Kevin felt a quick cold stab of fear. Didn't she care for him as deeply as he'd come to care for her? In any event, he'd frightened her again, and that was the last thing he wanted to happen. "I'm not talking about a summer fling." He drew her close once more, cradling her against him, falling back on the easy teasing banter she seemed to enjoy, but it took an effort of will that was almost physical to keep his voice even and not too intense.

"Weren't you?" she asked.

Kevin felt her smile as she rested her cheek against his shoulder. He relaxed a little, but at the same time he couldn't stop his body from reacting to her closeness. He wanted to kiss her so badly he could taste it, taste her. The memory of their earlier kisses was sweet on his tongue. He cupped her lovely stubborn chin in his hands and looked down into the liquid gold of her eyes. "I think you're afraid I might want to stick around for more than a one-night stand."

"What makes you think that?" Lisa wound her arms around his neck, still uncertain, still frightened of the intimate direction their conversation had taken, but too entranced to pull away. She liked the way the hard planes and angles of his body seemed to fit all her softer feminine curves. She could feel his desire, unfamiliar and exciting, as he pressed her close. She moved against him with a boldness she'd never before displayed. She was amazed at the intensity of his response. He tightened his hold, lowered his head to kiss her quick and hard. She kissed him back, despite the nervous clamoring warnings of her wary heart. Kevin Sauder was not a man to lose control. She was safe in his arms, as long as she wanted to be safe.

Kevin's eyes sparkled with devilry and mischief at her question, and if she didn't look too deeply, she could pretend not to see something more, something heated, seeking, and very, very male.

"All seemingly liberated, independent women," he said, "secretly want to be thrown over some strong, great-looking guy's shoulder to be carried off into the night and ravaged over and over." Kevin's marvelous sexy smile changed to a leer.

"Where did you come up with that crazy theory?" Lisa couldn't help it. She had to laugh at his exaggerated lustful expression. And frankly, the theory didn't sound so crazy if Kevin Sauder was the man doing the abducting.

"I read it somewhere." He looked as innocent as a choirboy. "In one of those weighty psychological tomes. Uh, *Playboy,* I think."

"An unimpeachable source." Lisa shook her head. "However—"

Suddenly Kevin was tired of playing games. "However, you're sidestepping the issue, Lisa."

"I haven't thought about any kind of relationship, Kevin." She was lying. She'd thought about being with him, being his, countless times. "I . . . my life is here. I'm dug in. My roots are here. And you're very vulnerable right now."

"Hey, that's supposed to be my line."

Lisa reached up and laid her fingers across his lips. "Shhh, let me speak. It's the truth. You were running away when you came here. It's too soon. You can't know for sure you've found what you were looking for."

"I've found you." He kissed the tips of her fingers as he spoke. Lisa outlined the curve of his jaw, feeling the scratchy roughness of a day's growth of beard, wondering what that roughness would feel like caressing her breasts. She lowered her hand abruptly.

"I can't just follow my heart, Kevin." She said it as much for her own sake as his. "I have to consider my brother and my sister in each and every decision I make. That won't be any different when it comes to choosing the man I love."

"We don't always get to choose who we love."

"Oh God, I know." The tears came then, suddenly, unexpectedly. Two great crystal drops that traced a glistening trail down the curve of her cheek. A picture of Brad swam into view behind her closed eyelids. So dear, so funny, so much in need of her love and guidance. She wouldn't trade his gentle affectionate company for anything on earth. But neither could she find the courage within herself to want to bring another such fragile human being into the cold hard world. That was the truth that lay at the bottom of her refusal to commit herself to Kevin Sauder. For Lisa, commitment meant love and marriage and family. Kevin would make a wonderful husband and father. But it wasn't fair to offer him her love, and her less-than-perfect body to mother those children.

"Lisa, I know that loving you means loving Katie and Brad."

She nodded, looking up at him with tear-drenched eyes. It also meant not having children of his own. No matter how hard he tried to downplay his pride and interest in his brand-new nephew, Lisa could sense how much the baby meant to him. He deserved children of his own. She couldn't give them to him. She should say so, now. But where to begin? She knew so little of men and how they felt, how they reacted to things of this nature. All she could really think of was how much she wanted to experience what it was like to love this man, physically, emotionally, with all her heart and soul. Not how to tell him he couldn't stay in her life.

"I'm no green kid. I know what I want." Kevin's heart thundered in his chest. He wanted Lisa now and forever. Everything else would fall into place from that moment on. He could build a future for them, for all of them if she was by his side. He could conquer anything, partial blindness included, if Lisa loved him. "I know what I want. I want you and I can wait until you know that's what you want, too."

"And if I don't want you?" Lisa would never know where she found the courage to ask that question.

Kevin's eyes darkened almost to black. He lowered his head and kissed her again, slowly, intimately, thoroughly. He molded her tightly to the lean hard length of his body, leaving no doubt as to how much he desired her. "If you don't want me, all you have to do is say so."

He seemed to tower over her, blocking out the light from the single lamp in the corner of the room. She wasn't afraid, not physically. If she told him to leave—leave the room, leave her life—he would. As long as he was convinced that it was what she wanted him to do. But Lisa wasn't a fool. She was much too poor a liar to attempt an outright denial. Yet if she didn't send him away now, she was sealing her fate. She decided to try to compromise, but the ploy was doomed to failure before the words left her mouth. Kevin Sauder would take all she had to give, or none of it, but he'd never settle for only bits and pieces of her love. "I need a little time," she said.

He continued to hold her close. "You don't need time if you want me out of your life. All you have to say is go I will. It will be harder than anything I've ever done in my life, but I'll go." His eyes held her will as surely as hi hands held her body. He demanded an answer, and she could do nothing less than comply.

It was easy, after all. Lisa made her own leap of faith, although at the time she didn't see it as such. She only knew he required her answer and she gave it to him.

"No, Kevin, don't go. Stay with us for as long as you can." She lifted her face for his kiss.

"LISA, WAKE UP." Lisa buried her head in the soft pillow, trying to block out her sister's insistent voice, trying to hold on to the fraying edges of her lovely dream. "Lisa, wake up. I'm home. Sorry it's so late. You didn't have to wait up for me." Katie's voice seemed to come from a long way off. Lisa kept her eyes tightly shut. It was no use. Kevin's image faded, the touch of his hands and his mouth on her hair, her lips, her breasts, receded. She sat up.

"What time is it?"

"It's after one." Katie was standing at the foot of the couch. Matt Swensen was beside her. There was a smudge on Katie's cheek, grease marks on the front of Matt's light blue cotton jacket.

"Was there an accident?"

"I had a flat tire on the truck," Matt explained sheepishly.

"And the spare was flat, too." Lisa gave him a disgusted look. "We had to walk a mile to Gilson's carrying the darn thing to put some air in it. It was even too flat to roll on the road."

"Hey, I carried it, not you." Matt flexed his broad shoulders as if they ached.

"It'll remind you to check on the spare once in a while. Anyway, somebody had to be on the lookout for bears."

"Good grief." It was Matt's turn to look disgusted.

"I tell you, Lisa, it's not safe out there after dark," Katie went on, not missing a breath.

"I'll remember that." Lisa brushed her hand through her hair. She touched a curious finger to her lips. They still felt tender and swollen from Kevin's kisses. She smiled a little to herself.

"Anyway, I wanted to come in with Katie and explain why we're so late," Matt said.

"Thanks, Matt. I appreciate it."

"I'd better be on my way. My folks will be climbing the walls. I'm surprised they haven't called here already, wondering where I am."

"Good night, Matt." Lisa stood up. She smiled absently in his direction. She didn't notice the speculation in Katie's bright hazel eyes.

"I'll walk Matt out to the truck."

"Aren't you afraid a bear might get you?" he said.

"The noise that truck makes scared off anything within a mile of this place. When are you going to get a new muffler for that thing, anyway?"

"Shhh, you two. Brad's asleep."

"Sorry."

"Sorry, Lisa." They headed out the back door arm in arm, still bickering, but with lowered voices.

Lisa went into the kitchen for a glass of water. Her head continued to spin with the aftereffects of her dream. Kevin had been making love to her, slowly, passionately, thoroughly. And she had been able to love him back without reservation. She hadn't been clumsy or awkward or inexperienced. She had been a woman, complete, with no fear of not being able to please the man who was so expertly pleasing her.

The dream had been marvelously detailed and erotic. It might also have actually happened if Brad hadn't come

ome when he did. Lisa couldn't decide if she was glad
eir escalating lovemaking had been interrupted by her
ounger brother's return, or sad. Her mind might not
now how it wanted to react to the curtailment of her and
evin's time alone together, but her body did. Now, hours
ter, it still sang with frustration and longing.

Lisa filled her glass with icy spring water. She turned her
ead and saw her sister and Matt silhouetted against the
ale cab light of his truck, locked in one another's arms.
Then the kiss ended, Matt hopped in the truck and pulled
ut of the driveway with a wave of his hand. As Lisa
atched, the red glow of his taillights was swallowed up by
e night. Seconds later Katie came back in the house.

"I'm starved," she declared from the kitchen doorway.
"How about a glass of juice?"

Matt's and Katie's interest in each other was open and
sual. They'd been dating steadily all summer. Katie al-
ady seemed far more grown-up than Lisa had been at
at age. Yet she knew the teenager's apparent sophisti-
tion was misleading. Katie had led a very sheltered life.
er experience of the world didn't extend far beyond
arquette, except for what she saw and heard on TV and
ad in books and magazines. Yet even here, drugs and
cohol and teenage pregnancy were problems that con-
rned parents as they did all over the country. Lisa trusted
atie's judgment and common sense. But she also knew
e time had come to tell her young sister what weighed so
avily on her own mind.

"Not juice. How about cocoa and toast?" It was one of
atie's favorite late-night snacks. It had been ever since she
as a little girl.

"That does sound good," Lisa agreed.

"I'll make it. You look bushed. Sit down," Katie dered. "Do you have to go into Marquette in the mo ing?"

"I have to be at headquarters by eight."

"Ugh." Katie made a face. "I'm going to sleep noon."

"Sounds like heaven." Lisa rested her chin on her fist she watched Katie pour milk into a saucepan and put br in the toaster.

"Hey, what's going on out here?" Brad stood in doorway, his hair standing up in spikes, his almond-shap eyes still heavy with sleep. He was wearing an old Gr Bay Packers T-shirt and a pair of running shorts. It was favorite warm-weather sleeping attire.

"We're having cocoa and toast. Want some?" Ka asked.

"Sure thing. Four slices."

"Two." Katie wagged her finger at her brother. "Yo end up looking like the Goodyear blimp if you eat like t all the time."

Brad made a face but didn't object. Katie got out other cup and spooned cocoa powder into it with a g erous hand. Brad buttered the toast as it popped out of toaster and stacked it neatly on a paper plate.

Lisa took a sip of steaming cocoa from the cup Ka handed her. Brad dunked half a slice of toast into his coa and stuck most of it into his mouth. The room quiet after Katie took her place at the table. They ate silence. Even the frogs and crickets seemed to have cal it a night.

"I know about the driving lessons." Lisa let her wo drop like tiny bombshells into the silence. Brad stop chewing and looked at Katie for some clue as to how

hould react. Katie looked at Lisa, who kept her face
oncommittal.

"Is that what you and Kevin were arguing about?" Ka-
e's question caught Lisa off guard. Katie waited for Lisa
o answer as she dipped her toast into her cocoa and took
bite.

"Yes." It was at least partly the truth. "He let the cat
ut of the bag purely by accident. He didn't mean to be-
ay your confidence."

"What?" Brad was unfamiliar with her last words.

"He didn't rat on purpose," Katie translated.

"Oh." Brad's face creased in a grin. "I knew Kevin was
n okay guy."

"Why didn't you two tell me what you were doing?"
isa asked, suspecting she hadn't kept all of her hurt feel-
gs out of her voice.

"We didn't want you to worry."

"I can do it, Lisa." Brad jumped into the fray. "I know
can. I'll get my learner's permit. You can go in the car
ith me. You'll see."

"But it's very difficult, Brad. There are so many rules
nd regulations, tests to pass, careless drivers on the road."

"If I don't pass the first time, I'll try again. Right, Ka-
e?"

"Right. We didn't mean to go behind your back, Lisa.
e just knew you'd worry too much. Like you're doing
ow."

"I'm not worrying. Now." Lisa grinned and held up her
ands in surrender. "I can't say I won't worry when I see
ou behind the wheel."

"It'll be great," Brad assured her with another infec-
ous grin. His anxious smile showed clearly and precisely
ow very hard he was trying to make his point. "No more
ding my bike to Gilson's in the rain. I can drive myself.

When Katie gets her car. Right?'' He glanced anxiously
his sister.

"That won't be for a while," she reminded him.

"I know. But I'll be ready."

Lisa smiled and ruffled his hair. "I just think you m
be."

"More toast?" Brad asked, his pleased grin almo
splitting his face.

"No." Katie was firm.

"Then I'm going back to bed." He took a last huge gul
of his cocoa, swiped a paper towel across his lips and stoc
up, giving Lisa an affectionate hug on his way out of t
kitchen.

Katie remained seated. She circled the rim of her c
with the tip of her fingernail. "He'll do fine, Lisa. Real
he will. He's not planning to take off for New York
anything like that, you know. Gilson's and his scho
McDonald's and the mall are just about the limits of l
world."

"I know." Lisa swallowed a sudden lump of tears.
just don't want him to be hurt."

"We won't let it happen." Katie suddenly sounded
very grown-up.

"Katie." Lisa's heart began to pound high in her throa
making it hard to breathe. "There's something we need
discuss."

"You aren't going to tell me I can't go on the campi
trip? It's only a few days away."

Lisa had almost forgotten her worry over the co
campout in view of all the other emotional upheavals
her life the past several days. "No, you can go. I talked
Nancy's folks and Matt's. They don't like the idea all th
well, either. But they trust their kids and I trust you."

"Thanks, Lisa. We'll behave. And we'll be careful—" he gave her sister a saucy look "—in the woods, I mean."

"No open fires." Lisa pretended to look stern and professional.

"No open fires, Officer Emery. It's sure not very romantic sitting around, necking in front of a Coleman stove, though."

Lisa drew a sharp breath, then laughed and shook her head. "Katie, what am I going to do with you?"

"Tell me what's bothering you. Fire safety isn't what we started to talk about, is it?"

"No, it's not. Katie, it's about us. All of us. You and me and Brad." Katie nodded encouragement, although she wasn't yet certain what Lisa was talking about. "I probably should have told you when we had that discussion about..." Lisa paused to clear her throat and order her thoughts.

"Not the birds and the bees again." Katie looked dismayed. "We've been through all that, remember?"

"Only in a way." Lisa looked down at her almost empty cup. The milk had cooled, leaving a scum on top. She pushed it away and picked up a spoon to have something to occupy her hands. "Katie, you know that Down syndrome is a genetic defect."

"Yes. It's caused by an extra chromosome in a cell. It throws everything off balance." She shrugged. "You know biology isn't my strong point."

"The type of Down syndrome that Brad has is very rare. It's hereditary, Katie. I'm a carrier. You probably are, too."

"A carrier?" Katie frowned and tilted her head. "What does that mean exactly?" She looked at Lisa, her gaze steady, unwavering.

"It means that our children will have a very good chanc
of being affected. Either with the disease, like Brad or b
passing on the condition in their genes to another genera
tion."

"How long have you known this, Lisa?"

"Since you were little. When I was about your age. B
fore Grandfather died, Mother found out she had an olde
brother like Brad who died when he was small. When Bra
first went to Ann Arbor to school, they suggested he b
tested, and the results confirmed the diagnosis."

"I see." Katie stood up and began to gather cups an
saucers to put in the sink.

"It means you'll have to be very careful about som
things, Katie." Was she doing this right? It had been suc
traumatic news for her at Katie's age.

"Like birth control." The teenager nodded her hea
wisely. "Don't worry, Lisa. I'm not in any hurry to fin
out what all the mystery is about." Lisa was glad Katie wa
standing at the sink and had her back turned for the mc
ment. She knew her face must be registering shock at th
frank comment.

"I'm glad you feel that way." Lisa felt knots of tensio
unwind from somewhere deep inside. It was over, don
Katie knew the truth. "Being an adult comes soon enoug
without rushing it faster than necessary."

"I suppose I should have this test someday." Katie b
gan to rinse the cups as though their talk was mundar
everyday conversation.

"If you decide to get married. I'm sure that's soo
enough."

Katie shut off the water. "What do you mean, if I d
cide to get married? Why shouldn't I?" She turned aroun
and motioned for Lisa to hand her the saucepan from th
stove. "I know this is something I have to deal with, bu

hey're always coming out with new tests and discoveries.
And neither of us knows for sure if we would have a baby
ke Brad. It's something I'd have to discuss with my hus-
and, isn't it?''

"Yes, it is." Once again, Lisa was surprised at the depth
f her younger sister's wisdom and calm acceptance of the
acts.

"Lisa, if you were in love, you wouldn't let this stand in
our way, would you? I mean, not if he loved you as much
s you loved him. You could work it out." Katie had
urned away again. She sat the saucepan in the sink very
arefully. Her voice was earnest, filled with thoughts and
motions she was trying to put into words. She looked up
nd caught Lisa's eye in the reflection of their faces in the
indow above the sink.

"No, Katie. I'd never let it stand in the way of loving
omeone." Suddenly Lisa wanted to cry. Katie wanted and
eeded her assurance on this point. Yet Lisa knew she was
ing. She was letting her fears stand in the way of happi-
ess with Kevin, and she couldn't seem to stop herself.

"Then neither will I." Katie smiled, and even in the faint
eflection, Lisa could see that for Katie all the world was
right again. "Neither will I," she repeated.

Chapter Ten

"I for one," Kevin said with real feeling, "will never agai[n] volunteer for any project your sister proposes."

"At least you've got an excuse for doing something s[o] dumb. You haven't had to deal with her all your life, an[d] so you didn't know what you were in for." Katie straight[en]ed up from her crouched position under the long buil[t] in workbench that ran the length of the big old garag[e]. "Brad and I should have known better." She brushed h[er] forehead with the palm of her hand, leaving a dust[y] smudge above her left eye. "She always makes it sound lik[e] a piece of cake. 'If you haven't got anything else to do t[o]day, why don't you take an hour and clean out the ga[r]rage?'" Her imitation of Lisa's voice was delightful[ly] accurate. "What an understatement. We've been here a[ll] day." She upended a cardboard box of odds and ends int[o] a plastic garbage bag. "Finally! That's the last of the jun[k] down here."

"I'm finished, too," Brad declared taking a swipe u[n]der the workbench with his broom. "What's next?"

"Upstairs?" Kevin lifted his arms above his hea[d] grasping one of the low rafters, stretching his long ran[gy] body to relieve the constriction of several hours of ben[d]ing and stooping.

"There's not much up there that I remember," Katie said thoughtfully. "We hardly ever go up there. Still, if it will keep my big sister happy, we can shove a few more boxes around. C'mon, Brad." She waved her brother toward the steep ladderlike stairs leading into the loft. "She's been in a snit the past two days."

"She's tired," Brad said, coming to the absent Lisa's defense.

"It's those two fires that broke out over near the national forest. She's been saying it would happen all summer. Now it has."

Kevin scowled down at his shoes, letting his upraised hands support most of his weight, only partly aware of what Brad and Katie were saying. Lisa, while not actively involved in fighting the two small fires nearby, had still spent most of the past few days and nights in the vicinity. They'd had very little time together. Last evening he'd insisted she come out in the canoe with him, if for no other reason than to get away from the phone and the radio receiver. She'd agreed, settled on a cushion between his knees, commented on how nice the sunset was and didn't he think it looked like rain, and promptly fell asleep with her head on his thigh.

He hadn't attempted to wake her, just let the canoe drift along with only an occasional dip of the paddle to keep them on course. The night grew heavy and still around them. Stars winked to life high above. Deer came to the water's edge to drink just beyond Enoch's cabin, undisturbed by their presence. A bald eagle made its way across the small cove directly in front of Lisa's house, just as it did most evenings as the sun slipped behind the horizon. He couldn't see the big raptor's victim, but Kevin knew from the slow beat of its wings and its low altitude that it held a fish in its talons.

Kevin's headaches were mostly gone. The feeling of emptiness and loss had receded to be replaced with the first faint stirrings of new hopes and dreams. He had made peace with himself. He felt new energy, wanted to get on with his life. He'd even found himself cleaning and inspecting his cameras and lenses. He didn't think he was ready to start using them again, and maybe he never would use them in the same way as before, but they no longer represented failure and the end of who and what he was.

Kevin still hadn't made any hard decisions about the future. But whatever he chose to do, he wanted it to be here, in the north country he was coming to love as deeply as Lisa did. Ideas for projects and new business opportunities were beginning to squirrel around in his head, insinuating themselves into his thoughts and dreams.

None of them had quite taken on substance and form, but he didn't have to make up his mind about anything today, this minute. He had time, all the time in the world. Except for one very important task. One that couldn't be accomplished soon enough. He intended for Lisa Emery to be his wife, the mother of his children, a permanent and very important partner in his new life.

"Kevin. Quit daydreaming and come on up here," Katie ordered. She was already halfway up the stairs. "You wanted in on this little cleanup detail. You're not backing out now."

"Hey, you can't talk to a paying guest that way."

All he got for that unwise remark was an inelegant snort and a disdainful toss of Katie's auburn curls as she disappeared into the loft.

"Ready, buddy?" Kevin motioned for Brad to precede him up the steep steps. Brad handed him his broom.

"I guess so." He spread his hands in a gesture of defeat.

"There's no fightin' 'em." Kevin grinned and slapped Brad on the shoulder.

"Women." Brad nodded his head, at one with Kevin in the inability to understand the workings of the female mind. "She's just in a big hurry to get done and leave on her camping trip. That's all she talks about anymore. I'm glad I'm spending the night in town with the Westons."

Kevin was already aware that Brad would be away for the weekend. He knew the boy was looking forward to seeing his friends from the sheltered workshop and school he attended in Marquette. They were going bowling and to the movies, then out to eat. He had his weekend planned down to the minute. He was happy, and Kevin was happy for him.

Kevin was also making plans of his own. The fires that Lisa had been monitoring so closely the past few days were small and nearly contained. Unless something unexpected happened, he and Lisa would be alone together a great deal of the weekend. He intended to make the most of that.

He was still grinning when he stepped onto the wooden plank floor of the loft. "Great—" he couldn't hold back a groan of protest "—this is going to be a real penance." The only area of the big open space that would accommodate his height was in the exact center of the room. The ceiling sloped steeply from the peak to low walls on either side. Katie was kneeling beside an upended box of tangled fishing lines and old rusted minnow buckets.

"This family never throws anything away." She sat down hard against a cupboardlike door built into the low wall. The latch that held it shut tore loose, leaving the padlock that secured it hanging useless on the outer frame. Katie looked over her shoulder. "I wonder what's in here?" She rose to her knees and tugged at the wooden knob that served as a handle. It opened reluctantly, throwing her off balance. She picked herself up off the floor with an unladylike exclamation and looked inside. "It's dark in here. Brad, run downstairs and get a flashlight. Help me drag this stuff out, will you, Kevin?" She scooted out of his way.

He bent almost double to reach the low wall, then dropped to his haunches. As far as he could see, the small space underneath the eaves was empty except for two big canvas bags.

"What's in there?" Katie demanded. "Open them." Kevin did as she asked, pulling out, one after another, a dozen carved and painted mallard-duck decoys.

"They must have belonged to Granddad," Katie said, disappointment obvious in her voice and in her posture. She took one of the lightweight wooden decoys when Kevin handed it to her, but spared it barely a glance. "He used to work at one of the big private hunting clubs they had down around Detroit. He moved up here when they sold off the land and closed it down. That was when my mom was a little girl. He died just before I was born and Brad was only little. Lisa's the only one who remembers him. Our place used to be his."

"Everybody says he was a real neat guy," Brad said, shining his flashlight into the cubbyhole. "It's empty now." He shut the door. Kevin handed him a decoy, too. "These are neat." Brad inspected the carving carefully.

"This wouldn't look too bad on the mantel," Katie admitted grudgingly, "if it wasn't for this big hunk of metal on the bottom."

"That's an eye to fasten a rope and weight to," Kevin told her as he opened the other bag. Inside there were a dozen more decoys—pintails, mergansers, and several more mallard drakes. "When you have a set of decoys like this, it's called a rig," he explained, recalling Enoch Spangler's goose decoys.

"Let's put them back. There's enough stuff up here without adding more. I'll keep this one to show Lisa."

Kevin took it out of her hands. "I think we'll keep all of them to show her." He didn't know a damn thing about duck decoys, but he had read a magazine article once that told how valuable some of them had become. "It might be a good idea to have Enoch take a look at them, too."

"Enoch was Granddad's friend. He tells me stories about him sometimes. I like this one." Brad turned the mallard drake over and over in his hands. "Its eyes look so real. How can they look so real, Kevin?"

"They're glass eyes, Brad." Kevin watched as the boy stroked his fingers down the length of the bird's back.

"And this looks like real feathers," Brad continued, totally intrigued by the carved decoy.

"These decoys are nice," Katie conceded. She held out her hand to put the one Brad was inspecting back into the canvas bag. "Let's get this place straightened up, okay? I have to pack. Matt's picking me up at four."

Brad released his carving reluctantly. "I'll go to Enoch's with you, Kevin." He looked up at Kevin as he stood and swung the bag into his arms. "The Westons aren't coming for me until seven-thirty."

"Okay, buddy. We'll take off as soon as we're finished here."

"Can't you two shove those boxes out of the way while you're talking?" Katie stood with her hands on her hips. Kevin laid the second bag with the first, near the opening to the stairway, and turned to give her a mock salute. "Yes, ma'am."

Brad did the same. "Yes, ma'am."

"I BROUGHT MY CAMERA," Brad said, sliding onto the car seat beside Kevin. "I only have two...exposures left on this roll." He looked pleased when Kevin indicated he'd used the correct terminology. "Enoch has an owl. I'll take his picture."

"What kind of owl?"

Brad shrugged his shoulders, trying to remember if he had ever heard it called by a name. "It has big yellow eyes and ears. At least I think they're ears. It sleeps all day and keeps Enoch up at night."

"Sounds like a great horned owl," Kevin said, sifting out the pertinent facts in Brad's description.

"Great horned owl." Brad nodded. "That's what Enoch said." He fiddled with his camera, watching the telephoto lens advance and recede as he pushed the button that controlled it. "I can't wait to see my pictures. How much does it cost to get them developed?"

"Don't worry, buddy. I'll take them into town with me the next time I go. You save your money for this big blowout of a weekend."

"Blowout." Brad repeated the word several times. He laughed out loud. "I like that. Blowout. I have twenty dollars to spend on a blowout." He frowned. "That doesn't go far on a date."

"Date?" Kevin eased the car along the narrow lane leading to Enoch's cabin. It was shady and cool under the trees. Kevin left his sunglasses in his pocket.

"I have a girlfriend," Brad announced. "Her name is Gina. We go to school together. She works at a restaurant. I might get a job there, too. We bowl together. She's nice."

"And she's your girl?" Kevin wondered if Lisa knew about this Gina. It was another facet of the young man that Kevin had never considered. Had Lisa told her brother about sex?

"She's my friend. We hold hands sometimes."

"Have you kissed her?" They pulled into Enoch's overgrown yard. Kevin killed the engine and twisted in his seat to face Brad.

He looked down at his camera and shook his head. "Lisa says she's too young. She's sixteen. Maybe someday?" He shrugged. "Lisa says we don't have to kiss to be going together. We can just hold hands and tell jokes and be friends." He looked up with a big smile. "Lisa knows how to do everything good."

"She's something special." Kevin got out of the car and opened the trunk where he'd put the bags of decoys. Each day that passed he found himself more and more impressed with the way Lisa Emery handled her responsibilities. She was raising Katie to be a mature and successful young woman. She was helping Brad to grow, even exceed the limits of his handicap. Now if she would only let herself go, let herself love him, Kevin, give as much of herself to him as she did to the others she loved, he would be a very happy man.

"What's this? Company?" Enoch Spangler asked from the open doorway of his cabin. Tall and broad, his ginger-colored hair and beard grizzled, liberally sprinkled with white, he filled the opening. Dressed in faded Levis, secured by red suspenders, and a red-and-black checked shirt, he looked exactly like Kevin's childhood memories of Paul Bunyan. "Welcome, welcome." His voice boomed off into the woods. From a large wire flight cage under the shelter of a big birch tree, the great horned owl Brad had described opened its big yellow eyes and gave its familiar hooting call. "Quiet, Luciano."

"Luciano?" Kevin held out his hand as Enoch walked toward him with hand outstretched in greeting.

"The bird reminds me of Pavarotti. Hoots for hours at a time, just like an Italian tenor."

"I see." Kevin swallowed a grin.

"To what do I owe the honor of this visit?" Brad had already wandered off toward the owl's cage.

"We have something we'd like you to see." Kevin gestured toward the two canvas bags in the trunk of his car. "Katie found these while we were cleaning the loft in the garage." Enoch looked surprised, but didn't comment on the fact that Kevin had been helping with Emery family chores. He opened one bag and pulled out two mallard decoys, one a drake, the other a duck.

Enoch let out a long low whistle. "Well, I'll be damned. Where did you say you found these?"

"In a locked cupboard underneath the eaves in the garage loft." Kevin picked up a pintail drake and examined it closely, ignoring the hazy blurring of his injured eye, concentrating on seeing it with his weaker but unaffected right eye. The carved form was graceful, suggesting life and movement, the painting subtle and attractive. "I know antique decoys are popular with collectors—"

Enoch laughed. "Popular. My boy, you have a gold mine here. These are Mason Premiers. I'm no expert, but then there's no mistaking the quality. And look here." Here pointed to the back of the decoy. "See how the paint is swirled, the deep texturing? That marks them as Masons, no doubt. How many are there?"

"Two dozen."

This time Enoch's laugh was more a roar of delight. "Does Lisa know about this?"

"No. We only found them a few minutes ago. We hoped you'd be able to tell us more about them."

"They're from the Mason Decoy Factory of Detroit, made in the early part of the century, or I miss my guess. Mason was one of three factories operating at the time, although the word 'factory' is deceiving. Everything but the bodies, which were lathe-turned, was handmade. They're works of art, the top of the line like these." Enoch explained as he went through the contents of the two bags, turning the decoys over in his big scarred hands, shaking his head in delight.

"Beauties, every one. Lisa's grandfather must have brought these up from the south with him when he moved back in the fifties. Some of the big private gun clubs were going under around then. DDT was wreaking havoc with the birds. The Depression and the war had done away with a lot of their wealthy members. He told me about burning load after load of decoys before he left. He must have taken these. Maybe they were the best of the lot, and he couldn't stand to see them torched." He stopped talking, let out his breath in a low whistling sigh. "We'll never know. But Harold Kinsey, Lisa's grandfather, was an honest man. I never saw these decoys, and he never spoke of having them. His conscience must have bothered him for taking them in the first place. Or maybe he simply forgot they were there."

"Are you telling me these decoys are worth more than what an antique dealer might give Lisa and the kids to sell them as mantel curios?"

"Curios." Enoch turned on him, moving quickly for so bulky a man. "If we find the right buyer, the right collector—" he paused, spreading his arms wide for effect "—even the right museum, we can just about guarantee enough to get Katie a real good start on her college education." He paused again, then laughed and added, "To say the very least."

Kevin looked down at the carved and painted decoys in his trunk. "I had no idea they were so valuable."

"At an auction in Maine a couple of years back, a hand-carved pintail drake by one of the East Coast masters sold for more than three hundred thousand dollars." He drew each word out to enormous lengths.

Kevin was suitably impressed. "I'll be damned," was all he could think of to say.

"These aren't in that league, of course. But for lathe-turned birds, well, you can't get much better than this. And two rigs. The variety." He slapped Kevin on the back so hard he stumbled against the fender of his car. "This calls for a celebration. Can I interest you in a beer?"

"Sounds great."

"Kevin," Brad called. He was still standing by the owl cage. "Look, the owl's awake and I'm out of film."

Maybe it was the excitement of the news he had for Lisa when she got home. Maybe it was just that the time to try to work again had come. He didn't stop to analyze his feelings. He just did what came naturally. Leaning into the trunk, he pulled his favorite camera out of the specially made, insulated, suitcase-size carrying case. He grabbed a lens and fitted it on the camera as he walked toward the cage. The older man disappeared into the cabin, returning a few minutes later with two cans of beer and a soft drink.

Enoch motioned Brad over to take the soft drink and they both watched Kevin at work. It wasn't easy. He felt awkward, out of practice, clumsy and slow, as he used his uninjured eye to focus and compose. While he worked he asked Enoch questions about the owl. A female, it had been hit by a car, Enoch disclosed, and taken to a vet in Marquette. Her wing was broken. She'd never fly again, so the vet had contacted him, knowing he was licensed by the state and federal governments to care for injured raptors. That was six months ago. Luciano had been making his life miserable ever since. Brad laughed loudly at the last self-pitying and obviously facetious statement.

"It doesn't bother you that you named a female owl Luciano?" Kevin asked, moving in for a tight close-up of the owl's face, the big yellow eyes staring intently into the camera lens.

"She doesn't care," Enoch said as if he'd discussed the point with the owl on numerous occasions. "Come, drink your beer. You can snap shots of her anytime you like."

"She's hardly ever awake during the day," Brad pointed out as Kevin straightened from a squatting position in front of the cage.

"I'm done." To Kevin's surprise he'd gone through an entire roll of film. He slipped the camera strap around his neck. It felt familiar, yet strange. Once it had been almost a part of him, his livelihood, almost his life. Now it was part of him again, but in a different, more subtle, less urgent way. He took the beer and hunkered down on the grass, while Enoch and Brad shared the bottom two steps leading up to the cabin door.

They talked a little about the two fires to the south, both freak accidents—one the burning household trash, the other an engine fire in a logging truck—that had started them within hours of each other, the pure bad luck of it, the good chance that they'd both be contained before the day was over. Then Enoch abruptly changed the subject.

"How long are you planning to stay?" He looked Kevin straight in the eye without apology for the personal nature of his question. "I know a lot about what's going on in the Emery clan. Brad visits me almost every day, don't you, friend? The girls stop by often, too."

"I come here every day I have time," Brad said for Kevin's benefit. "When I get my car, I can even come if it's raining."

"All in good time." Enoch slapped him on the shoulder, far more gently than he'd done with Kevin. "Are you studying your driving laws?"

"Every day." Brad took a big swallow of his soda. "Katie says I'm getting them down pat. Whatever that means." He frowned down at the drink in his hands.

"Since Luciano's awake, why don't you get her a mouse to snack on?"

"Okay." Brad hopped up. "Poor little mice," he said, shaking his head. "Luciano won't eat anything that isn't alive."

"Actually," Enoch said twirling his beer can between his hands, "she eats frozen rabbits regularly. But she needs the exercise."

Brad let the small gray mouse loose in the cage. The owl watched it, twisting its great head, its yellow eyes wide and alive with interest. It spread its wings, the crippled one held awkwardly away from its body and swooped down on the mouse, dispatching it quickly and efficiently, then hopped back up on its perch. "Yuck." Brad shivered in exaggerated reaction. "That's gross." He continued to watch the owl eat, despite its less-than-appetizing meal.

"Lisa and Katie have worked miracles with that boy," Enoch said. "Their mother loves him, too. But she could never see beyond the heartache, beyond the sorrow of knowing her son could never have the kind of life that he might have had if he'd been born normal. It's his sisters who've made him what he is today, who've grown with him, grown because of him, into fine, caring women."

"I know." Kevin took a swallow of his beer, hoping to swallow the lump in his throat, too.

"You've been involved in the conspiracy to keep the driving lessons a secret from Lisa, I understand."

Kevin took another quick swallow of beer. Enoch Spangler seemed to know a great deal about the Emery family. He was also making it his business to know what part Kevin intended to play in their lives.

"My intentions were good." Kevin rubbed his hand over his cheek, remembering the slap. "Lisa didn't appreciate my interference."

"She thinks with her heart, not with her head, sometimes, where Brad and Katie are concerned."

"I'm aware of that, too."

Enoch looked at Brad, still engrossed in the owl's activities. "You still haven't answered my first question, Sauder. How long are you staying here, eh?"

It was the first time Kevin had heard Enoch use the familiar north-country intonation. Was it a deliberate reminder that Kevin was an outsider, a transient, just passing through like thousands of other tourists before him?

Kevin decided to stop beating around the bush. "I'm staying as long as it takes." The sun was beginning to tilt into the west. He put his hand into his pocket and took out the sunglasses but didn't put them on.

"These kids mean a lot to me," Enoch said, not pretending to misunderstand, "Lisa most of all. She's all tied up in her brother and sister, in her work. She's never had time for herself, for her heart. I've seen you two together out on the lake. I've heard that special note in her voice when she talks about you. Her father saved my life in Korea. Her grandfather was my friend, too. They're not here anymore to help her out. Her mother is fifteen hundred miles away." He stood up, cleared his throat. "Don't trifle with her, Sauder. She's not like the women you're used to."

Kevin stood up, too. He topped Enoch by two or three inches, but the older man was broader and thicker, outweighing him by forty pounds. Enoch crossed the few steps of dry grass that separated them until they were standing toe to toe. Kevin held his ground. "You're wrong, Enoch. Lisa is very much like the women in my life. The ones I admire and respect. The ones I love."

Brad chose that moment to tire of watching the owl. "It's going back to sleep," he informed Kevin as he crossed to stand beside the two men. Enoch stepped back. Kevin did the same. "What time is it?" Brad asked, squinting up at the sun. "I forgot my watch."

Kevin glanced at his wrist. "Almost three. We'd better be getting back."

"Lisa promised to be home before I leave. We have to check over the clothes I'm taking along. Let's go, Kev. So long, Enoch." He waved over his shoulder, already trotting off toward the car. "I'll be back soon."

Enoch folded his arms across his chest. "And you, Sauder, will you be staying long enough to pay us another visit?" His sharp brown eyes held Kevin's in a steady demanding gaze. The sun was bright in the yard now, but Kevin neither flinched nor looked away.

"I'll be staying." He held out his hand. Enoch hesitated a long moment, then grasped it in his own.

"For as long as it takes?"

"You can count on it, eh?"

Chapter Eleven

"I had no idea these were stored in the loft." Lisa traced her finger over the crested head of a wood-duck drake. She touched the lifelike glass eye. "Granddad never spoke of them."

"Enoch thought he might have taken them from the private club he worked for when the land was sold. Maybe he was supposed to destroy them and couldn't. Maybe he just put them up there in the loft and forgot about them." Kevin was standing in the kitchen doorway drying his hands on a dish towel. He and Brad had fixed supper for her before Brad left for his weekend with the Westons. Katie was already gone. She and Kevin were alone in the house. Lisa looked at him over her shoulder as she replaced the decoy on the mantel. He tossed the towel onto the counter and crossed the room toward her, unrolling the sleeves of his shirt as he walked.

"Granddad had a stroke two years before he died. It affected his speech and memory. He might have forgotten they were there. I'm sure he never suspected they might be so valuable one day. Thousands of dollars?" She shook her head in wonder, still unable to assimilate the magnitude of their good fortune.

"We'll know more after Enoch contacts his friends. They'll be able to give you a more concrete figure of what the decoys are worth."

Lisa walked over to the back door and looked out into the darkening southeast sky. "My grandfather might not have been able to foresee how much the decoys would appreciate in value, but he always admired beauty and fine craftsmanship. I'm sure that's why he couldn't destroy them."

Lisa lifted her face for a moment. Was that smoke she smelled? She wondered. The topmost branches of the trees were barely moving in the fitful sunset breeze. Kevin came up behind her and slipped his arms around her waist. It was an easy natural gesture. She leaned against him, grateful for his support, eager for his touch.

"I photographed all of them today. Tomorrow I'll take the film into town and get it developed, so that Enoch can get letters off in the afternoon mail."

Lisa tipped her head back against his shoulder in order to see his face in profile. "Kevin, you didn't have to do that." She held her breath. It was the first time he'd mentioned using his camera. Did that mean he was coming to grips with his handicap, working past the barriers he'd thrown up between himself and his work? Did it mean he was going to leave them even sooner than she'd feared?

"It was time," he said simply. "I have to start somewhere."

Lisa didn't say anything more and stared out at the dying day. The breeze stirred and strengthened. She could feel the cool touch of it on her bare arms. Again a hint of wood smoke reached her nostrils. She shivered, hoping it was only her imagination.

"Are you cold?" Kevin asked, brushing the top of her head with his lips so lightly Lisa didn't think it could be termed a kiss. Yet the butterfly touch sent another shiver, this time one of sweet excitement slipping over her skin. She liked the way his voice rumbled low and deep in his chest. She liked to lean against him and feel the smooth play of muscles beneath the soft cotton of his shirt, the hair-roughened expanse of his skin.

"I thought I smelled smoke." She made it just enough of a question that he could deny her response if he wanted to. Kevin remained silent. He wouldn't soothe her, she knew, with useless platitudes, with well-meant evasions of the truth. He would treat her as a woman. Why couldn't she react as something other than a frightened young girl? "Maybe the odor is still in my hair..." she added. She'd come home tired and dirty, her uniform ruined, full of tiny holes caused by flying cinders and hot ash, her eyes burning and her throat scratchy from the smoke she'd inhaled.

"No. Your hair smells of lemons and forest ferns, but not of smoke." He pulled her tighter into the comforting circle of his arms. She was wearing a simple short-sleeved ivory-colored blouse and a full skirt in an abstract pattern of khaki and black. Her skin was warm and soft beneath the thin cotton material. He ached to touch her more intimately, have even this slight barrier no longer between them. Kevin lifted his head, looking out into the dusk at the softly swaying tops of the pines at the edge of the clearing. Soon. Soon she would be his.

"The fire's coming closer." Lisa didn't want to admit the truth, but she couldn't lie to Kevin or herself. "We were so close to having both of them contained." One of the two small fires burning near the boundary of the national forest directly south of her home had been brought under control during the night. The second fire had unexpectedly jumped a firebreak along an old logging road and gained a foothold in a boggy area that made it almost impossible to use any kind of motorized vehicle to help slow its path.

"There's nothing we can do now but wait," he said.

"I hate waiting." She hugged her arms around her waist. Kevin put his hands over hers and bent his head to lay his cheek against the softness of her hair.

"So do I. But I'm learning not to fight it. Sometimes we have to wait. This is one of those times." He was thinking of his eyes. Of the months, possibly years, that would pass before he could have the surgery that would restore his sight completely. Lisa squeezed his hand to show that she understood. But when she spoke it was about the fire.

"It's too close." All day the flames had hopscotched toward the northwest, defying ground assaults, as well as water and chemical retardant dropped by low-flying planes. If she closed her eyes she could see it, hear it. Smoldering and slow moving in the damp peaty undergrowth of the string bog, the wildfire could flare into life at the merest hint of a breeze, streaking for a hundred yards or more at a time through scrub brush and mature trees, faster than a man could run. At this point it was simply too unpredictable and inaccessible to be stopped.

"For weeks I've been worried about lightning, carelessly tended campfires, even discarded cigarettes. Then, within twelve hours, two freak accidents. An engine fire in a logging truck and somebody burning old newspapers in their backyard threaten to make an inferno of this part of the Upper Peninsula." The trash fire, being the one nearest homes and private property, had been the first reported. It also merited the greatest concentration of firefighting equipment. But it was the second fire, caused by an overheated truck engine, that threatened her home most directly. Only a bulldozed firebreak and the county road eight miles south of the one her home was situated on stood between the runaway fire and everything she held dear.

Eight miles as the crow flies. Only hours away if the wind became stronger and steadier. She'd gone up in a fire-patrol plane that afternoon to see for herself the perimeters of the burn and to check on the whereabouts of two moose cows and their calves known to have wandered into the area. The animals were part of a small experimental herd, all wearing radio collars, that had been reintroduced into the Upper Peninsula from Canada three years before. The department was concerned for their safety.

Lisa had been able to locate both cows and calves in a relatively sheltered marsh, surrounded on three sides by broad slow-moving streams. Since the fire was patchy, not yet burning in a large continuous block, most wildlife wasn't seriously threatened. Still, she saw an unusual number of white-tailed deer moving out into open areas they usually avoided during the day, and even a couple of black bears ambling along the rusted overgrown track of an abandoned railroad, disturbed by the smell of smoke and man and the noise of low-flying aircraft and heavy equipment.

"I was under the impression that your supervisor sent you home to get some rest." Kevin kept his voice low but firm. He turned her to face him.

"He did." Lisa sighed, then raised her hands to lay them on his chest. "I can't. If the wind starts to pick up, the fire will move faster. If it jumps the county road it could be here in a matter of hours." Kevin covered her hands with his own for a moment, then pulled her back into the circle of his arms. "Or they'll confine it to the bog and it will never get any farther. You need to relax."

"I can't seem to do that, either."

He could think of one very wonderful way to relax her, but the sudden familiar wariness in her eyes warned him to go slowly. "How about a canoe ride along the shore? There's a moon tonight."

Lisa greeted his suggestion with a tired apologetic little smile and a shake of her head. Her arms went around his waist, and she leaned back to study his face. "I don't think so."

"We could go for a walk. Watch for deer to come down and drink at that narrow strip of land where Enoch's road jogs off to his cabin." A year ago he would have laughed at anyone who told him that sharing such simple pleasures with a woman would be so important to his happiness.

"They might not come as usual." There was sadness in her voice. She let him pull her closer, mold her to the length of his body. He held her lightly, comfortingly, yet the intimacy of their position couldn't be denied. Lisa wet her lips with the tip of her tongue. The unconsciously sexy act sent Kevin's blood racing through his veins. "If I can smell smoke in the air so can the deer. They'll be nervous, more cautious than usual."

Just as Lisa was herself. Kevin wasn't going to make the mistake of comparing her to a doe or fawn. She wouldn't thank him for it; she'd probably give him a piece of her mind for even daring to mention it aloud. Still in some ways she did remind him of those gentle forest creatures. She was wary of loving him, of giving herself to him physically and emotionally. There was a streak of passion hidden deep within her. The kind of passion that could drive a man to the edge of distraction. But the vein was deep and well hidden. He thought it might take a lifetime to unearth all her secrets, and that suited him just fine.

"All right. Let's just sit in front of the fireplace."

Lisa looked as if she wanted to protest the suggestion. Kevin stopped her by touching the tip of his finger to her lips. "Sans fire tonight, I think. What I really want to do is hold you in my arms."

"I . . . I want that, too."

"Do you, Lisa?" He looked at her for a long heart-stopping moment. She wanted to turn away, run away. Yet she wanted to be closer still, to know all of him and to have him know her. But how best to say that, to let him know how she felt and still not reveal herself as less than a woman?

"Very much."

"Good. That's settled." Kevin smiled. "Do you have any candles?"

"Candles?" Lisa wondered if she would ever know this man well enough to find him predictable.

"We don't want a fire, but that doesn't mean we can't sit on the couch and be lost in the luminous flickering glow of myriad burning tapers—"

"Kevin!" She couldn't help but exclaim at his exaggeration.

"Too much, eh?" He grinned down at her, unrepentant.

"Just overly dramatic." She smiled, too. "I like the idea. There're some emergency candles in the kitchen."

"They'll do fine. Where?" Kevin kissed her on the tip of the nose. Her cheek. Her hair. Her nose. When, dear heaven, she thought, was he going to kiss her mouth?

"Second shelf on the right. But—"

"No buts." He gave her a push toward the couch. "Go. Sit like a good girl. Take your shoes off. Relax."

How could she relax? Lisa knew as well as he did where this night was leading. What would he think of her inexperience? Would it amuse him? Bore him? Would he wonder if there was something wrong with her because she'd reached the advanced age of twenty-six without ever making love?

But there was something wrong with her, something terribly and forever wrong. Lisa sat on the couch and stared at the dark TV screen. Maybe if she turned it on, something would be interesting enough, intriguing enough to distract him from his seduction.

She wasn't so naive that she couldn't see what he was doing. She wasn't so strong, her feelings so uninvolved, that she could remain untouched by it. She wanted to be seduced by the tall blond man who'd come quietly back into the room to kneel beside the dark empty fireplace. She wanted to be his. All except one small miserable part of her mind. That cautionary whispering voice would not be stilled, would not completely fade away.

Lisa watched as Kevin positioned a dozen squat white candles on the grate well back on the stone floor where they could burn softly. Moving as if in a dream, she knelt beside him, helped to light the last few tapers. "Very nice." She couldn't keep a touch of surprise out of her voice. The candles looked lovely. The flames danced and curtsied in the slight draft of the open fireplace. Shadows flitted across the ceiling, played over the strong lines and angles of Kevin's face as he stared into the flames.

His hands rested lightly on his knees as he rocked forward on the balls of his feet. The pale green shirt he wore was new; she hadn't seen it before. He'd rolled the cuffs just above his wrists. She watched the play of light over his hands, the sleek hardness of his thighs, the wide expanse of his chest. She looked up, found him watching her and felt heat rise to her cheeks.

"Kiss me," she said in a rush before her brain could censor her tongue. She had considered, agonized, argued with herself for days. The truth couldn't be changed, couldn't be denied any longer. She loved Kevin Sauder. She loved him as a woman loves a man, with all her heart and soul. And she wanted to love him with her body. If she didn't speak of commitment, of happy-ever-after endings, neither would he.

"Lisa." Kevin put his hands on her shoulders. She was trembling. "Are you sure this is what you want?" He'd given her his word. He wouldn't use the strength of his own feelings, the sheer force of his will, his need for her, to coerce her into commitment. His body ached for fulfillment. He wanted to feel himself sheathed deep within the soft heat of her. He wanted to tell her with words and with his body how much he loved her, wanted her, needed her now and the rest of his life. That kind of happiness came only once in a man's life. He could wait for it if necessary, but it was the hardest thing he'd ever done.

"This is what I want." Lisa wrapped her arms around his neck, leaned into his embrace. Her breath touched his lips, his cheek. Her eyes held his. They were the color of darkest amber in the dim wavering light of the candles. Kevin didn't ask any more questions. She did want him. He could see it beyond the faint uneasiness that lingered in her gaze, the tension in the set of her jaw, the straight line of her shoulders. He stroked her back. She pressed closer. Her breasts were crushed against his chest. Now it was he who couldn't breathe. "I want to be with you tonight."

Kevin stood up, pulling her with him. "Which is your bedroom?" he asked, his voice was low and rough. He scooped her into his arms. She felt a tight spiraling warmth spring to life inside her. She had never been carried by a man before. She liked it. She liked the strength of his arms around her, the slow steady thud of his heart against her side, the width of his shoulders beneath her hands. She buried her face in the crook of his neck and gestured toward her bedroom door, her mind filled with images of a far more intimate embrace.

She felt small and light in his arms. She was still trembling, but Kevin sensed it wasn't entirely from passion. Was she afraid of him, of making love, of making herself too vulnerable emotionally? He didn't know which of those reasons it might be, or if it was a combination of all three. He only knew he intended to put her mind at ease, protect her physically. And set her body on fire.

Inside her bedroom Kevin kissed her again slowly, tenderly, letting her legs slide down the length of his body, cradling her against him again as soon as her toes touched the floor. No more hesitation, no more walking tiptoe around the issue. He spoke his mind. "I love you, Lisa. I've never told any woman that before. I'll never tell another woman that as long as I live." He started to unbutton her blouse.

"Oh, Kevin." Her voice was barely more than a whisper in the darkness. He couldn't make out details in the faint wavering light of the candles in the fireplace. Their light barely reached past the open door. The bed was behind Lisa. There was a dresser and mirror along the far wall, a table and rocking chair beneath the single window. The floor was carpeted. Those details registered at the back of Kevin's awareness. More immediate was the feel of her small firm breasts as they filled his hands, the scent of her shampoo, woodsy and fresh, the scent of her body, heated and sweet. He skimmed her skirt and panties down over her hips, lifted the covers, pushed her gently down onto the bed.

Lisa grabbed for the sheet, covered herself, but then watched in fascination as Kevin, after going out to the fireplace grate and returning with two of the candles and small holders, which he placed carefully on the dresser, shed his own clothes. His body was long and rangy, perfectly formed. His shoulders were broad, his hips narrow. Lisa caught her breath. Now it was too late, there was no backing away. He would know she had never made love before, that no other man had found her attractive enough to talk, cajole, caress his way past the protective walls around her heart.

Kevin tugged the sheet out of her hand and lay down beside her. He drew her into his arms. She lifted her arms, encircled his neck, returned his kiss. "I love you." Kevin repeated the words as much as a talisman against his own uncertainties as an opening for her to tell him the same. He moved over her. She stared up at him wide-eyed and apprehensive. "You don't have to tell me you love me back, Lisa."

He smiled, but there was none of the teasing warmth in his voice she so loved to hear. He sounded sad, hurt, empty. She loved him, too, desperately. Why couldn't she say so? The answer came as quickly as the questions: because of all the things that remained unspoken between them.

Kevin rested his weight on his elbows. His lower body pressed against her, full and hard. Their legs were tangled together. He moved against her and her body responded as if it had a will of its own. He kissed her. In a moment he would enter her and he would know. He waited for her to relax, kissing her mouth, her eyelids, her throat.

Her body responded, opening to his touch. Her breath came quick and light, but still she lay passive beneath him. Kevin thought his heart would break. This was what hell must be like, to have the thing you wanted most in the world at your fingertips and be denied. "Lisa—" the words came out ragged and scratchy "—I love you. I want to make love to you, with you. But if you don't love me back it's all right. It will still be beautiful and glorious and I'll cherish the memory for the rest of my life. I've told you again and again. I won't press you for what you can't give."

Lisa choked on a sob. "I love you." She got the words out in a rush. "I love you. But I..." She felt as if she were confessing to a crime. "I've never made love before." She closed her eyes, refusing to look into his, see the dancing silver flecks of amusement, or worse yet watch them harden in pity or dismay.

"You're a virgin?"

"Yes." She kept her eyes closed. "You don't have to make it sound like a crime, you know." She felt his hands in her hair. She could feel him staring down at her.

"Lisa, open your eyes." It was a command, low and sensual, but a command nevertheless. Lisa hesitated, felt the brush of his lips on her eyelids. She did as she was told.

"Don't laugh at me." She meant the words to be strong, measured, defiant. They came out sounding soft, whispery and a little forlorn.

"Laugh?" Kevin tightened the pressure of his fingers on the sides of her head, holding her still so that she could see nothing but his face, focus on nothing but his heated gaze. "You're offering me the most precious gift in the world. Why should I laugh?"

Lisa was embarrassed and exhilarated at the same time. Her heart beat hard and light high in her throat. "It's not precious. I'm just...a late bloomer, that's all, and—"

Kevin cut her protestation short. "It is a precious gift." He let his weight rest even more heavily against her soft rounded curves. Her world narrowed down to the feel of his body, so heated and hard next to hers. "There's only one thing I'll treasure more. Lisa, I want you to be my wife.''

"Kevin." Agony and joy warred within her. "I don't know."

"Shhh." There was a smile in his tone. "Just say yes. We'll argue about the details later." It was back. That lazy, marvelous teasing note in his voice. Lisa couldn't resist it. She hadn't been able to from the first day they'd met. She couldn't resist her heart, either, or the clamoring of her senses, the searing current of desire coursing through her body.

His mouth lowered to hers, his body moved over her. He began to show her with his lips and his hands what she'd only dreamed of experiencing before. "Say yes, Lisa," Kevin demanded as he caressed her, cajoled her body into readiness to receive his love. "Just say yes."

She wasn't afraid any longer. She wasn't thinking of past sorrows or future fears. She was thinking only of love and being loved. "Yes." It was easy, after all. "Love me please, Kevin. Now."

He rolled away from her for a moment, fumbled in the pocket of his jeans. He took her in his arms again holding her close as he whispered his promise to protect her. Kevin entered her then. The discomfort was slight and fleeting. The pleasure was beyond anything she'd imagined in her most private fantasies. But this wasn't a fantasy. It was real. It was love. The sharing, the oneness that made a lifetime commitment worth the risk. To feel Kevin within her, around her, joined with her, made Lisa realize that with love anything was possible.

Or at least to dream all that was possible. Even as Kevin drew her with him into completion, one small cold kernel of logic refused to be burned to cinders in the glory of fulfillment. Love was real—that much she knew for certain now. But she also knew that for her marriage and babies were still an impossible dream.

THE MUTED RINGING of the telephone woke Kevin several hours later. He came out from the hazy depths of sleep slowly and reluctantly. Only when Lisa uncurled herself from beside him, depriving him of her warmth and softness, scooting across the bed to answer the incessant jangle, did he come fully awake. It was very late, probably closer to dawn than midnight. He knew time had passed because the candles on the dresser were reduced to only guttering flares. He reached out to touch the warm soft curve of Lisa's bare thigh. Her hand closed over his fingers for a brief instant before she picked up the receiver and turned away.

The phone was on a table at the far side of the bed. "Emery." Lisa's voice was throaty and slurred with sleep. Kevin bunched the pillow behind his head and sat up. He'd never liked being awakened in the middle of the night by a telephone. Tonight was no exception, even if it did give him another opportunity, when the intrusive caller had been dealt with, to make love to Lisa before dawn.

Kevin smiled and leaned over to kiss Lisa's shoulder blade. He moved his hand over the sweet seductive curve of her waist, letting it rest below the swell of her breast. She covered his hand with her own. A woman's voice came faintly from the receiver. Kevin couldn't make out the words, but she sounded elderly. And excited. Lisa listened patiently. Kevin rubbed the sleep from his eyes with his fist. His thoughts left the warm hazy dimension of lovemaking and sharpened into reality.

"Stay put, Maggie," Lisa ordered after listening to the cracked voice for a good three minutes. "I'll be right there. Don't let them know you're still in your house." Lisa paused for a breath, then demanded to know why the old woman, Maggie, had not moved away from the danger zone. "The fire can't be more than four or five miles away from you."

Again Kevin heard the agitated voice pour a torrent of words into Lisa's ear. He felt a tightening in his gut. Something was wrong. "Don't open the door to anyone but me," Lisa instructed in a no-nonsense voice. "Maggie, do you understand? No one but me." She waited for confirmation from the woman before continuing. "Okay. I'm leaving now."

Lisa scooted off the bed. Her naked body glowed like ivory in the darkness. She was so beautiful. And she was his. Kevin sucked in his breath, felt his body stir and harden. And she was headed out into the night and into danger. He forced his thoughts away from the sweet heated memories of her response to him and focused on the darker reality of here and now.

"What's up?"

Lisa looked over her shoulder. "Poachers," she said, making the word sound like a curse. She picked up the telephone again, began to dial, then slammed it down with a muttered "Damn." She ran her fingers through her hair and turned to open the closet door all in one lithe fluid movement.

Kevin swung his legs off the bed and started to hunt for his clothes. Lisa went on talking as she dressed. "That was old Maggie Lesatz. She lives by herself down a dead-end road about three miles from here."

"Three miles closer to the fire?" Kevin asked as he pulled on his pants.

"Yes." Lisa's voice was grim. "I had no idea she was still in her home. She should have left hours ago, but she's so stubborn." Kevin could hear the exasperation and affection in her tone, even though she'd turned her back to him as she dressed. "She broke her hip last fall. She has trouble sleeping. That's why she was awake. She saw a car pull up in the open meadow near her place. Shine three deer..."

"Shine?" Kevin asked, his voice muffled as he leaned down to tie his shoes.

"Shine," Lisa explained, as she pulled her hair into a knot of curls on top of her head, "means that someone with a high-powered spotlight shines it on deer while they're feeding in the open. The light seems to paralyze them, and they don't run. Very often they won't even move. It's like they're frozen."

"Then our avid sportsman with the spotlight sticks a gun out the window and shoots them where they stand."

"That's about it." Lisa sat down on the edge of the bed to tie her shoes.

"And you're going after these poachers now, in the middle of the night. Alone."

His voice was sharp, his tone demanding. Lisa looked up, startled to find him standing very close. "Ordinarily, no. As a matter of fact I'll probably get my pedigree read for going out alone. But there isn't another C.O. within twenty miles tonight. Most of the sheriff's deputies are on fire alert. It'll take the best part of an hour to get someone out to Maggie's to back me up." Kevin was working on the buttons of his shirt while she talked. She was a little surprised to find him already dressed, but she was relieved at the moment not to have to face him without clothes. She found his body endlessly fascinating. She didn't think she'd ever get enough of holding him, touching him, but now she needed all her concentration focused on the business at hand.

"Get some backup, Lisa." Kevin refused to consider the idea of her going after armed miscreants alone.

"No time. Maggie says they're field-dressing the deer. Gutting the carcasses," she said bluntly "right out in the open where they fell. That takes one hell of a lot of nerve."

"How many are you talking about?" Kevin didn't move. Lisa stood up, but she would have to push him out of her way to get out of the room.

"Two. Possibly three, if it's who I think it is. Maggie isn't positive how many. But she recognized the vehicle. Remember the man I told you about? The one I testified against last week? It's his truck."

"Then we're not talking about some poor out-of-work stiff with a family to feed, are we?" Kevin held her by the shoulders, his eyes searching hers in the near darkness.

It wouldn't have done any good to lie to him, to try to protect him, by keeping the seriousness of the situation to herself. "No. We're talking about a professional poacher who sells the meat to trendy restaurants down south who pass it off to their customers as legally harvested venison. There's a big market for it in the cities." She reached up, took his hands from her shoulders, held them between her own. "Kevin, I have to go. It's my job. It's my duty." She sighed. "I have to catch him red-handed with the gun and the deer carcasses in his possession. If I do, there's a good chance the judge will be able to stand by her word and send him to jail. It'll be a lesson to every poacher in this part of the state. It'll be a victory for all of us who love and value wildlife." She had thought it would make her uncomfortable to voice her feelings, but it did not. She could tell Kevin all this, explain her feelings about her job and her love of this half-tamed wild country. It felt good. It felt right.

"I understand." Kevin stepped aside. Lisa was relieved to have made her point without an argument. She reached up on tiptoe and let him catch her close against him for a quick hard kiss. "Why don't you go back to bed. Get some sleep. If I miss them, I'll probably be back by first light. If I make the arrest, the paperwork will keep me busy until noon."

"I'm not going back to bed," Kevin said flatly.

"Then make yourself some coffee and breakfast." Lisa hurried into the living room, switched on the light and took her shotgun down from the rack beside the door. She didn't look to see if Kevin had followed her out of the bedroom. Her attention was centered on checking her equipment. She didn't see him reach for the black sweatshirt he'd been wearing earlier in the evening.

Lisa loaded the gun, put extra shells into her pocket and grabbed a high-powered flashlight from her desk. She paused in the doorway, unwilling to give Kevin another chance to try to talk her out of going after the poachers alone, but equally unwilling to leave him without saying goodbye. She didn't turn around. "Kevin, whatever happens, I'll call you as soon—"

"That won't be necessary."

Lisa whirled around. Kevin was only a few steps away, his hands shoved into his pockets, his expression unreadable. His jaw was set in the hard stubborn line she already knew too well. "You don't have to call to let me know what's going on. I intend to be right behind you every step of the way."

Chapter Twelve

"No, Kevin. It's out of the question." Lisa grabbed the car
keys from the nail by the door and walked out into the
night. The moon had set long ago. The stars were still
bright, but there was the expectant hush of dawn in the
cool air. Lisa spun on her heel. Kevin was right behind her.
"I can't take an unarmed civilian along. It's too dangerous."

"Dammit, I know it's dangerous. But if I stay here, so
do you." He reached out one long arm, closing his hand
round her wrist.

"Let go of me." Lisa tried to keep her voice steady.
Time was running out. She had fifteen, maybe twenty
minutes in which to work. "You're interfering with a law-
enforcement officer in pursuit of her duties. I could arrest
you right here. On the spot. Handcuff you to the trunk of
that tree and leave you to rot." She matched him stare for
stare. Golden eyes clashed with green. Kevin looked away
first, hesitated for the space of two heartbeats, then called
her bluff.

"Try it." He didn't move an inch. He was an intimidat-
ing figure in the darkness. He could prevent her from
going after the poachers and the effort wouldn't even leave
him breathing hard. Yet he held her wrist with only enough

strength to enforce his will; he caused her no pain. Lisa
knew it was fear for her safety that prompted him to act so
rashly, and she was touched. But she was also in a hurry.

"Kevin, I know my job. I'll be careful. I won't take any
unnecessary risks. Willie Gleason is a bully and a fool.
He's big as an ox and not too bright. I can handle him. I'll
be fine." She wanted to lift her hand to smooth away the
deep furrows in his forehead, but she couldn't. She was
holding a shotgun in one hand and Kevin held the other.
She tried to smile, to reassure him, but her nerves were so
on edge she didn't bring it off well. And Kevin didn't smile
in return. He looked grim, single-minded and very determined.

"I know you'll be fine, because I'll be with you." His
tone didn't leave any room for negotiation.

"All right." Lisa gave in without a great deal of grace.
She tilted her head, caught and held his gaze, narrowed her
eyes in frustration. "Damn you, Kevin Sauder. I don't
have time to argue with you." She jerked her hand out of
his grasp. "Get in the car."

He did as he was told. Moments later they were speed-
ing along the dark deserted road, heading for the turnoff
to Gilson's, then straight on toward the pale glow in the
horizon. Except that they were headed south, not east, and
the glow wasn't red-gold of dawn but of fire.

"It's closer," Kevin said, his words falling like stones
into the heavy silence between them.

"I know, but only a little closer, thank God." Lisa
snapped off the headlights, then reached under the dash
and flipped a switch. Kevin didn't ask what she was doing,
but she told him any way. "That switch bypasses the taillights. If we have to chase Gleason or his pals down, or pull
off the road or sneak up on them the red lights won't give
us away."

"Sounds like an old moonshiners trick." Lisa heard the echo of his special smile in the words.

"Let's just call it an old game warden's trick, okay? Kevin, please, for your safety and my peace of mind, do as I say from now on." She took her eyes off the road, turned her head in his direction. "Please. I'm in enough trouble already just having you in the car. But if anything happens to you, if you get hurt . . . I couldn't live with myself.

Kevin was staring straight ahead. He didn't see the anguish in her eyes, nor hear the tremor in her voice. "I'm no hero, Lisa. I'll do what you say, but I sure as hell wish I had something in my hand. How about a billy club?" He was half joking, half serious.

"Under the seat," came her immediate reply. "And there's another lantern in the glove compartment. He reached down and pulled a smooth blunt-ended club from under the seat. He tested its weight against his palm, then located the flashlight, and flicked the switch to check the battery. That was a mistake. Kevin realized it the moment the bright white light flared into life. Blinded, he switched it off again and stared, blinking, into the star-spangled darkness. Lisa seemed not to notice his discomfort. She was still talking, detailing her plans, trying to prepare him for any eventuality.

"I'll cut the engine at the top of this hill and coast down. Maggie's cabin's at the bottom. It'll hide us from view. If we had time I'd track down their vehicle and disable it. But that's the problem in a nutshell. We don't have time. Instead we'll head straight for the spot Maggie described when she called. It's about a hundred yards beyond her cabin. The deer gather there in the winter. That's probably why they came back here when the fire drove them out of the woods. Stay close and watch your step."

By the time they were ten yards into the thick scrub trees beyond Maggie's place, Kevin regretted more than ever turning on the light he carried in his hand. His night vision was far more limited by his injury than he liked to admit. Now he couldn't see a thing beyond the pale glimmer of Lisa's hands and the back of her neck in the darkness. Thirty feet farther on Kevin could make out the sound of human voices in the distance. Lisa held up her hand, came to a halt. The men continued talking, making little effort to remain quiet. Kevin felt some of his tension drain away. The culprits had no idea they were being tracked. It was also apparent they were nearly finished with their grisly task.

Lisa tugged on the sleeve of his sweatshirt. Kevin bent his head so that her lips were scant inches from his ear. It wasn't until he caught the faint intoxicating scent of her skin that he realized the smell of wood smoke tainted the air around them.

"They're just beyond the trees. Three of them." He nodded his understanding. "When I tell you to, turn on the flashlight and shine it straight into their eyes. It works with deer. It'll work with men." She put her hand on his sleeve. "If they open fire. Drop."

"Like a stone," Kevin promised. He kissed her cheek. "Don't be a hero."

"Ready?" Her voice was more sensation than sound. Should he tell her he couldn't see? No, Kevin decided looking up at the sky. It was better now. He could make out one or two stars through the lacy pattern of tree branches. Once beyond the cloaking darkness of the foliage he would be all right.

He touched her arm quickly, lightly. "Go."

Lisa stepped out of the shelter of the trees. There were indeed three men, and they were bent over the carcasses of three white-tailed deer. One man had already slung the body of a field-dressed doe across his shoulders. He wasn't holding a gun, but Lisa kept a wary eye on him just the same. It was Willie Gleason, the man she'd testified against a week ago, just as she'd suspected it would be. He was a giant of a man. Even field-dressed, a deer the size of the one he had slung so casually over his shoulders would weigh at least one hundred and fifty pounds, and yet he handled the weight as if it were nothing.

Willie wasn't carrying a gun. Lisa said a short prayer of thanks. With any luck there would only be one rifle between them. Willie Gleason had a high-powered rifle that Lisa suspected was equipped with a silencer. That would certainly explain why they were able to kill three deer so close together. She scanned the ground around the area of the kill. There was no telltale glimmer of starlight on gunmetal. She began to breathe a little easier. Still, it wouldn't do to relax her guard. Each of the trio carried a razor-sharp hunting knife, a dangerous weapon in the hands of a cornered man. She felt Kevin's presence like a warm solid shadow behind her. She took comfort from his nearness while at the same time she felt anxiety for his safety.

"Now." She tightened her grip on the handle of her square lightweight flashlight. The powerful beam streaked out in front of her. At her side Kevin did the same. She swung the light up and to the left, blinding one of the men kneeling on the ground. A heartbeat later Kevin's beam held the second squatting poacher in its glare. "Gentlemen," Lisa said in a loud clear voice, "I'm the game warden and you are under arrest." Because she was making the apprehension under a provision of the game laws, she didn't have to read them their rights and they knew it. A flurry of groans and curses greeted her announcement.

Kevin felt his heart pounding against the wall of his chest. None of the men changed position, but their tension, hostility and fear were so strong the emotions were almost tangible.

"Is that you, Ms. Emery?" One of the men asked, his tone incredulous. The question ended with a nervous whine.

"Sure is, Nat Benchly, and as you can see I'm not alone," Lisa replied, obviously recognizing the culprit illuminated by Kevin's flashlight. "Jake," she said, indicating the second kneeling man, "move over there by your brother." She motioned with the beam of her flashlight.

The brothers looked at each other, weighing their options, sizing up the opposition. How long would it be before they realized Lisa's companion wasn't another law-enforcement officer and recognized their advantage? Kevin tensed. If they decided to rush them, or bolt and run, Lisa would be hard put to control the situation. The only thing Kevin could hope to do was bring one of them down with a blow of the billy club.

"Jake, Nat—" Lisa's voice was friendly, almost casual "—you two haven't had a violation in two years. The judge'll probably go easy on you if you cooperate with me. It's Willie I'm after." The two men on the ground didn't move. Kevin waited as seconds ticked past.

"Hell, Jake. I'm not goin' to jail for Willie, eh?"

"Me, neither." The two men stood up and raised their hands. Lisa handed Kevin her flashlight. A pair of handcuffs appeared in her hand.

"Cowards!" The third man's voice was a roar. Kevin swung the beam of light so that it impaled him, still standing with the butchered doe across his shoulders. Kevin blinked in disbelief. Dressed in a filthy camouflage jumpsuit, wooly-haired and wild-eyed, with the dead animal draped over his shoulders, Willie Gleason was a sight to behold.

"Keep your hands where I can see them, Willie." Lisa's tone was no longer quite so friendly.

"That damn old woman in the cabin squealed on us, didn't she? I shoulda known she'd still be sittin' down there, too stubborn to cut 'n' run from the fire."

"Save the talk, Willie. Just start walking toward me, nice and slow." Lisa gestured with the barrel of her gun.

Suddenly the big man moved. It happened so quickly Kevin was caught off guard. "Damn fool woman. You aren't going to take me in again." He lifted the dead deer over his head and threw it at Nat Benchly who was standing directly in front of Kevin. The man went down with a startled grunt, arms and legs flailing. Kevin couldn't side-step quickly enough. He landed in a sprawling heap, but managed to maintain his hold on the flashlight. The billy club went flying off into the night. He could hear running footsteps as Willie Gleason made his bid for freedom.

The sound of a shell being loaded into the chamber of Lisa's shotgun was loud in the night. The gun went off, shattering the normal unobtrusive forest sounds with its violent concussion.

"Hold it, Gleason." Lisa ducked into a half crouch, then raised her voice to carry over the sounds of pain and confusion around her. She didn't know who was moaning in the darkness. If it was Kevin, she didn't think she could ever forgive herself for allowing him to follow her into danger.

"Kevin?" she lowered her voice, all the while straining to see if the fugitive had obeyed her command.

"I'm right here." There was a grunting curse, another moan, and Kevin was on his feet beside her.

"Are you okay?"

"Fine." His words were strong, his voice steady. He wasn't hurt. Lisa bit her lip in relief. Obviously it was Nat Benchly, still lying under the body of the dead deer, who was moaning in pain. The cowering figure next to him was his brother, Jake.

"We have to pin Gleason down with the lights. Ready?"

"Ready." Kevin's tone was clipped, devoid of emotion, cold. If Lisa had had the time to analyze it, she would have said he sounded as distant and angry as he had the first night they met.

"As far as I can tell, he's in front of you and a little to the right."

Kevin didn't answer but swung the beam of light in the direction Lisa had indicated. A running crouching figure appeared for a moment in the light, then disappeared again. "Too far. A little to the left. There."

"Got him." Kevin sounded darkly satisfied.

Lisa raised her voice again, "Hold it, Willie. Put your hands behind your head and turn around." When the poacher made no move to obey, Lisa levered another cartridge into the chamber of the shotgun. "There's four more shells where that one came from. One of them's bound to bring you down."

"You don't have the guts," the cornered man growled, but he did as she told him, raising his arm to fend off the glare of the flashlight. He stood still, not attempting to run a second time. "You wouldn't shoot an unarmed man," he yelled back, but the defiance had gone out of his voice.

"Don't count on it," Lisa advised him. "This way. Move."

When Gleason and the other two were safely handcuffed, Kevin helped the still-moaning Nat Benchly to his feet. A quick examination of his injuries turned up nothing more serious than scrapes and bruises. Lisa pronounced him fit enough to drag his doe out of the meadow, which would be kept as evidence. An hour later, with no more trouble out of the three poachers, they were on their way back to Marquette. Lisa drove Willie Gleason's pickup, the culprits handcuffed in the back. Kevin drove her car.

Lisa worked her way through the formalities of turning the men over to the sheriff's department, the tedium of entering into evidence Willie's high-powered, illegally silenced rifle, filling out the seemingly endless reports and paperwork that accompanied the arrest. When those tasks were finished, she had to face the inevitable encounter with her supervisor who praised her initiative and threatened to dock her a day's pay for her foolhardiness. All in all, Lisa was ready to call it a day by nine in the morning.

Kevin was waiting for her, sprawled in the front seat of her car, one foot propped on the dash, his eyes closed against the glare of the bright morning sun. There were two deep grooves running between his nose and chin on either side of his mouth. A dark blond stubble of beard roughened his chin. He'd taken off his sweatshirt and tied the sleeves around his shoulders. The collar of his pale green shirt was open at the throat. Lisa thought of kissing him there, of feeling the smoothness of his tanned skin, the hard warmth of bone and muscles beneath her fingers, and closed her eyes against the rush of desire that coursed through her veins. He opened his eyes, looked at her as if she were a stranger and closed them again.

Lisa was shaken. She hadn't been bothered by the morose silence of Willie Gleason and his henchmen. But Kevin's cold detachment was a complete surprise. It was as if their night together had never happened, as if he'd never told her he loved her, wanted to marry her, initiated her into the physical pleasures a man and a woman who meant everything to each other could share.

He was a stranger again.

They were halfway home before Kevin spoke. "One of the sheriff's deputies recognized your car," he said in that carefully controlled, distant voice she hated. "He said to tell you he was going out to pick up Maggie and her cats and take her to her granddaughter's in Ishpeming."

"Good. I left word when I turned our three friends over to the deputies that it would be best to evacuate her as soon as possible. She is eighty-seven, after all, even if she is the most stubborn self-sufficient woman I've ever met."

"He also said to tell you the fire line is holding for the time being, but there's a weather front due to move through Sunday night or Monday."

Lisa sighed. She was tired and uncertain and discouraged. The man sitting on the seat beside her was someone very different from the lover who had held her in his arms just hours before. Something had happened during their encounter with Willie Gleason and the Benchly brothers, something that had changed him back into the angry, bewildered man he'd been when he first walked into her life. "That means the wind will pick up," she said, reacting only to his words, not his attitude. "How fast the front moves through will determine when that will happen."

"And how long it will take to turn the fire back on itself," Kevin said, well aware of the effect his coldness was having on Lisa.

"We know only one thing for certain," Lisa said. Her voice, sounding hoarse and rough, clearly gave evidence of her effort to hold back tears. It tore at Kevin's heart. She continued, "The wind will increase out of the south before it switches around to the west."

She didn't need to say any more. When the warm moist wind from the south was funnelled ahead of the advancing weather system, it would push the fire before it, almost certainly bringing it within range of her home. And when that happened he'd be no more help to Lisa than he'd been out there in the woods. Kevin let the anger he felt at his failure eat away at him like acid on metal.

What kind of fool was he to think he had this thing licked? He was half-blind, a has-been wildlife photographer, without prospects, and he'd let his own macho self-image put the woman he loved in danger. What right did he have to ask Lisa to love him, to marry him, to bear his children? He couldn't even take care of himself.

The steady beat of pain that had been escalating inside his head since sunup kept tempo with his inner rhythm of doubts. The sooner he got out of her life, the better. He might as well leave today, fire threat or no fire threat. What the hell good could he do her, anyway?

The car came to a stop. Kevin, pulled out of his dark thoughts, looked around, blinking painfully in the strong morning sunlight. They were parked in front of his cabin. He turned in his seat. "I'm bushed," he said, clipping off his words. "You look like you could use some sleep, too."

He saw Lisa's flush, the color rising to stain her cheeks a dusky red. He was being deliberately cruel, because it was the only way he could hide his own pain. How in hell did he think he could just walk away, never look back and keep from losing his mind, if she kept looking at him like she'd lost her best friend?

"Kevin?"

"Catch you later." He opened the door, bolted out of the car and headed for the cabin.

Lisa climbed out of the car, too. She left her hat and jacket on the seat. Her hair spilled across the shoulders of her sage-green shirt like autumn leaves on grass. She pushed it behind her ears with distracted fingers. If he thought he could just turn his back and walk out of her life—because she was absolutely certain that was what he meant to do—he had another thing coming.

"Kevin, wait."

Lisa never stopped to consider that it would be easier if he left now, today, before both their hearts were so deeply committed they couldn't pull back. Letting him go, sending him away, was a noble gesture, to be sure. It worked in theory, but not in practice. She'd already passed the point of no return where loving Kevin Sauder was concerned. She didn't know if they could work out a future together. A sad mocking little voice inside her kept insisting they could not. But she wasn't going to accept defeat without a struggle.

He pretended not to hear her. Lisa ground her teeth. "Kevin!" she yelled. If he left her, it would be because he couldn't accept the reality of who and what she was. It wasn't going to be because he thought he'd failed her back there in the woods, because he feared he was less a man ever since the injury to his eye. "Kevin, wait!"

Kevin hunched his shoulders and continued into the cabin. Lisa hesitated a fraction of a second, then followed. He was rummaging in a cupboard when she opened the door. He took down a bottle of prescription medication, shook two capsules into his hand and turned to find her standing in the doorway. "I've got one hell of a headache. I forgot my sunglasses when we left in such a rush last night. I'll catch up to you later." He opened the refrigerator and turned his back on her again.

"Kevin, I want to talk."

Kevin shook his head and regretted the movement instantly. He studied the contents of the refrigerator:

ketchup, mustard, a dozen eggs and two light beers. He grabbed one of the cans to wash down the pills.

"You aren't going to mix alcohol and pain medication, are you?" Lisa's tone was incredulous. He resisted an urge to smile.

"Why not?" Kevin really hadn't been paying attention to what he was doing. The pain in his head increased with each surge of blood through his veins. Lisa was slamming cupboard doors. He slammed the refrigerator door and wished he hadn't. "Cut out the noise." He pressed the heel of his hand into his eye. What had ever made him think he was beating this thing? he asked himself again. He hadn't been able to help Lisa out there in the woods, not really. And now he could barely help himself.

"Here." Lisa was shoving a glass of water into his hand. "Give me that beer. You'll make yourself sick."

"One beer isn't going to make that much difference."

His continued stubbornness was beginning to make her angry. She picked up the bottle of pain medication and glanced at the label. "Mixing alcohol with this stuff can make a big difference." Her voice softened, took on a cajoling, wistful note. "Please Kevin, tell me what's wrong."

He swallowed the capsules and set the glass on the counter. Still facing the sink, he spread his legs and rested his hands on the edge of the counter. He dropped his head, rolling it from side to side, trying to work out the stiffness, the discomfort, both physical and mental, that he was experiencing. "Nothing's wrong that getting a few hours of sleep won't cure." He turned his head, glaring over his shoulder.

Lisa folded her arms across her chest. "You're not getting rid of me this easily, Kevin Sauder. If you're feeling sorry for yourself because you think you didn't pull your weight with Gleason and the others, don't. I shouldn't have taken you with me in the first place, but since I did, I want you to know how much I appreciated having you there to back me up. I was scared. But more important, I would have had to let them go if you hadn't been with me. The odds against me were too high."

Kevin gave a disgusted snort. He was still standing at the sink, his head bowed. "All I did was get knocked on my can. If Nat and Jake had been anything more than a pair of bumbling cowardly losers, they'd probably have beat me to a pulp."

"I doubt that." Lisa kept her tone deliberately light, let him hear the hint of challenge in her words. "I imagine you could hold your own in a fight if you had to." He'd bunched his hand into a fist. She reached out, touched his knuckles very lightly, brushed the tips of her fingers over the back of his hand, the hair-rough skin above his wrist.

"You're not going to let me enjoy my misery in peace, are you?" The pills were beginning to work, or perhaps it was Lisa's touch that lessened his pain.

"No." Lisa shook her head, swallowing hard against the sudden lump in her throat, against the surge of pleasure touching him produced deep inside her.

"I was afraid of that." A ghost of a smile touched the hard curve of his mouth. He turned around, leaned back against the sink, drew her into his arms. He looked down at her face, memorizing each line and curve. He loved her so very much. "I could have gotten you killed," he whispered, his voice rough with emotion.

"I could have gotten you killed." Lisa lifted her hands to frame his face between her palms. She pulled his head down, touched her lips to his lightly, fleetingly. "Don't blame yourself like this. Don't dwell on what you couldn't do because of your eyes. Think about what we did right. What we accomplished together."

"I'd rather remember what we accomplished earlier—in your bed." Kevin's words, the dark heated look in his eyes, took her breath away. "I told you we'd argue later. I just didn't think it would be about catching poachers." He smiled wryly.

"I don't want to argue about catching poachers, either." Lisa pressed herself against him. She closed her eyes, recalling the taste and shape and feel of his naked body against hers. "I don't want to argue about anything. I want to make love."

Her eyes flew open. Had she really said those words aloud? Apparently she had. Kevin pulled her closer still, fitting their bodies together, moving against her until she thought she would explode into a thousand pieces of desire.

"Do you love me?" His hands skimmed her breasts, her waist, the curve of her hips. "I need to hear you say it." He was watching her closely. She looked deep into the jade depths of his eyes. She saw her own face reflected there, taut with growing desire. She didn't know herself. The woman she had become was a stranger.

"I love you." She smiled in acknowledgment of the truth of her words and was herself again. Kevin held her so tightly she could scarcely breathe. He kissed her eyelids, her cheek, the tip of her nose.

"Stay with me," he murmured. "I want to make love to you. Long and slow. Again and again."

"I'll stay," she replied. He didn't say anything else about marriage. Lisa didn't know whether to be happy or sad. She couldn't marry him without telling him her secret. Yet he was still enough of a stranger that she couldn't be certain how he would react to what she was keeping from him. She had never felt so torn in her life.

"You'll stay with me forever." It was a statement, not a question. Kevin bent his head to capture her mouth with his. His kiss was demanding, exciting, an invitation to a joining even more intimate and fulfilling. When he freed her from his embrace to lead the way into his bedroom, Lisa's head was a whirl of conflicting needs and emotions. She couldn't think; she could only feel. And what she felt was wonderful beyond her loveliest dreams.

"I'll stay with you for as long as you want me."

Chapter Thirteen

Kevin leaned one hip against the stainless-steel counter in the camera shop's darkroom, folded his arms across his chest, pursed his lips and let out a long low whistle as he studied the five-by-seven color prints strung out on a wire along the wall. Luciano, the great horned owl, stared unblinkingly back at him. In one shot she was looking back over her shoulder. In the next, unimpressed by his attentions, she had spread her wings, the injured one held stiffly away from her body, mantling in a proudly defiant gesture.

It was good work. Kevin nodded, satisfied. He *could* get his touch back. Maybe he'd never again be able to spend six months swinging from a harness a hundred feet above the floor of the Brazilian rain forest, but he could still take pictures, damn good pictures.

The simple truth of the matter was that he no longer wanted to spend his life isolated for months at a time in some far-off corner of the earth. His world was happily encompassed by this half-wild land that was Lisa's home. He wanted it to be his. He wanted her to be his. They had spent all of yesterday and last night giving and taking and giving love again. He'd never experienced as much intensity of emotion and sensation with any other woman. Yet

it was as if he and Lisa could only exist in the here and
now. She wouldn't talk of the future, and Kevin didn't
press the subject for fear he would startle her into pulling
back inside the barricades still in place around her heart.
Time was growing short. He was going to have to make her
choose between loving him and protecting whatever secret
she held close to her heart.

Kevin slammed his fist on the counter in frustration. He
spun around and immediately felt his anxiety and preoc-
cupation with his private problems drain away. On the
opposite wall of the small square darkroom, which he'd
been given permission to use this quiet cloudy Sunday
morning, was another row of color prints. They were all
Brad's work. It was hard to describe what he saw in the
simply composed shots of everyday things. Perhaps it was
a touch of soul? Perhaps one of the gifts Brad had been
given to compensate for his handicap in vital areas of his
life was the ability to find beauty in ordinary things.

Ordinary subjects. There were the two shots of Luciano, of course, both of them taken when the owl had her
huge yellow eyes closed. Kevin spared them little attention. It was the remainder of the exposures that gave him
food for thought. Brad always seemed to find a great deal
to interest him in what to others seemed to be small un-
important details. Kevin had seen Lisa's brother, camera
in hand, looking intently at the pattern of a flower's petal,
or the veins of a leaf, and wondered what the boy was
seeing, conditioned as he himself was to look for life and
form and movement in animals.

Now he could see what Brad saw. It was the pattern of
leaves glistening with subtle hues against the forest floor,
a white butterfly poised on a cane of ripe red raspberries,
sunlight making even more delicate patterns on the al-

ready-fragile fronds of a maidenhair fern. Small things in a limited environment, yet a world worth preserving.

He understood Brad better now. But he understood himself even more. For years he'd been searching, seeking, looking for something beyond himself, but now he was no longer driven. He no longer felt compelled to change the global conscience, influence the way people treated the environment and other living creatures sharing the planet. At least not on the scale he'd always envisioned. He might be far more successful saving one small corner of that larger world, as Lisa and Enoch were working so hard to do. And in the bargain he might also save his soul, find peace and contentment, happiness with the woman he loved.

WHEN HE FINISHED at the camera shop, Kevin stopped at McDonald's, where the Westons had made arrangements for him to pick up Brad. Reports of the fire, its movements and the fire fighters inability to bring it completely under control, had worried Lisa's brother very much. He'd phoned before breakfast to say he wanted to come home early. Kevin had already spoken to Lisa's friend, the owner of the camera shop, about using the darkroom, so he volunteered to pick up Brad and bring him home. However, he'd spent so much time at the camera shop he was late. Brad was sitting on a picnic bench outside the restaurant with his canvas duffel beside him, eating a hamburger.

"I'm sure glad to see you. I told the Westons they didn't have to wait with me, but I didn't think you'd be this late. Do you want something to eat?" he asked, climbing into the passenger seat of Kevin's car.

"No, I had a big breakfast."

"Then let's go home. They keep saying how close the fire is getting to our lake. I'm worried about Lisa."

"She was fine when I left," Kevin assured him.

"I still want to get home." He squinted up at the sky as a rumble of thunder echoed off in the distance. Rain would be welcome, but Kevin knew a wildfire the size of the one that threatened them wouldn't be stopped by even the heaviest downpour. Their only hope was for the wind to shift and push the fire back on itself where it would die of lack of fuel to feed its flames.

They drove most of the way in silence. Kevin watched the trees bend and sway in sudden intermittent gusts of wind, still blowing from the south, and wondered where the fire line was. Smoke rose into the sky like a wall of gray stone around some ancient castle fortress. It stretched to the south and east for as far as the eye could see. It was also much closer than it had been when he'd traveled the same route that morning.

Kevin guessed it wouldn't be long until the authorities would be urging them to evacuate the area around the lake. Lisa was probably already stowing her most important possessions in her car. He had very few things outside of his clothing and cameras to worry about. He'd have plenty of room in his trunk for whatever Lisa needed him to carry.

Brad didn't mention the fire, but talked sporadically about his weekend and looked over the stack of prints Kevin had given him to examine. Yet every now and then, from the corner of his eye, Kevin caught him looking at the billows of smoke climbing high to merge with the low-hanging gray clouds.

"I did a pretty good job with the camera, didn't I?" he asked as he studied the photographs. "Except this picture of Lisa didn't come out very good."

"You were too far away for the flash to be effective," Kevin explained, as he glanced at the shots of Lisa and

Katie that Brad had taken along with the others. Katie looked fresh and mischievously pretty sitting on the dock, splashing a handful of water in Brad's general direction. Lisa, on the other hand, looked startled and under-lighted. She didn't photograph exceptionally well, just as he had suspected in the beginning. Still, with the right lighting and makeup, her body relaxed and languid, as boneless and supple as a cat's, as their lovemaking had shown him it could be, she would be a striking study.

"Too far away." Brad filed the information away for later reference. "How can I tell what's too far away?"

Kevin searched his mind for an easy rule of thumb to help Brad visualize the best working distance for the automatic camera's limited flash range. Suddenly inspiration hit. "How tall are you?"

"Five feet, nine inches," Brad said sitting up straight in his seat.

"Okay. When you go to take a flash picture, do this. Imagine you just fell flat on your face in front of whoever or whatever it is you're trying to shoot. If you don't hit them with your head when you fall, you're too far away."

Brad slapped his thigh with the flat of his hand. "That's good. I can remember that. Fall flat on my face." He laughed loudly. "That's good."

"I picked up some more film for you," Kevin said, indicating a sack on the seat between them. "The more you practice, the better you'll get."

"How much did the film cost?" Brad asked, wrinkling his forehead in a frown. Kevin told him. "That much?" He sighed, looking down at his hands. He was still holding the prints. He ran his finger around the edge of the top one. "I can't afford that much money till I get a job."

Kevin didn't make the mistake of offering the film as a gift. "I'm buying the film for you as an investment," he said, choosing his words carefully, speaking slowly and clearly so Brad could understand what he was trying to convey.

"An investment? Like in business? I don't know anything about business."

"I want us to have a sort of a partnership." Kevin looked across at Brad and pushed his sunglasses on top of his head so that the young man could see his eyes. The sun had disappeared behind gray-edged, rain-heavy clouds some time ago.

Brad's face was a study in concentration. "Why?" he asked simply.

"I think I can sell a couple of your photographs to some people I know. They print calendars and greeting cards, stuff like that. I'll pay for the film and the developing, postage and paperwork. If they buy the shots, you can pay me ten percent. That's one dollar out of every ten dollars they pay you. I'll be your agent."

"Agent?" Brad looked impressed. "Like movie stars have?"

"Well—" Kevin grinned "—not like movie stars, exactly. But I guess you could call me your agent, yes. Is it a deal?" He took his right hand off the wheel and held it out to Brad to seal the bargain.

"It's a deal." He pumped Kevin's hand enthusiastically. "Wait till I tell Lisa."

But by the time they were almost home, business plans were the farthest things from their minds. When they turned off the highway at Gilson's corner, they found the south fork of the road blocked by earth-moving equipment, a fire truck and a dozen tired dirty men in sweat-stained, fire-blackened coveralls, hard hats and protective goggles.

Kevin slowed to a stop and rolled down the window. One of the men came over and poked his head in. "The fire jumped the county road in two places about an hour ago. We're bulldozing a fire break from here east. We've been at it most of the morning. But if that doesn't hold, we can't guarantee the safety of anybody who lives on the shore road. I'm sorry but you'll have to turn back."

"But we live on the shore road. My sister's there." Brad tripped over his words in his haste to get them out. His skin turned a pasty white, and he started to shake.

Kevin put his hand on Brad's knee. "It's all right, buddy." He turned his attention back to the exhausted fire fighter. Dark tired eyes looked back at Kevin from a grotesque mask, a macabre clown's face where white circles around the man's eyes contrasted starkly with the sweat and grime-blackened skin of the rest of his face. "How long do we have?"

"If the wind switches in time, we've got it stopped. If not—" the man shrugged "—an hour at the most.'

"It won't take us ten minutes to get to the Emery place, set the boy's mind at rest about his sister and get back here." Kevin spoke with quiet assurance. He was worried about Lisa, also, but he respected her abilities and he wasn't going to take any greater risk than necessary. Brad's safety was his first responsibility.

The fire fighter looked up at the billowing clouds of smoke. "You're right on the lake?" Kevin nodded. "You can get out by boat if necessary?"

"Yes."

"Get going." He motioned Kevin through the roadblock.

Gilson's big graveled parking lot was full of cars and people milling around. Kevin recognized Enoch's battered pickup but couldn't spot the older man in the crowd.

He did see Lisa's neighbors and their two small children huddled near their car. They'd hitched a small wooden trailer behind and it was piled high with possessions.

"There's Matt and Katie," Brad yelled, pointing excitedly at Matt's old green truck.

"Kevin! Brad! Over here." Katie was calling and waving as she ran toward Kevin's car. Matt was right on her heels. "I want to go back to the house. Get my things. Find Lisa." She started to sob. "Matt won't take me."

"The fire fighters said it wasn't safe." Matt looked defensive and harassed.

"You did the right thing," Kevin said, getting out of the car.

Matt looked relieved. "Thanks."

"I could see the smoke was getting closer even from the campground," Katie said. "I wanted to come home." She stopped sobbing, sniffed and dabbed at her eyes with the tissue Kevin had Brad fish out of a box in the glove compartment.

"Get in the car. We're going to check on Lisa right now." Kevin waved her questions aside. "I've got permission. Matt, will you stay here in case Lisa shows up?"

"If you don't need me at the house." He looked uncertain.

Kevin shook his head. "With three of us in the car we won't be able to bring out anything but what's absolutely essential. If for some reason Lisa's still there, it's probably because she has car trouble. Or there's some other problem..." He didn't finish the sentence. He didn't need to.

"Right. Be careful, Kate." Matt pulled her into his arms for a hard quick hug.

"I'm sorry I yelled at you."

"You always are. I'll be right here when you get back."

Katie climbed into the backseat, still sniffing back tears. Brad coughed. The smoke was getting thicker, making it hard to breathe. Kevin rolled up the window and turned on the air-conditioning. He hoped it was only his imagination that made him think he could hear, beyond the still-distant rumble of thunder and the keening of wind in the trees, the far more ominous crackle of flames.

"Lisa's not here," Brad said the moment they pulled into the driveway behind the house. "The car's gone. She left without us?" His voice was high and squeaky with fear.

"Stay calm, buddy. She would have been waiting for us at Gilson's if she'd evacuated like everyone else. There's some other reason she's not here. Maybe she left us a note."

The air in the yard was hot and dry despite the approaching rainstorm. Katie glanced apprehensively out over the trees in the backyard. Smoke rolled overhead. It was growing darker by the moment. Here and there, flames were reflected back from the low-hanging clouds. "Let me out of the car, Brad. I'll get the lockbox and Lisa's jewelry box with Grandma Kinsey's pearls. What else do you think we should bring with us, Kevin?"

Kevin climbed out of the car before answering. He pulled the seat forward so Katie could get out, too. "Photo albums, I think, and a few clothes. We might not get back for a while. Anything else that's small and means a lot to you or Lisa."

"I have my camera in my bag," Brad said, spurred into action. "Are your cameras safe?" He looked at Kevin, his almond-shaped brown eyes wide with fear despite his attempt to smile.

"They're in the trunk. Put yours in the case with them if you want to. It's unlocked. Let's get going."

Lisa had indeed left a note taped to the door. She'd been called to Munising to help search for two trout fishermen who'd been lost in the woods since Saturday afternoon. From the time she'd scribbled on the note, Kevin realized she'd left only about half an hour later than he had that morning. She'd had no way of knowing the fire was so close. And even now, if she was in a position to monitor the fire fighters' radio frequency, she was too far away to get back in time to help. Kevin sent Katie and Brad inside while he backed the car up to the door. He didn't want to waste time loading the vehicle. He'd told the fireman he'd only be gone ten or fifteen minutes. They'd been in the fire zone for nearly that long already. It was no longer only his imagination that he heard the pop and crackle of flames. Twice the explosive roar of pines igniting had shattered the unnatural silence that seemed to exist in advance of the still-muted, freight-train roar of the main fire. Occasional sparks rained on them. Cinders blew thick and gritty on the wind that still gusted obstinately out of the south.

"Why doesn't it rain?" Katie asked on a rising note of hysteria. If he didn't keep them busy, Kevin thought, the kids were going to crack.

"Move it, Katie. We don't have time for the vapors."

"Vapors! That's worse than your Ivanhoe bit." Five minutes later Kevin looked down at the hastily gathered array of clothing and mementos in his trunk. He slammed the lid.

"We can't stay here any longer. Get in the car."

Katie opened the passenger door but then slammed it shut and sprinted up the back steps of the house. Kevin made a grab for her hand and missed. "Katie, get back here. We have to go. Now."

"Not yet. We forgot those decoys. They're on the front porch. We can't leave them."

"We don't have room for them," Brad said, looking to Kevin for guidance.

"We'll make room. Shove that stuff on the backseat off onto the floor." Kevin suited action to words. "We'll squeeze them in back here. We can all three ride in front. It'll be crowded, but we'll make it, buddy."

He was jockeying the second canvas duffel of decoys into the cramped backseat when Enoch's pickup roared into the driveway in a cloud of dust and blowing ash. He jumped out of the cab, looking almost as grimy and dirty as the fire fighters.

"We're just pulling out," Kevin said with a grunt as he gave the duffel one last shove.

"It's too late," Enoch told him quietly. "The road's blocked behind me. I barely made it through. I was getting Luciano squared away in a shed at Gilson's. All those people and smoke were making her nervous. I'd just finished unloading my truck, stowing some of my carvings away, when the Swensen boy came up and told me what you three were up to." He took a deep breath, running his fingers through his grizzled red hair. "I came to help, but I was too late. Most likely it was a top fire that jumped the break. Two trees came down across the road damn near on top of me. I radioed the fire trucks on my CB, but to tell you the truth, right now we're all trapped here."

Brad started to cry. Katie put her arms around him and murmured reassurances, but the hazel eyes she turned to Kevin for guidance and her own reassurance were wide with fear.

"We're trapped as far as getting out in the car," Kevin said, dragging the duffel out of the backseat, "but not as far as the water's concerned." He spared a moment to wish that Lisa's runabout was tied up at the dock. It was bigger, faster and had room to carry cargo and four human beings more safely than the fishing boat that was now their only means of escape. "Just remember to keep the weight evenly distributed in the bottom and we'll be fine. Got that?"

Katie nodded. Brad stopped crying and did the same, but he looked puzzled. "Don't worry," Katie said patting his shoulder. "I'll show you where to put everything."

Enoch laid a hand on Kevin's shoulder. Kevin looked at the older man, saw his desire to speak privately and walked a few steps away from the car as Katie and Brad disappeared toward the lake with their first load of possessions.

"There's a good chance the fire won't get a real hold on this side of the lake. Ground's not a peat bog like where it's been burning for the past week. It's a genuine goddamned swamp out there. A little dry on top now—sure, what isn't—but plenty wet underneath where a fire likes to get a stranglehold on the land."

"What are you getting at, Enoch?" Kevin wasn't in the mood for a natural-history lesson at the moment.

"What I'm getting at is that, no matter what happens along the rest of the lakeshore, there's a damn good chance this house is going to go up in flames. Harold Kinsey was my best friend, but he was a fool when it came to trees. There's too damn many pines close to the buildings. They're dangerous in a fire. They don't burn—they explode. We're not in any immediate danger, but I suspect the phone and electric lines are already down. We're on our own. I'm going to fire up Lisa's standby generator for the well pump and start hosing down the roof of the house. What do you think?"

"I wish to hell I'd thought of it," Kevin said, shaking his head.

"No, you shouldn't have thought of it." Enoch's voice was rough and dry like the wind swirling in hot gusts around the yard. "You had your priorities straight. Those kids, the things they hold dear in this world. And those marvelous decoys." He grinned then, a wide white slash of teeth in his dirty bearded face. "Buildings come last. A long way behind people."

Kevin didn't waste any more of his time or energy on self-pity. Enoch was right. He had his priorities straight. "You get started with the hoses while I help finish loading the boat."

"Sure thing." Twenty feet behind the garage a big half-dead pine exploded in a shower of sparks and debris as though to illustrate Enoch's point. Kevin forgot about everything else as flaming twigs rained on the yard. He raced into the house and grabbed a big woven cotton throw rug off the floor. He ran back outside and beat at the dry grass that was already starting to smolder and burn. He couldn't do much about the tinder-dry roof of the garage. In the length of time it would take him to get a ladder from inside, set against the wall and climb onto the roof, any of the dozen smoking shingles he could see from where he stood would be ready to ignite. *Keep your priorities straight.* Saving the house was most important. He didn't look at the garage again, just kept working to contain the flames on the far side of the driveway.

Behind him Kevin heard the generator sputter to life in the pump house. As Enoch suspected, the electricity had already been cut off, probably when the trees fell and blocked the road. Without the generator to power the pump used to bring water up from the well, they'd be powerless to fight the flames.

Kevin rested a moment, his hands on his knees, as he tried to draw oxygen into his laboring lungs. The air was smoky and hot and gave no relief. He needed a damp handkerchief or towel, anything wet and cool to tie over his nose and mouth, but he couldn't spare the time to find something. He tried to protect his face with his arm. He was thankful he was wearing a cotton shirt and denim pants. He hated to think what it would be like standing unprotected among falling twigs and red hot cinders in man-made fabric, which would melt before it burned.

Tongues of fire licked at the roof of the garage and raced through the treetops in the distance, but for the most part, the swampy ground behind the buildings prevented the fire from marching straight ahead as Enoch said it would. Kevin wiped stinging sweat from his eyes. He turned his head. Brad and Katie were lugging his camera case around the side of the house. He felt a tight hot lump in his throat that had nothing to do with thirst or how much smoke he'd inhaled. They were saving his cameras at the expense of some of their own valued things. He wanted to shout at them to forget the damn cameras, he'd buy new ones. But he didn't have the extra breath to yell. Sparks showered from the now fiercely burning garage roof. His shirt sleeve started to smolder. He slapped at it with his bare hand.

Time ceased to exist. Kevin continued to beat at the grass fires in the yard until his rug was a charred rag. Katie appeared at his elbow with another, and blessedly a wet cotton scarf. He bent his head and she tied it around the lower half of his face. He was wearing his sunglasses to protect his eyes from flying debris. "You look like one fierce bandido," she yelled over the wind and flames. She tried to smile.

"I feel like hell."

"I'm moving your car and Enoch's truck around to the front yard. It'll be the safest place for them."

"Thanks." It came out more a croak than an intelligible word, but Katie seemed to understand.

"Enoch says it's going to rain any minute." She had pulled a cotton jacket over her head to keep sparks and cinders out of her hair. She smiled. "The wind's starting to change."

Was it? He couldn't tell. Kevin went back to beating at the flames. More time passed. His back ached from bending over. His arms and shoulders burned from swinging the rug. Suddenly a spray of icy water showered over him. Kevin gasped, then turned to face Enoch who had the hose directed straight on him. "Your hair's on fire," he yelled. "Fall back." For the first time Kevin felt an uncomfortable stinging sensation on the back of his neck. He swatted at the cinders that were lodged in his hair, retreated to the other side of the gravel drive, then dropped to his knees. Was the air less thick with smoke? Or was that only wishful thinking? Enoch turned the hose back on the house. Still, a gentle patter of drops fell on his head. Kevin looked up at the sky. It was raining. Thunder growled directly overhead. Lighting streaked down from the black rolling clouds.

He glanced to the right, wondering for the first time how the cabin where his belongings still were had fared. Surprisingly, no smoke issued from that direction. It was then he noticed the wind *had* shifted. The sparks and flames as the garage roof caved in on itself rose straight up and then flew back to the south, in the direction of the areas already burned.

The walls of the garage continued to burn, but presented little additional threat. The area around the building and directly behind it was charred black and lifeless. The little white fish house was gone, and he hadn't even noticed that it had caught on fire. Kevin got to his feet and moved under the shelter of several big birches. It was raining hard enough to penetrate their thickly intertwined branches, and the soot and cinders couldn't reach him there.

Kevin glanced at his watch. It was still running. The hair on the back of his hands was singed. There were a dozen small burns and blisters on his fingers and wrists, but the long sleeves of his shirt had saved his arms, chest and back. He rubbed dust and ash off the face of his watch. Two and a half hours since he'd left the dirty exhausted fire fighter back at the roadblock. Kevin looked down at his own blackened hands and filthy clothes. He'd bet nobody could tell the two of them apart now.

The walls of the garage fell in on themselves. With grim satisfaction he watched the smoke and sparks rise skyward and veer off to the south and east. The wind would blow steadily out of the northwest now that the front was passing through. The fire would be easily contained, although hot spots would probably burn in the soft peaty soil for weeks to come. Too bad about the garage, he thought, as he closed his eyes and leaned back against the tree trunk. Heat from the flames carried all the way across the yard. Enoch came over, still carrying the garden hose and held it out. Kevin took it, letting the clear cold water run over his head and neck, into his mouth. Nothing had ever tasted so good.

"The worst of it's over now." Enoch took a drink from the hose. "Too bad we couldn't save the garage."

"Too bad," Kevin agreed, but there was no self-condemnation in the words. He had helped save Lisa's home and its contents. He hadn't failed. The injury to his eye hadn't hindered his performance. He could live with his handicap if necessary. He could certainly endure it until the doctor determined it was time for the surgery.

"Kevin. Enoch. Are you too tired to come and see what Brad did with the decoys?" Katie had pulled on a plastic poncho to keep off the rain, coming down in buckets now. Soot streaked her face. Her mascara made a raccoonlike mask around her eyes, still red from crying and the acrid sting of smoke. Kevin just hoped she didn't decide to look in a mirror until they got all their things back in the house. He estimated it would take her at least an hour to repair the damage to makeup and hair. "There wasn't room for them in the boat. While I was trying to get stuff covered to keep off the rain he came up with a solution all by himself. Come see." She beamed on both of them.

Enoch shrugged and threw down the hose. "Lead the way, Kate." He reached out a hand and helped Kevin to his feet.

Brad was sitting on a cement block on top of the concrete retaining wall near the dock, his hooded red jacket a brave bright spot of color against the stormy gray sky and equally stormy gray lake.

"See." Katie pointed proudly at the bobbing line of decoys bouncing and jostling each other at the end of a long yellow nylon rope. Brad got up from his seat smiling broadly.

"I thought of it all by myself," he started out in a rush, then slowed down. "I took the ski rope that was hanging on a nail by the porch. I strung them on it through—" he struggled for the correct word "—the eyebolts underneath. I tied the other end to a cement block just like this one." He gave the heavy square block a nudge with the toe of his shoe. "I threw it as far out into the lake as I could. They just floated out to the end of the rope and stayed there. I knew they would be safe." He finished his recital with a wave of his hands.

"I would never have thought to save them that way," Katie said beaming with pride at Brad's accomplishment.

"Do you think Lisa will think I did a good thing?"

"She'll think you're a hero."

"That's right, buddy. A real live hero." Kevin's words ended in a spasm of coughing.

Enoch looked at him with concern. "Are you all right?"

"Fine," Kevin said. "Just swallowed too much smoke, I guess."

"We all did. Let's get this stuff under some cover and then get cleaned up. Katie, do you think you could rustle us up something to eat?"

"Sure. It's a good thing we have a propane stove and hot-water heater. As long as the generator keeps running we're all set. I can't wait to wash the smell of smoke out of my hair." She made a face. "I must look like a scarecrow."

"You look like a raccoon," Brad said truthfully but unwisely. Kevin grabbed a plastic bag stuffed with clothes out of the boat and handed it to him before he could say anything else that might alert Katie to her true appearance.

"Come on, buddy," he said hastily. "The sooner we get done here the sooner we get cleaned up. And," he added to clinch the argument, "the sooner we get to eat."

Brad took the sack and headed for the house without another word.

Chapter Fourteen

Lisa pulled into the parking lot at Gilson's an hour before sundown. It had stopped raining. The sun was a brassy sullen ball above the horizon. There was still smoke in the air. She could smell it all around her. The atmosphere was hazy with its residue. But the wind was blowing steadily out of the northwest, and by tomorrow the odor, too, would be gone. The fire had been turned back on itself. In a matter of hours it would be contained and controlled. In a few days it would cease to be a threat, but the scars of its passing would remain on the land and in human memories for a long, long time.

The fire had reached the lakeshore in one or two places in what the professionals termed a light surface burn. That much she'd learned from monitoring the frequency the fire fighters used on her car radio during the long lonely drive home. Some property damage had been noted from aerial reconnaissance flights by a Park Service spotter plane. There were civilians thought to be in the area of the breakout, but no injuries or fatalities had as yet been reported.

Injuries or fatalities. The phrase kept repeating in Lisa's head. She pulled the car into an empty space at the edge of the graveled parking lot and folded her arms on the wheel, resting her chin on her hands. People were everywhere, walking from car to car, talking in small groups. The county emergency unit was stationed directly in front of her and to the left. Children were running up and down the front steps of the store, splashing in puddles, tracking sandy mud over Gilson's porch. She saw Matt Swensen's familiar green pickup, her neighbor's car with a trailer full of plastic-draped household items and furniture hitched on behind. Her heart dropped into the region of her stomach. She searched frantically, her eyes darting from one vehicle to the next without seeing either Kevin's sedan or Enoch's disreputable old truck. Real terror began to squeeze the breath from her lungs.

Dear God, where are they? Please let them be safe. Lisa climbed out of the car. She grabbed her dark green baseball cap from the seat, pulled it on and shoved her hair underneath. She hadn't even taken the time to comb out the bits of twigs and leaves that had snagged in the windblown curls as she'd searched through heavy brush and alder thickets for the two lost fishermen. All the way back from Munising she'd been hoping against hope that the breakout in the fire was farther along the shore road, where it came to a dead end and there were only a few ramshackle summer cottages that might be destroyed. But all the while, deep inside her, she'd known what she would find. Her home in ruins.

She could accept that loss if only her brother and sister, her friends, the man she loved, were safe and unharmed. Now she couldn't even be certain that prayer was answered. A tall familiar figure appeared in one of the knots of people gathered around the ambulance unit. "Matt," Lisa called, waving. "Over here." He came toward her at a trot. "Where are Brad and Katie? Is Kevin with them? And Enoch. Were they trapped by the fire?"

Matt looked as upset as she was. His hair was standing up in spikes; he'd obviously been running his fingers through it in worry. "They were here. They were safe. But they went back. Kevin told me they'd only be gone as long as it took to make sure you were okay."

"Me?" Lisa made a steeple of her hands and pressed them to her mouth to keep from moaning in anguish.

Matt nodded. "Nobody knew where you were. They were already sealing off the road when Brad and Kevin got back from town. The flames jumped the firebreak so fast nobody had time to check on every place along the road. Katie and I were here—arguing—over what to do next. She wanted to go home, but I wouldn't let her."

Lisa couldn't hide the small sad beginnings of a smile. "Oh, Matt, did she give you a hard time?"

"She nearly took my head off."

"You did the right thing, keeping her here."

"That's what Kevin said. But Brad was frightened, too. Kevin talked to the head guy. One of the fire fighters they brought in from out west, I think. He said it was okay to go check on you and get some of your important stuff if they came right back. He thought they had enough time." Matt shrugged broad shoulders. "Maybe this fire was different." He shook his head, running his splayed fingers through his hair again, over the top of his head to clasp them wearily behind his neck. "Anyway, he was wrong. They got trapped."

Lisa looked out over the parking lot again. "Enoch, too?" she asked, guessing why his truck was gone, hoping that she was wrong.

"He took off after them to help bring stuff out. Near as we can tell, some trees fell across the road, cut them off. They still haven't got the road open. But the sheriff just headed in that direction to check it out, so I don't think it'll be much longer till we can get to your place.''

"My God." Lisa's knees grew weak. She sat down hard on the bumper of somebody's truck. "They went back to look for me." She shook her head, unbelieving. She would never be able to forgive herself if something had happened to them, any of them.

"They could get away in the boat easy enough. Out on the water they'd be safe. That's why the sheriff and the fire fighters wouldn't let anyone try to rescue them.'' Matt looked mutinous and sheepish at the same time.

"Oh, Matt, did you try to go after them, too?"

"I didn't get very far. The sheriff took the keys to my truck. He's still got them." He scowled and gestured off down the road in the direction of Lisa's house. There was a moment of silence, then Matt spoke again. "Where were you, Lisa?" He sat down on the bumper beside her.

"Out in the boonies, chasing after two fishermen who couldn't read a compass and got lost."

"Find them?" Matt asked, momentarily diverted.

"Yeah." Lisa looked at him and grinned. She must have pulled it off satisfactorily because he smiled back. At least it was more of a smile than a grimace. "We found them. Five miles from their car, wandering around in circles. Dirty, thirsty, and half-eaten alive by mosquitoes."

"Probably from down below, eh? City people, I bet."

"Cincinnati, I think," Lisa said, studying the mud on her hiking boots. Her fatigues were stained and dirty. She was grimy and sweaty and ached with weariness, yet her senses were working at full speed. She could hear bits and pieces of conversations going on around them. She could hear the sound of a piece of heavy machinery coming up the road long before it rounded the bend and came into sight. The sheriff's car preceded a big yellow Caterpillar bulldozer. Lisa and Matt were up and running for her car before most of the others milling around the parking lot realized the road was open and they could go home.

"LISA! LISA!" Katie was laughing and crying and trying to hug her sister through the open window of the car, even before Lisa had turned off the engine. Her hair was damp and curled in wisps around her face. Her face was scrubbed clean of makeup. She was pale and tired looking. Her eyes were red from tears and smoke, but otherwise she seemed fine. "Oh, Lisa, you can't imagine." Katie threw her arms around Lisa's neck the moment her sister was out of the car. "It was awful. The garage and fish house burned down."

"So I see." Lisa glanced at the still-smoking ruins as she held Katie in a tight hug. When her sister stepped out of her arms and ran to Matt's, she turned her gaze back to the first thing she'd seen when she turned into the drive. Her home, standing just as she'd left it that morning, four-square and solid against its backdrop of trees and sky and the restless gray lake.

The leaves on the trees nearest the drive were scorched and withered. There were one or two places where the grass in the yard was charred and burned, but the house itself was intact. In fact it had never looked so good. Lisa blinked back sudden tears.

"Kevin and Enoch saved the house," Katie said more quietly from the circle of Matt's arms. "Kevin worked like a madman to keep the fire from jumping the driveway. Enoch got the generator going and kept the roof hosed down so that sparks and cinders wouldn't set it on fire. We knew the fire trucks couldn't get through."

"Lisa!" Brad rushed down the back steps. He was wearing a damp T-shirt and jeans. His shoes weren't tied.

He was carrying a towel in one hand that he'd evidently been using to dry his hair. "We don't have any electricity. And the telephone's dead, too. We tried to call Gilson's to tell everyone we were all right, but we couldn't get through." He stopped talking when Lisa held up her hand to slow him down. He took a deep breath, laughed and launched himself into her arms. "I missed you. I was scared of the fire, but Kevin and Enoch kept it from getting to the house." He pulled away from her embrace and straightened his shoulders. "I saved the decoys."

"What?" Lisa was crying and didn't care who saw it. "How did you do that?"

"I threw them in the lake. Come and see." He draped the towel around his neck and pulled her along by the hand. "They're still in the water. Enoch said he'd help me get them out after he gets back from checking to make sure his place is okay. Kevin's sitting out on the dock, 'exchanging the smoke in his lungs for real air.'" He screwed his round face into a grimace. "Whatever that means."

Kevin. Lisa's heart skipped a beat. Her feet missed a step. A great deal had happened since he'd left her that morning. She loved him so much, there was a tight aching constriction around her heart. She wanted to be free of her doubts and fears so that she could become his wife, with no regrets, no hesitation. Yet that wasn't possible as long as she was keeping the knowledge of her body's shortcomings from him. Would not having children make a difference to him? Or if they did have a child, a child like Brad, could Kevin love him? Or would he blame her and break her heart?

"Lisa, do you see them?" Brad was tugging on her sleeve impatiently. Lisa blinked tears out of her eyes and looked at the row of crowded-together decoys bobbing at the end of their tether.

"I'm so proud of you." Lisa hugged him again, as much to give herself time to get her emotions under control as to show him how much she loved him. "I'm proud of all of you."

"C'mon, Brad," Katie urged, watching Lisa carefully. "Let Lisa go talk to Kevin alone. We'll wait for the fire engine to get here. They'll be down to check on us now that the road's open."

"Okay." Brad looked at Lisa, puzzled, then switched his inquiring brown gaze to Kevin, sitting alone at the end of the dock, apparently lost in thought.

"The two lovebirds want to be alone," he said slyly.

"Brad." Lisa was shocked. "Where did you get such an idea?"

"I'm not blind, you know," he said, looking at her with exaggerated owlish innocence. "Men talk about that kind of stuff."

"Brad," Katie urged more forcefully, "come on. Matt doesn't want to miss the sheriff if he comes by. Apparently he's got the keys to his truck."

"How'd that happen, Matt?" Brad asked as he obediently followed the young couple.

"It's a long story," Lisa heard Matt say as they disappeared around the corner of the house, but already her attention was moving away from her brother and sister to focus on the more serious problem of her relationship with Kevin.

HE FELT THE VIBRATION OF HER FOOTSTEPS along the wooden planks of the dock. Somewhere in the back of his mind he'd registered the sound of voices, rising and falling, but he'd paid no attention. He couldn't remember ever being so tired before. He didn't even have enough energy at the moment to drag himself over to the cottage to shower and change clothes. The best he'd been able to manage so far was getting his hands and face clean and eating the sandwich Katie had made for him. His clothes reeked of smoke, his hair was full of ashes and there were holes in the bottom of his shoes where he'd stepped on hot cinders.

"Kevin?" He opened bloodshot eyes. Lisa was kneeling in front of him. He regarded her from behind his sunglasses. She looked very young and pretty, with curling wisps of hair straying from beneath the baseball cap. She was wearing her fatigues, the dark green color giving her hair the color of cinnamon and the texture of silk. He studied her more closely. She looked tired, too.

"Hi." His throat hurt from breathing in so much smoke. The word came out in a hoarse crack.

"Are you all right?" She reached out and brushed back a lock of dusty-gold hair that had fallen across his forehead.

"I feel like I've been run over by a truck," Kevin said with all honesty. "It's been one hell of a day."

"Brad and Katie and Matt told me all about it. Thank you for saving my house." She sucked in her breath. "Kevin, your hands are burned."

"Nothing serious." He shrugged off her concern. "I'm sorry we couldn't save the garage."

"I don't give a damn about the garage," Lisa said, and meant it. She ached for his pain, and the intensity of her compassion frightened her.

Kevin took off his sunglasses. He didn't need them anymore. The sun was low on the horizon, a big red ball in the dark blue, rain-washed sky. He rested his hand on his bent knee and let the sunglasses dangle from the ends of his fingers. "You would have cared if the decoys had still been inside.'' He waited for her reaction to the leading statement.

Lisa shook her head. Her gold-brown eyes flashing with indignation. ''Those decoys were in that locked cupboard for years before I was even born. You can't miss something you never knew you had. On the other hand—'' she paused, bit her lower lip and finished the sentence in a rush of words ''—if I'd lost Brad or Katie or—''

''Or what?'' Kevin interrupted, tilting his head to better see the expression flitting across her expressive features.

''Not or what,'' Lisa corrected him softly. ''Who. If I'd lost you today, I don't think I could ever love again.''

Kevin looked down at the hand holding his sunglasses. It was trembling slightly. He folded the sunglasses carefully and stuck them into his shirt pocket. He was tired of waiting for Lisa to find the courage to tell him what was in her heart. She had said last night that she loved him. But for Kevin that wasn't enough.

''What do you mean by that, Lisa?'' She sat back on her heels, looking surprised and wary as she so often did when he pressed her. This time Kevin ignored the voice inside his brain urging him to be cautious. ''Tell me.''

''I . . . I love you.'' Her hat was too tight. It was making her head hurt, making her dizzy. Lisa pulled it off. Her hair tumbled down around her shoulders, catching the last coppery rays of the setting sun.

''Enough to marry me?'' Kevin couldn't take his eyes from her face. She looked lovely and wild and half-tamed, like the country she loved so much.

''I . . .'' Again Lisa's voice faded away into silence. She folded her hands together in her lap, crushing the soft cotton fabric of her hat. She looked away, closed her eyes briefly, as if against some quick hurting pain, and then opened them again, looking him straight in the eye. "I don't think I'm ready for marriage. I need time. I need a chance to get used to the idea." Her eyes slid away from his. She looked down at her hat again.

Kevin took it away from her. "What are you suggesting? That we live together?" Kevin kept his tone deliberate and even. He wasn't going to tease her into agreeing with him tonight. What they had to decide was too serious, the consequences too far-reaching to be resolved by banter and innuendo.

"Well, no. Not exactly. I mean Brad and Katie are at such a vulnerable age . . ." Lisa let her words stumble to a halt.

"But I take it you have no objections to me, say, staying on in the cottage? You could sneak out of your window a couple of nights a week, spend a few hours with me." Kevin frowned and clasped his hands behind his head, appearing to consider the idea seriously. "Sort of a variation on the old kept-woman theme. Only I'd be a kept man. Of course, we'd have to come up with some alternate plan when the snows come. It won't take Brad and Katie long to figure out what's up if they see a fresh set of tracks in the snow every morning when they leave for school."

"Kevin." She laughed, but it came out sounding nervous and jittery. Lisa chewed on the inside of her lip. "You're teasing me." It was more a hopeful question than a statement.

"No, Lisa, I'm not. I'm dead serious."

"It would give us time to learn to know each other."

Kevin shook his head. "I'm too old to play house. Loving and marrying someone is a risk, I admit, but one that's well worth taking. I love you. I want a wife and lover and a partner." He reached out and took her hand in his before she could pull away. "I want everything that goes with that commitment. A home. Here." He stabbed his finger onto a plank of the dock. "I worked my butt off today to save this place, because I love it, too. I want a family. Katie and Brad, to start. And kids of our own. Two, three, four. We can work that out later."

"Kevin, stop!" Lisa jerked her hand away and jumped to her feet. Kevin was too fast for her. He moved with deceptive smoothness to block her escape. Tears pushed against her eyelids. She blinked them back. "I need some time."

"No, that's not good enough. There's something else standing between us, and I wish to hell you'd tell me what it is. If I kiss you, make love to you, will that prove I mean every word I've said, with all my heart and soul?"

"Kevin, don't."

He pulled her into his arms and kissed her long and lingeringly, as if it might have to last him a lifetime. Lisa kissed him back. She couldn't help herself. He was everything she wanted in life, and he deserved so much more than she could give him. The kiss went on and on. Her senses spun. She was weak in the knees when he finally lifted his mouth from hers. She couldn't stand alone, and she clung to him, her arms around his waist. He smelled of smoke and sweat and that elusive essence that was Kevin himself.

"I don't know what it is you won't tell me, Lisa. Whatever it is, it won't make any difference in how I feel. I love you, today, tomorrow, till the end of time. If you want to take the risk of loving me in return, I'll be waiting for you. There's only one problem, though." He lifted her chin with the tip of his finger so that she had to look at him.

"What?" The single word was a whisper on the wind.

"I'll love you all my life. But I can't wait forever for you to find the courage to love me back."

He turned and walked away, leaving her standing alone in the fading twilight. There was no one but a late-flying gull to see her tears, no one but the wind to hear her cry. Or so Lisa thought. She never saw the slender auburn-haired figure in the shadow of the trees. Neither did Kevin, although both of them passed within a few feet of her hiding place. But Katie was there, had been there all along. She'd heard every word spoken, analyzed every gesture and come to a few conclusions of her own. She waited where she was until she was certain Brad and Matt were occupied in the kitchen and Lisa had shut herself into the shower to cry her eyes out in private, and then she slipped off down the path to Kevin's cottage, determined to see the matter of her sister's happiness settled to her own satisfaction.

THE SOUND OF A CAR DOOR slamming woke Lisa from a light restless sleep. She lay still, staring up at the ceiling, wondering for a moment just what it was she had heard. Then the sound of a trunk closing carried through her open bedroom window. *Kevin.* Lisa sat straight up in bed, her hair in wild disarray, faint shadows beneath her eyes from a restless night spent tossing and turning until long after the first golden light of the new day had brightened her room. Kevin was leaving just as he said he would when she'd avoided giving him her unqualified love last night.

Lisa swung her long legs over the side of the bed. He was leaving. She couldn't let him go. She'd tossed and turned all night, weighing the alternatives, the consequences of her actions and omissions, and she'd come to a decision. She loved Kevin and he loved her. They would take the good with the bad. Together. She pulled clothes out of the closet, heard the sound of a car's engine come to reluctant life and almost panicked.

Throwing her clothes aside she grabbed the soft, linen long-sleeved robe that matched her floral-printed nightgown and raced to the door, barefoot and breathless. She hurried along the path between the house and the cottage, tying the belt of the robe tight around her waist as she ran, clutching at the long full skirts to keep from tripping and falling flat on her face.

She burst into the clearing around the cabin in a swirl of lace and linen. Kevin was standing in front of the car with the hood up and an oily rag in his hand, a startled look on his face.

"Lisa." He looked down at the oil stick he was holding, closed his eyes in a quick silent prayer of thanks. He replaced the metal rod with calm deliberation, wiped his hands on a clean rag and closed the hood of his car.

"Kevin, I...I heard your car." Lisa stood where she'd stopped running, her breasts rising and falling against the thin material of her gown, her hair a silky mass of curls framing her face. She brushed at several wisps of hair, pushing them behind her ears. Her eyes were wide and full of pain. He walked toward her, his face carefully expressionless, but the set of her softly rounded jaw was strong and determined. "I...I don't want you to leave."

Kevin stopped walking and looked at her closely. Obviously Lisa thought he was going back to Bartlow, when in reality he'd only been going out to photograph some of the burned areas around the edge of the lake. During a night every bit as restless and wakeful as Lisa's must have been, it had come to him that it would be useful to have a photographic study of the fire's devastation. Then a season-by-season pictorial log of nature going about her miraculous healing process. The idea interested him; it was a long-term project, and it took a small portion of his thoughts away from the problem of how he was going to extricate himself from the ultimatum he'd given Lisa the night before. He had a lot of things to reconsider after the talk he'd had with Katie. Now that he knew the reasons behind Lisa's reluctance to commit herself to their love, he was willing to wait as long as necessary for her to find the courage to be his wife and the mother of his children.

"I thought I might—"

"I love you," Lisa burst out. "I want to marry you. Don't go." She stepped into his arms, and he pulled her close. Holding her was what he wanted most in the world. They stood there quietly for a long time. Lisa was crying. He could feel her tears wet the front of his shirt. He felt the sobs shaking her body. "I haven't told you something very important about myself, Kevin. That's why I acted the way I did last night. I—" This time it was his turn to interrupt.

"I know about Brad's condition being hereditary."

"You do? How?" Lisa looked up, her eyes the color of molten gold as they shimmered with tears.

"Katie overheard us last night out on the dock. She came to the cottage. She told me the facts and offered quite a lot of advice on how to court her sister, as well." He shook his head, smiling wryly at the memory of the teenager's visit.

"Oh, Katie." Lisa smiled through her tears. "I don't know who is raising whom in this family. But Kevin, you do understand why I hesitated. I'm afraid to have a child. I've always been afraid, ever since I learned that what happened to Brad might happen to my children, too. I'm still afraid. I probably always will be. Can you accept that?"

"Yes. I understand and I accept. But will you promise me something, also?" Kevin framed her face in his hands, threading his fingers through her hair, tracing the high sloping angles of her cheekbones. "That if you change your mind you'll let me know right away. A lot has happened in genetics research in the past ten years. There are new tests, new medical advances all the time."

"But we could never be sure."

"There are only three sure things in this life."

"Three?" Lisa looked at him, puzzled.

Kevin smiled. "Death. Taxes. And the fact that I love you more than anyone has ever been loved before."

Lisa grasped her courage in both hands. She looked deep into his eyes, searching for any sign of doubt, of pulling back. She saw nothing but love and need and wanting. "Could you love a child like Brad? Could you sacrifice all the time and energy it takes to give such a child the best life he can have?"

Kevin's voice was low and steady, a verbal caress. "Together we can do whatever we have to. Brad has brought you as much love and satisfaction as heartache. He's a unique individual, despite his restrictions. I'd be willing to take the risk of bringing such a child into the world, if you are, because I know how very much he would be loved."

"You're so certain I possess all the right qualities to make a success of being a wife and a mother," Lisa whispered, shaking her head. "I can't be so confident."

"I have enough confidence for both of us." He tipped her head back, lowered his mouth to hers and proved the truth of what he said without further use of spoken words.

"I love you, Kevin Sauder."

He scooped her up in his arms so swiftly Lisa didn't have a chance to object. "And I love you, very-soon-to-be Lisa Sauder." He grinned down at her as he started walking back toward the cottage. That marvelous special smile he saved for her alone. "I might as well tell you the truth about where I was going so bright and early this morning."

"Kevin." Lisa wiggled in his arms, realizing she'd been outmaneuvered again. "You weren't planning to leave me, were you? I came running over here in my nightclothes, without shoes, my hair sticking out all over my head, for no reason."

"I don't know about that," Kevin countered with a grin more wicked than charming. "I can think of one very good reason for you to be dressed like this."

"What's that?" Lisa asked suspiciously, knowing full well what he was going to say.

"So I can undress you more easily, of course." With Lisa still in his arms, Kevin opened the screen door and strode into the small pine-paneled bedroom of the cottage. He lowered her onto the bed, following her down, covering her body with his.

He kissed her long and deep and endlessly. She kissed him back. Her hands were busy with buttons and zippers. His hands were busy with lace and ribbons. He touched her breast. Lisa sighed. She pulled him into the silky heated depths of her body. Kevin sighed. Joined, they began to move in the ageless ancient rhythms of love. Lisa looked into his eyes and smiled. Her thoughts were scattering, her whole body focusing itself on the building wave of desire drawing her with him into the eye of the storm. There was something more she had to say.

"Kevin," her voice said falteringly, then grew strong again as he moved deep within her, "you are right. We can do it. I can do it. If it's always like this between us. If we're always together." His arms tightened around her. Their bodies moved as one.

"Always together," Kevin promised. His voice was dark and rough, somewhere between a growl and a purr. He lowered his head to kiss her again. A tiny fluttering spasm started deep within her, spiraling out of control, catching him up in a whirlwind of sensation with her, carrying them toward completion.

"Always together." Lisa smiled and closed her eyes against the intensity of her release.

Later, floating back to reality, she savored Kevin's weight, heavy and comforting, resting against her. She felt the warm faint stirring of his breath against her cheek. He was asleep. She repeated the two words that were both a promise and a prayer. "Always together." She smiled and held Kevin tight. "Together with you I'll find the courage to make all our dreams come true."

Epilogue

"Merry Christmas, squirt," Kevin said, coming up behind Laurel as she stood at the foyer window in the afternoon twilight, watching the snow coming down outside their parents' home. He put his arms around his sister's waist and rested his chin on the top of her head.

"Merry Christmas, big brother. And don't call me squirt." She gave him a playful poke in the ribs with her elbow.

Kevin grunted in feigned agony. "Say, you're beginning to pack a wallop. Has Seth been teaching you some of his old Secret Service moves?"

"Don't be silly," Laurel giggled, and the sound reminded Kevin of sleigh bells and twinkling crystal stars in the night sky. "The new muscles come from lugging around fourteen pounds of infant son all day long." She bent her arm and made a fist to show off a bicep. Kevin obligingly squeezed the slender arm beneath her fuzzy oversized pink sweater.

"Impressive."

"Umm." Laurel went back to watching the snow.

"I'm glad you're home for Christmas this year, Kev. I'm glad we're all together and well and happy." She turned in his arms, tilting her head back and a little to the side to see him better. "You are happy, aren't you?"

"I'm very happy." Kevin smiled down at his petite brown-haired sister. "Very happy."

"And content. I can see that, too, and I know whereof I speak."

Kevin tilted his head in the opposite direction of Laurel's. "Didn't you think your big brother could be happy living in the Great White North?"

Laurel was suddenly serious. "No, I was afraid you might never find anywhere that you wanted to call home. I was afraid I'd always be waiting on Christmas Eve for long-distance calls from outlandish places instead of spending the holidays with the people I love most in this world."

"My wandering days are pretty much over." Kevin lifted his eyes to look out over the familiar small-town neighborhood he'd grown up in. Bartlow would always be his hometown, but now Lisa's beautiful half-tamed north land was his home, simply and forever. "If it hadn't been for that tree branch cracking me on the head, I might never have had the time to slow down and find out what I was missing. There really are blessings in disguise, and silver linings in the darkest clouds, and—"

Laurel laughed again. "All right, all right, enough heart to heart. Lisa said you're working on a new book."

"I am. A composite, a little bit of this and a little bit of that. I've got thousands of shots I've never used. Carrie Granger—you remember Carrie, don't you?" Laurel indicated that she did. "She's going to help with the text, as usual. It'll be a good book."

"I know it will."

"And if you promise to keep it a secret, I'll tell you something else."

"I don't keep secrets from Seth," Laurel said, lifting her chin.

Kevin waved her objection aside. "I told him earlier this afternoon."

Laurel looked as if she were going to protest, then decided against it. "What?" Her brown eyes danced with excitement.

"I've been contacted by a California production company about making a series of how-to videos on wildlife photography. All the way from buying a camera to outfitting an expedition. How does that sound? Can you see your big brother as a video star?"

"Of course, I can," Laurel stated with conviction.

"Funny, that's just what Lisa said."

"I'll bet."

Kevin felt his neck and face turn red. What Lisa had really said was much more provocative and had ended with their making love with passionate abandon.

"Why, big brother, I do believe you're blushing."

"Change the subject, squirt." Kevin knew his deliberate use of Laurel's detested childhood nickname would do the trick.

"Kevin . . ." His sister's tone held a warning note.

"Better be nice to me, squirt, or I won't give you your present in the morning."

"Is it something you brought from up north with you?" Laurel asked, instantly diverted.

"Could be. You'll just have to wait and see, won't you?"

"I want to know now. Tell me, is it one of Enoch Spangler's carvings, like the loon and chick he gave you and Lisa as a wedding present? If it is, you can call me squirt to your heart's content. Is it?" she demanded, impatient as always.

"Could be," Kevin hedged, then broke into a smile adding, "but you're going to have to wait until morning like everyone else—squirt."

"Kevin!" Lisa stretched up on tiptoe to give him a hug. "You are absolutely the world's greatest big brother."

"Hey, I've known that for years." Kevin swung her high in the air. Laurel laughed in delight. Her figure was slightly rounder, more mature than he remembered. She looked happy and fulfilled, content with her marriage and her life.

Kevin felt that way, too. He'd been to the doctor earlier in the week. The deterioration of his vision had halted. For the first time the doctor had ventured a guess as to when he might be ready for surgery to remove and replace the damaged lens. The date was still some distance in the future, but he had far too many plans for his time to be discouraged by the additional wait.

"Kevin!" Laurel's voice was breathless. "Put me down!"

Kevin came back to reality in a hurry. "Sorry, sis." He set her down. "You're just such a little wisp of a thing I got carried away."

Laurel sniffed. "I'm not that little anymore. And I never was a wisp of anything in the first place." She made a face.

"Laurel?" A man's voice called from the swinging door leading into the kitchen. "The candlelight service and cantata start in twenty minutes. The others left fifteen minutes ago. We have to get a move on, or we'll be late." Their cousin Elinor's teenage son, Sam, had volunteered to take Katie and the older Sauders in his car; Brad would ride with Seth and Laurel. Elinor had promised to save them seats. Lisa and Kevin were to baby-sit little Sam and attend Christmas morning service instead. Laurel had planned the evening as if it were a military maneuver. The only problem was that Laurel herself was inevitably late.

"I'm getting my coat." She made a face and stepped out of Kevin's arms.

"She's ready any time you are," Kevin assured his impatient brother-in-law as he grabbed Laurel's coat from the hall closet.

"Good." Seth came striding into the foyer. "Here's Sam's bottle." He handed it to Kevin. "I just finished feeding him his supper. Brad's got him in the living room right now. You're sure you and Lisa won't have any trouble with him?" Dark-winged brows drew together in a frown over Seth's startling blue eyes.

"Sam will be fine. Kevin and Lisa will be fine," Laurel said, turning her back to her husband so that he could help her into her coat. "Stop fussing, Seth."

Kevin wasn't paying attention to the marital give-and-take. As he watched through the archway that separated the living room and foyer, Brad very carefully placed Kevin's roly-poly nephew in Lisa's arms. Kevin's heart turned over in his chest. His wife was wearing a pale blue dress with long wide sleeves and a full skirt that fell in folds to the floor. Her hair was loose on her shoulders, held back by mother-of-pearl combs. She looked young and lovely in the soft glow of the firelight, and she would make a wonderful mother, he thought. He could see her sitting in a rocking chair in their home, candlelight catching the auburn fire in her hair, holding his child to her breast, the way she was holding Sam.

Brad leaned over the back of Lisa's chair and ruffled Sam's soft brown hair. He adored the infant. Kevin had been slightly apprehensive about Lisa's brother being thrust into the noisy, crowded, competitive storm center that his parents' house always seemed to be during the holidays. He needn't have worried, for Brad took it all in stride. When, on the first evening after they arrived, Seth and Laurel had placed their son in his arms to hold and Brad had accepted without a moment's hesitation, Brad had become their friend for life.

"See you later, little guy. Bye, Lisa." He gave his sister a hug. "I'm ready to go," he said, smiling at Laurel and a little shyly at Seth, and then grabbing his coat from the clothes tree by the front door. "So long, Kevin," he said.

"So long, buddy." Kevin patted his parka-clad shoulder. Brad was now working two afternoons a week at the same restaurant as his girlfriend, Gina. Kevin had also recently sold several of his photographs to a company that printed calendars and postcards. Brad was saving up for a car. He'd passed his driver's test just a week before they'd started south.

"Let's get the car warmed up, Brad," Seth said, motioning the young man to precede him out the door. "Laurel, you have exactly ninety seconds to find your gloves and get your fanny out to the car," Seth commanded, then spoiled the effect of his stern words by smiling indulgently at his distracted wife.

"Bully." Laurel made a pet name of the word. She searched her pockets, then her purse. "Found them." She waved the gloves triumphantly in his face. Seth shook his head in defeat and walked out the door.

Laurel looked at Kevin as she pulled on her bright blue fuzzy gloves. "I wish we had more time alone together to talk. The house will be packed to the rafters with people from dawn until midnight tomorrow. Couldn't you take a late plane to Florida?"

Kevin shook his head gently but firmly. "No. We promised to spend some time with Lisa's mother and stepfather. Lisa and the kids haven't seen much of them for the last few years. Besides, you know you're spending tomorrow afternoon and evening with Seth's family."

"I know." Laurel bit her lip. "You will stay with us a few more days before you head back to Michigan?"

"You can drive us to the airport tomorrow and pick us up when we fly back from Florida to make sure we don't slip away."

"It's a deal." The sound of the car horn made Laurel glance toward the door. "There's Seth. I have to go."

"I'll wait up for you tonight," Kevin promised. "We'll have a long talk."

"I'd like that." Laurel laid a hand on his arm. "I'm so glad you found Lisa to love as much as I love Seth." Her great brown eyes were misty with emotion.

"So am I, sis." Kevin looked into the living room at his wife. Lisa's head was bent over the sleeping infant. She kissed him, touched his cheek wonderingly with the tip of her finger. As if she sensed Kevin watching her, Lisa looked over at him and smiled. His breath caught in his chest, his heart jerked out of rhythm, then settled into a slow drugging beat that spread warmth throughout his body. "Last night," he said with quiet exultation, wanting to let Laurel share a little of the great happiness he felt, "we talked about starting a family of our own."

Harlequin Regency Romance™

Romance the way it was *always* meant to be!

The time is 1811, when a Regent Prince rules the empire. The place is London, the glittering capital where rakish dukes and dazzling debutantes scheme and flirt in a dangerously exciting game. Where marriage is the passport to wealth and power, yet every girl hopes secretly for love....

Welcome to Harlequin Regency Romance where reading is an adventure and romance is *not* just a thing of the past! Two delightful books a month, beginning May '89.

Available wherever Harlequin Books are sold.

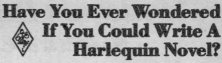

Have You Ever Wondered If You Could Write A Harlequin Novel?

Here's great news—Harlequin is offering a series of cassette tapes to help you do just that. Written by Harlequin editors, these tapes give practical advice on how to make your characters—and your story—come alive. There's a tape for each contemporary romance series Harlequin publishes.

Mail order only

All sales final

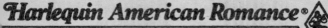

Harlequin American Romance®

COMING NEXT MONTH

#289 FULL HOUSE by Jackie Weger

Justine's house was full . . . of complications. She had plenty to do just adjusting to life after divorce, making a new home for her kids, and struggling to keep her mother and ex-mother-in-law from tearing what security she'd managed to build to bits. But Tucker, her handsome neighbor, was a complication she found hard to resist—especially when she found out about the dilapidated old house's other occupant: Lottie Roberts, a 159-year-old ghost.

#290 HOME TO THE COWBOY by Bobby Hutchinson

The new vet in Bitterroot, Montana, Sara Wingate, was up to her ears in muck and squealing pigs when she first met rancher Mitch Carter. A former rodeo hero, Mitch had reluctantly returned to work the family spread. How long would it be before wanderlust hit him again? Or had Mitch come home for good?

#291 TOGETHER ALWAYS by Dallas Schulze

The moment he'd set eyes on the pale, pretty child, Trace Dushane knew why he lived. Over the years he'd kept Lily from harm, fed her, sheltered her. Now he had to convince her she no longer needed him. That was the hardest part of all—for the first time facing a life without Lily.

#292 ROBBING THE CRADLE by Anne Henry

Lots of women dated younger men, but could thirty-year-old Dallas caterer and mother of two small boys, Pam Sullivan, do it? Persistent Joel Bynum was "that nice young man at the supermarket." He was a college kid, for heaven's sake! Could Pam throw caution to the winds?

COMING IN MARCH FROM

Harlequin Superromance

Book Two of the
Merriman County Trilogy
AFTER ALL THESE YEARS
the sizzle of Eve Gladstone's
One Hot Summer continues!

Sarah Crewes is at it again, throwing Merriman County into a tailspin with her archival diggings. In *One Hot Summer* (September 1988) she discovered that the town of Ramsey Falls was celebrating its tricentennial one year too early.

Now she's found that Riveredge, the Creweses' ancestral home and property, does not rightfully belong to her family. Worse, the legitimate heir to Riveredge may be none other than the disquieting Australian, Tyler Lassiter.

Sarah's not sure why Tyler's in town, but she suspects he is out to right some old wrongs—and some new ones!

The unforgettable characters of *One Hot Summer* and *After All These Years* will continue to delight you in book three of the trilogy. Watch for *Wouldn't It Be Lovely* in November 1989.

SR349-1

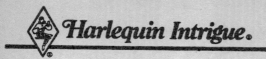

Harlequin Intrigue.

They went in through the terrace door. The house was dark, most of the servants were down at the circus, and only Nelbert's hired security guards were in sight. It was child's play for Blackheart to move past them, the work of two seconds to go through the solid lock on the terrace door. And then they were creeping through the darkened house, up the long curving stairs, Ferris fully as noiseless as the more experienced Blackheart.

They stopped on the second floor landing. "What if they have guns?" Ferris mouthed silently.

Blackheart shrugged. "Then duck."

"How reassuring," she responded. Footsteps directly above them signaled that the thieves were on the move, and so should they be.

For more romance, suspense and adventure, read Harlequin Intrigue. Two exciting titles each month, available wherever Harlequin Books are sold.